OPEN CITY

New York City, Spring 2001
Number Twelve

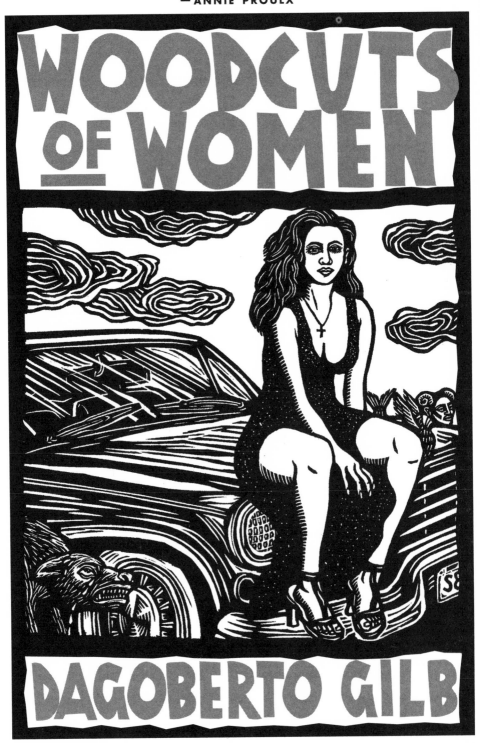

WOODCUTS OF WOMEN

DAGOBERTO GILB

Grove Press   Distributed by Publishers Group West

CHRISTIAN MARCLAY

20 JANUARY – 17 FEBRUARY

SOPHIE CALLE

24 FEBRUARY – 24 MARCH

CÉLESTE
BOURSIER-MOUGENOT

24 MARCH – 28 APRIL

SHERRIE LEVINE

24 MARCH – 28 APRIL

ANDRES SERRANO

5 MAY – JUNE

PAULA COOPER GALLERY

521/534 WEST 21ST STREET NEW YORK NY 10011

TEL 212.255.1105 FAX 212.255.5156

OPEN CITY

LINCOLN PLAZA CINEMAS

Six Screens

63rd Street & Broadway
opposite Lincoln Center
757-2280

ROBERT JACK
WEBS AND FLOW
February 10 - March 31

PIOT BREHMER
JULIANNE SWARTZ
LANDING ~ THE BUBBLE
April 10 - May 31

Tel: 212 219 1482   www.123watts.com   123 Watts Street
Fax: 212 274 1726   gallery@tribecatech.com   New York, NY 10013

OPEN CITY

EDITORS
Thomas Beller
Daniel Pinchbeck

MANAGING EDITOR
Joanna Yas

ART DIRECTOR
Nick Stone

EDITOR-AT-LARGE
Adrian Dannatt

CONTRIBUTING EDITORS
Sam Brumbaugh
Vanessa Chase
Amanda Gersh
Laura Hoffmann
Kip Kotzen
Sam Lipsyte
Jim Merlis
Geoffrey O'Brien
Elizabeth Schmidt
Alexandra Tager
Jon Tower
Lee Smith
Piotr Uklanski
Jocko Weyland

EDITORIAL ASSISTANT
Alicia Bergman

READERS
Gabriel Marc Delahaye
Jim Higdon
Jennifer Stroup
Susan Tepper

FOUNDING PUBLISHER
Robert Bingham

A four-issue subscription is $32 in the U.S.; $40 for institutions; $36 in Canada and Mexico; $52 in all other countries. Make checks payable to: OPEN CITY, Inc., 225 Lafayette Street, Suite 1114, New York, NY 10012. *For credit card orders, see our Web site: www.opencity.org. E-mail: editors@opencity.org.*

Cover photograph by Miranda Lichtenstein,
"Untitled, #4 (Richardson Park)"
Front page drawing by Pieter Schoolwerth

Art projects in this issue curated by Jocko Weyland.

ISBN 1-890447-23-4
ISSN 1089-5523

We  Airplane Noise.

ANNA

150 E. 3rd Street at Ave. A
212.358.0195

photo by Hellin Kay

CONTRIBUTORS' NOTES

DAPHNE BEAL lives in New York City. She was recently a writer-in-residence with the Lannan Foundation in Marfa, Texas, and is currently finishing a novel set in South Asia.

JILL BIALOSKY is the author of *The End of Desire* (Alfred A. Knopf) and a forthcoming book of poems, *Subterranean*, to be published in spring 2002. She lives in New York City.

PAULA BOMER grew up in South Bend, Indiana, and now lives in Brooklyn, New York. Her fiction has appeared in *Nerve* and *Global City Review*. "The Mother of His Children" is from a collection in progress very tentatively entitled *Marriage and Babies.*

SAM BRUMBAUGH was born in Washington, D.C. He was a founding partner and creative director of SonicNet. He has been the talent executive and producer for a number of music-related shows for PBS and Canal Plus, and is currently producing a documentary on the life and times of Townes Van Zandt. He lives in New York City.

LEWIS COLE teaches screenwriting at Columbia University's film department. His last published book was *This Side of Glory* (Little, Brown and Company, 1995). "Push It Out" is an excerpt from his novel *Winner's Out.*

MEGHAN DAUM's essay collection, *My Misspent Youth*, will be published by Open City Books in March 2001. She lives in Raymond, Nebraska.

MARY DONNELLY was born and raised in San Pedro, California—L.A.'s answer to Bayonne, New Jersey. She has co-written two feature-length screenplays and works as a writer/producer in the precarious world of Internet television. She lives in Brooklyn.

BEN DOYLE's first book of poems, *Radio, Radio*, won the 2000 Walt Whitman Award and will be published this April by Louisiana State University Press. He lives in Iowa but longs so for travel.

ANN FAISON is a musician, singer-songwriter, video artist, and photographer who lately has been drawn to trees.

FORD MADOX FORD was born Ford Herman Hueffer in London in 1873. He founded and edited both the *English Review* and the *Transatlantic Review*, and was the author of over eighty books, including *The Good Soldier* and *Parade's End*. He was an officer in World War I and was badly gassed and shellshocked. He died in 1939. "Fun—It's Heaven" was first published by the British magazine *The Bystander* in 1915 and is reprinted here from *War Prose* (Carcanet Press Ltd., Manchester, 1999).

HENRIK HÅKANSSON was born in Sweden and currently resides in Berlin. He investigates the social constructs of nature by focusing scientific-observation strategies on biological matters. His latest exhibitions are "Whiteblue Light" at Galleria Franco Noero, Turin, and "Sweet Leaf" at Galerie Fur Zeitgenössische Kunst, Leipzig.

TORU HAYASHI is an artist and CEO of TravelAgency Garden, a fictitious company. He lives in New York City.

THOMAS HAUSER is an artist living in Berlin.

HUNTER KENNEDY is from Columbia, South Carolina, and is the founder and editor of *The Minus Times*. He has just completed his first novel, *Miss State Line*, and currently lives above a funeral parlor in Brooklyn.

HEATHER LARIMER's "Casseroles" is part of an unpublished collection of short fiction called *Someone's Wife*. She is a graduate of the University of Washington's M.F.A. program in creative writing. She recently relocated to Portland, Oregon.

CRESTON LEA's stories have appeared in *DoubleTake* and in the W.W. Norton anthology *25 & Under: Fiction*. He lives in Burlington, Vermont.

MIRANDA LICHTENSTEIN is an artist living in New York City. She is represented by the Goldman Tevis Gallery in Los Angeles. She will have a solo exhibition at the Whitney Museum of American Art at Philip Morris in July 2001.

GIUSEPPE O. LONGO was born in Forlì, Italy in 1941. He holds degrees in electronic engineering and mathematics and a Ph.D. in cybernetics and information theory. He is a professor of information theory at the University of Trieste. Longo has translated fifteen books from English and German and in 1991 was awarded the Monselice Prize for scientific translation. He has published four collections of short stories and three novels, and several of his plays have been produced. While his novel *L'acrobata* received the Laure Bataillon award for best novel translated into French, "In Zenoburg" is his first publication in English.

DAVID MENDEL retired as a cardiologist in 1986 after publishing the cult classic, *Proper Doctoring*. He then took a degree course in Italian and now writes, lectures, and broadcasts on the BBC about Italian matters. He is especially interested in Primo Levi, whom he knew and writes and lectures about.

EVIE McKENNA is a photographer who has spent the last several years documenting buildings that exhibit vernacular architecture. Many of her subjects have been found in the Catskill region of New York State, with sporadic rangings into the South and Southwest. Her mother considered moving a sport and those frequent real-estate visits may have been the inspiration for this work. She has been on the faculty of the School of Visual Arts in New York City and is represented by the Ricco Maresca Gallery.

MATTHEW MILLER lives in a farmhouse near Iowa City, where he recently received his M.F.A. from the Iowa Writers' Workshop. His poems can be found in recent or forthcoming issues of *Colorado Review*, *New Letters*, *Prairie Schooner*, and other journals. His collection of poems, *First Engine*, is currently making the rounds at the contests. He can be reached at godotnut@hotmail.com.

SARA OGGER is an assistant professor of German at Montclair State University.

SAM SAMORE lives and works in New York, Paris, and Tokyo. He exhibits internationally. His most recent solo exhibition, "Sam Samore: Pathological Tales/Schizophrenic Stories," was at the Casino Luxembourg, July–September 2000. His next book, *The Adventure*, a picture/storybook, will be published in spring 2001 by powerHouse Books. In New York, he is represented by Gorney Bravin + Lee.

MATTHEW SAMTON was born in New York City and lives in New York City, but, if he has any power over it, will die elsewhere.

PIETER SCHOOLWERTH is an artist living and working in New York. He has had recent exhibitions in Milan and New York, where he is represented by American Fine Arts, Co.

ELKE SIEGEL and **PAUL FLEMING** live in Charm City.

TIM STAFFEL was born in 1965 in Kassel, Germany. He studied theater arts and now lives as a freelance writer in Berlin. His first novel, *Terrordrom*, from which this piece is an excerpt, was published in German by Ammann Verlag in 1998. This excerpt is reprinted with their permission.

DAVID STARKEY lives in Santa Barbara, California. His chapbook, *Fear of Everything*, was winner of Palanquin Press's spring 2000 contest.

BENJAMIN von STUCKRAD-BARRE was born in 1975 in Bremen. He lives in Berlin and is an editor of the *Frankfurter Allgemeine Zeitung*. "Show

#7" is a chapter from his novel *Livealbum*, which was published in German by Kiepenheuer & Witsch in 1999. This chapter is reprinted with the permission of Joan Daves/Writer's House, Inc. on behalf of the publishers.

MUNGO THOMSON also makes his own graph paper. He lives and works in Los Angeles and is represented by the Margo Leavin Gallery.

WILLIAM WENTHE's book of poems is *Birds of Hoboken* (Orchis, 1995). He has published poems recently in *Orion*, *Southern Review*, *The Literary Review*, *Chelsea*, and other journals, and has won fellowships from the NEA and the Texas Commission on the Arts. He lives in Lubbock, Texas, and is the poetry editor of *Iron Horse Literary Review*.

RACHEL WETZSTEON lives in New York City and is the author of two books of poems, *The Other Stars* and *Home and Away*.

BRIDGE
STORIES & IDEAS

Come Across

Hey, you. Yeah. You.

Ask yourself: Why live in a world of fear? There's a whole other side to life, and all you need do is take those first, wobbly steps. We've got plenty of advertising space here, see. Wouldn't you like to help us fill that up? That certainly would be nice. Because then we'll be able to keep bringing you, our readers, work that represents the high-water-marks of the *Bridge* standard. Get on the beam, Jackson.

Take a minute if you need to. Think it over.

Then call us about advertising at 773-395-8454. Or email us at mworkman@bridgemagazine.org

We thank you.

FEED

www.feedmag.com

Contributors include:

Sam Lipsyte, author of Venus Drive

Geoff Dyer, National Book Award finalist

Roger Ebert, "Roger Ebert & The Movies"

Alex Ross, The New Yorker music critic

Sven Birkerts, author of The Gutenberg Elegies

Denise Caruso, New York Times columnist

Lisa Carver, author of Dancing Queen

Jenny Offill, author of Last Things

Esther Dyson, cyber-guru

"Some of the sharpest writing on-line or off . . . . Unfailingly original, insightful and refreshing."

—*The New York Times*

And **FEED** Magazine co-founders

Steven Johnson

and **Stefanie Syman**

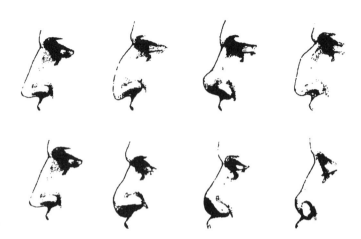

OPEN

Stories by Mary Gaitskill, Hubert Selby Jr., Vince Passaro. Art by Jeff Koons, Ken Schles, Devon Dikeou. (Vastly overpriced at $200, but fortunately we've had some takers. Only twenty-eight copies left.)

ISSUE # 1

Stories by Martha McPhee, Terry Southern, David Shields, Jaime Manrique, Kip Kotzen. Art by Paul Ramirez-Jonas, Kate Milford, Richard Serra. (Ken Schles found the negative of our cover girl on 13th St. and Avenue B. We're still looking for the girl. $100)

ISSUE # 2

Stories by Irvine Welsh, Richard Yates, Patrick McCabe. Art by Francesca Woodman, Jacqueline Humphries, Chip Kidd, Allen Ginsberg, Alix Lambert. Plus Alfred Chester's letters to Paul Bowles. (Our cover girl now has long brown hair. $150)

ISSUE # 3

Stories by Cyril Connolly, Thomas McGuane, Jim Thompson, Samantha Gillison, Michael Brownstein, Emily Carter. Art by Julianne Swartz and Peter Nadin. Poems by David Berman and Nick Tosches. Plus Denis Johnson in Somalia. (A monster issue, sales undercut by slightly rash choice of cover art by editors. Get it while you can! $15)

ISSUE # 4

CITY

back issues

Change or Die
Stories by David Foster Wallace, Siobhan Reagan, Irvine Welsh. Jerome Badanes's brilliant novella, Change or Die (film rights still available). Poems by David Berman and Vito Acconci. Plus Helen Thorpe on the murder of Ireland's most famous female journalist, and Delmore Schwartz on T. S. Eliot's squint. (A must-have at only $17!)

ISSUE #5

The Only Woman He's Ever Left
Stories by James Purdy, Jocko Weyland, Strawberry Saroyan. Michael Cunningham goes way uptown. Poems by Rick Moody, Deborah Garrison, Monica Lewinsky, Charlie Smith. Art by Matthew Ritchie, Ellen Harvey, Cindy Stefans. Rem Koolhaas Project. With a beautiful cover by Adam Fuss. (Only $10 for this blockbuster. Free to the first six people who request it.)

ISSUE #6

The Rubbed Away Girl
Stories by Mary Gaitskill, Bliss Broyard, and Sam Lipsyte. Art by Jimmy Raskin, Laura Larson, and Jeff Burton. Poems by David Berman, Elizabeth Macklin, Steve Malkmus, and Will Oldham. (A reader from Queens chastises us for our shameful synergistic moment with indie rock. $10)

ISSUE #7

Beautiful to Strangers
Stories by Caitlin O'Connor Creevy, Joyce Johnson, and Amine Zaitzeff. Poems by Harvey Shapiro, Jeffrey Skinner, and Daniil Kharms. Art by Piotr Uklanski, David Robbins, Liam Gillick, and Elliott Puckette. Look for Zaitzeff's *Westchester Burning* in stores soon. ($10)

ISSUE #8

Bewitched
Stories by Jonathan Ames, Said Shirazi, and Sam Lipsyte. Essays by Geoff Dyer and Alexander Chancellor, who hates rabbit. Poems by Chan Marshall and Edvard Munch on intimate and sensitive subjects. Art projects by Karen Kilimnick, Maurizio Cattelan, and M.I.M.E. (Oddly enough, our bestselling issue. $10)

Editors' Issue
Previously demure editors publish themselves. Enormous changes at the last minute. Stories by Robert Bingham, Thomas Beller, Daniel Pinchbeck, Joanna Yas, Adrian Dannatt, Kip Kotzen, Amanda Gersh, Jocko Weyland. Poems by Tony Torn. Art by Nick Stone, Meghan Gerety, and Alix Lambert. ($10)

Octo Ate Them All
Vestal McIntyre emerges from the slush pile like aphrodite with a brilliant story that corresponds to the tatoo that covers his entire back. Siobhan Reagan thinks about strangulation. Fiction by Melissa Pritchard and Bill Broun. Anthropologist Michael Taussig's Cocaine Museum. Gregor von Rezzori's meditation on solitude, sex, and raw meat. Art by Joanna Kirk, Sebastien de Ganay, and Ena Swansea.($10)

Please send a check or money order payable to *OPEN CITY, Inc.* Don't forget to specify the issue number and give us your address. Send checks to:

OPEN CITY
225 Lafayette Street, Suite 1114, New York, NY 10012

For credit card orders, see www.opencity.org

Gorney Bravin + Lee

534 West 26th Street
New York, NY 10001

T 212 352 8372
F 212 352 8374

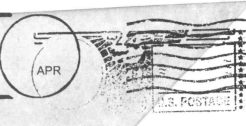

The Academy of American Poets announces

NATIONAL
POETRY MONTH
APRIL 2001

This spring, National Poetry Month will celebrate the **American Poet Stamp** series from the United States Postal Service. Visit **www.poets.org** to nominate a poet for a future stamp and sign a petition for more stamps featuring American poets. Visit the National Poetry Month website today!

National Poetry Month is sponsored this year by the following organizations:
**Benefactors: Bennett Book Advertising, Inc. • The Gale Group • Alfred A. Knopf, Inc.
Mead Coated Paper Co. • Merriam-Webster, Inc. • The National Endowment for the Arts
The New York Times Advertising Dept. • The New Yorker • Random House**

Sponsors: Harry N. Abrams, Inc. • American Booksellers Association • The American Library Association • The American Poetry & Literacy Project • Associated Writing Programs • The Association of American University Presses, Inc. • Bennington College Writing Seminars • Black Sparrow Press • BOA Editions, Ltd. • The Children's Book Council • City Lights Books • Coffee House Press • Copper Canyon Press • Council of Literary Magazines & Presses • Counterpoint Press • Curbstone Press • Dover Publications, Inc. • Farrar, Straus & Giroux • FIELD/Oberlin College Press • The Folger Shakespeare Library • Four Way Books • Geraldine R. Dodge Poetry Festival • Graywolf Press • Grove / Atlantic, Inc. • Hanging Loose Press • Harcourt Brace • HarperCollins • Henry Holt and Co. • Holy Cow! Press • Houghton Mifflin Co. • House of Ansani Press • Hudson Valley Writers' Center, Inc. • Kelsey St. Press • Ladan Reserve Press • Library of America • Louisiana State University Press • Miami University Press • Milkweed Editions • Modern Language Association • The Modern Poetry Association • The National Association of College Stores • The National Book Foundation • National Council of Teachers of English • New Directions • New Issues Press Poetry Series • New York State Council on the Arts • Northwestern University Press • W.W. Norton & Company, Inc. • Pearl Street Publishing • Penguin Putnam • People's Poetry Gathering • Persea Books, Inc. • Poetry Society of America • Poets House • Poets & Writers, Inc. • Robinson Jeffers Tor House Foundation • Sarabande Books, Inc. • Scholastic Inc. • Scribner • Small Press Distribution • Story Line Press • Teachers & Writers Collaborative • University of Akron Press • University of Chicago Press • University of Georgia Press • University of Illinois Press • University of Iowa Press • University of Massachusetts Press • University of Wisconsin Press • Urban Libraries Council • Utah State University Press • Wake Forest University Press • Wesleyan University Press • YMCA National Writer's Voice • Zoland Books
Media Sponsors: AGNI • American Book Review • The American Poetry Review • Another Chicago Magazine • The Bloomsbury Review • Bomb • The Boston Book Review • The Boston Review • The Christian Science Monitor • The Georgia Review • Harper's • Kenyon Review • The Nation • The New Republic • The New York Review of Books • North American Review • Northwest Review • Open City • Osiris • The Paris Review • Partisan Review • Ploughshares • Poetry • Poetry Calendar • Poetry Flash • Potomac Review • Publishers Weekly / Library Journal / School Library Journal • Seneca Review • The Sewanee Review • Tin House • The Writer's Chronicle • The Yale Review • ZYZZYVA

CANADA

359 Broadway (basement) NYC 212 925 4631
David Askevold Sarah Braman Aaron Brewer Karma Clarke-Davis
Robin Peck Jocelyn Shipley Anke Weyer Wallace Whitney

The world needs
more important things
than monster men,
flying saucers,
telephone psychics.
But everyone loves a mystery.
(Donnelly, page 151)

The Mother of His Children

Paula Bomer

THE CAR ARRIVED AND HIS WIFE HELD THE BABY ON HER HIP and waved to him as he trotted down their front steps. "Call me," she said, and he could still smell her coffee-mouth and sour, breast-milk smell as he slipped into the car. She looked old and beat-up, a bit of a double chin resting on her neck. One of her breasts was noticeably larger than the other; this had happened after the birth of their new son, Henry, when her milk came in. He waved back at all of them. Their three-year-old, Jake, bounced around on the sidewalk scream-ing, "Bye-bye Daddy! Bye-bye Daddy!" He would be gone for only two days. No matter; he was thrilled, thrilled to leave them, stinky, loud, and demanding, all of them. And he didn't feel guilty about it. He loved his family, how they were always waiting for him to arrive in the evening. They needed him. He had framed photographs of them on his desk at work. But they were not always that pleasant to be around.

Ted Stanton was the technology director of a Web site, thirty-five, balding, and with a limp tire of fat around his middle. He played bas-ketball on Sundays in Brooklyn, near his newly purchased house, with other men in their prime who worked in the online world. They played extremely aggressively, turning red and oozing noxious, booze-scented sweat. They never talked business, but every push, grunt, and jump was about whose IPO was fatter than the others. If he wasn't playing ball on Sundays, he sat. He sat on the subway to and from work, he sat at his desk in his office in a sleek loft in downtown

Manhattan, and he sat on the couch at home drinking a beer. He sat at the dinner table where Laura served him dinner almost every night. He then sat in front of the TV, and then sat up in bed and leafed through a magazine. Soon he would be fat. He was convinced Laura wanted him to be fat, as she always presented him with a pint of ice cream and a spoon while they watched TV at night. He hated her for this, but he also was relieved that she was there to take the blame, as he would never want to be responsible himself for putting on weight.

He had met Laura five years ago at a party. They discovered that they both lived in studio apartments on Mulberry Street. She was not at all remarkable looking, but her clothes were tight, and her trampy style was unique in his circle of Ivy Leaguers. They slept together that night, at her place. The next morning, deeply hungover, he had to look at a piece of mail on her kitchen counter to get her name. He had forgotten it, or never bothered to ask for it in the first place. They continued to drink a lot and sleep together, and when she accidentally got pregnant, they agreed to go to City Hall and get married. Two years earlier, he would have made her get an abortion. But Ted liked her, liked that she was his, and she cooked him dinner all the time. They had fit well together in bed, and while he knew she was no rocket scientist, he found her simplicity comforting. He had been thirty and eager to marry. He never had much confidence with women, and Laura had made him feel slightly good about himself.

She was just fine in every respect, really. Did he love her? This was a subject matter both Ted and Laura found embarrassing. It was something they had in common, this squeamishness about love. Once, after a particularly gymnastic and satisfying lovemaking session, he had blurted out "I love you." She answered him, her face muffled into the pillow, something that sounded like "ditto." This was good enough for him, but thereafter he restrained himself from saying anything in the heat of passion.

And now? Now, he was on his way to San Francisco, to a conference. He flew coach and could barely fit into his designated seat. But the flight left on time and no fat people sat next to him, in fact, no one sat next to him. He had a window seat. A pile of magazines and his laptop occupied the seat next to him. His flight attendant was female and despite the globs of makeup on her face, was relatively attractive and not too miserable seeming. He briefly imagined shoving his dick down her throat. Her tight, navy polyester skirt would rustle loudly as she pulled it up so she could get down on her knees; her shiny, lip-glossed mouth would part as she bent her head back to make room for his erection. It was something he did, imagined violating strange women whom he came in contact with. Once he had even fantasized fucking Larry Worth, the president of his company, in the ass. Larry, chubby, nasty-tempered Larry. Gasping from his smoking habit, the stink of old sweat coming off his dirty boxers as Ted ripped them down and shoved him over his very own desk. The tightness of his asshole, the little pieces of shit clinging to the dark threads of hair. He'd let out one angry scream as Ted stuck him like the pig he was. Larry had been a classmate at Harvard and Ted liked him, but resented him for making more money than he did. He didn't have kids to support. He didn't even have a wife! And definitely not a wife who perhaps defined herself entirely by what she bought.

Besides shopping and minding the children and house, Laura did nothing. In fact, minding the children and house had become a sort of shopping in and of itself. There was new underwear for Jake one day, diapers for the baby the next, and pork chops the day after. Ted knew that taking care of the children and the home was work, regardless of the weekly visits from a Caribbean housekeeper and a part-time babysitter. He wouldn't want to do what Laura was doing. It was thankless, and not only because he didn't really appreciate what she did—which was, in fact, true—but because no one did, not their little children, not the other depressed, defensive, and overeducated mothers she hung out with, not anyone. He was, of course, secretly glad she didn't have a career. But when the sitter came in the morning, Laura went out shopping. And usually, in the afternoon, she strapped the kids in the stroller and shopped some more. She bought nice stuff—Kate Spade diaper bags, Petit Bateau pajamas for the kids, a pair of Gap leather pants for herself. She bought shell steaks, fresh rosemary, organic baby food. She cooked nice dinners with the nice food she bought. But sometimes Ted wondered if there was anyone lurking beneath all that shopping. This kind of thinking made him anxious, and he tried not to go there. He didn't like hyper-intelligent women, but he also liked to think that Laura had a soul.

San Francisco, now there was a nice thought. Ted undid his seatbelt, breathed deeply. Out the airplane window was nothing, a whitish gray, cloudy nothing. Larry was meeting him at what was promised to Ted to be a very happening restaurant. Larry would bring a crowd of fabulously important schmoozers. There would be lots of parties to go to after dinner, lots of drunk, younger women with interesting jobs. But for some reason, despite the fact that Ted was doing quite well, all those loose party girls, all that fresh lemon pussy, the squeaky young recent college grads with their sixty-grand-a-year jobs, never came on to him. It wasn't because he was married. Plenty of his married colleagues had flings. In the past, his insecurity had made him invisible to women, that he knew. But now he felt as if it were something else. He felt it was because he actually pro-grammed Web sites, was a tech guy. All the young women wanted to fuck the creatives, as they were known. It was as if the nature of his job forced him into a monogamous lifestyle he no longer could bear. No one wanted to talk to him about code. Code was not sexy. He didn't want to talk about code either, frankly. It was just something he had a gift for, something he did for a living. And no women, young or old, did technical work. They all worked in marketing or production.

Did he want to divorce Laura? Hmm. Every day he left for work and she stayed home, he felt them grow apart. They grew eight hours apart every day. He, with adults and computers, participating in the world. She, primarily with young children, sinking into a dull, repet-itive existence. Besides shopping, she spent a lot of time picking up. She picked up underwear, dirty dishes, toys, old newspapers. She put away the bath towels, lined up the spices in the spice rack, took the old, bad food out of the refrigerator. Every night she sat cross-legged in front of the refrigerator, perusing its contents. Once, they had sex in common. That, and socializing. Sex, in many ways, was what had brought Laura and he together. Sure, they were both white, educated, and upper-middle class. They both believed in the superiority of all things New York. But it was their fucking that really clinched the deal, the negotiation which was their marriage.

"Something to drink?"

It was early. He knew the flight attendant really meant juice or cof-fee, but he ordered a Bloody Mary. There she was, with her full cart, leaning over to find a miniature bottle of vodka. She smiled at him. He wanted her to care that he was ordering a drink so early, he wanted her to feel his pain, see him as slightly on the edge. But what did she care if he had a drink first thing in the morning? He was nothing to her. She placed the little plastic cup with the rounded ice cubes onto a napkin, leaning again to do so, this time over his pile of stuff on the seat next to him. She had nice tits. She smiled, revealing a slight overbite. Perhaps the overbite was why he had imagined putting his dick in her mouth. The extra room there, the sexiness of the imperfection. Perhaps she secretly hated men who drank, he thought. Perhaps her father was a drunk who beat her, molested her. He wanted her to care.

The drink tasted good. Slightly horseradishy, very cold. The plastic cup was like a feather in his hand. He felt wild, free. He pushed the little silver button on the armrest and leaned back. Someone behind him coughed in annoyance and Ted looked back. Some guy with a job, like himself. Angry in his little seat, jowly face in his newspaper. Fuck him, Ted thought, and pushed the seat back further, as far as it would go. The back of his seat at this point, he knew, was in the guy's lap. Ted coughed back at him.

An ice cube from his drink fell in his lap. Ted felt it there, felt it cold and hard, making a dark stain on his trousers. He picked it up off of his pants and put it back in his cup. Then he downed his drink.

When they had decided to keep the baby, Laura had been thrilled. She glowed in those first few months, despite her upset stomach, she positively glowed. She quit drinking, smoking, and cut back on her coffee intake. She started watching lots of TV. As she grew larger, they both grew more anxious. Ted worked late at night. Laura began looking for a house in Brooklyn, as the tiny apartment in Manhattan would no longer work for them. She took a prenatal yoga class where she met other expectant moms. She bought baby clothes, researched strollers and car seats. Her life, which once was partying and flirting, turned into obsessive nesting activities. Ted continued to work late and became ambitious in a way he'd never been before. He asked for a huge raise and got it. He wanted a corner office. He, too, became obsessed, obsessed with making more money.

And sex? They continued to have sex, albeit more cautiously, less frequently, and toward the end of her pregnancy, not at all. The last time they had sex during the pregnancy had been late at night, under the covers. Laura's back was facing him as they lay side by side. It took about two seconds before he came. Her pussy had felt so swollen, and so thick with mucous, that it freaked him out. It had felt good, in a way, but alarmingly different and almost completely animal, or something. Like he was fucking a sheep. Overall, it was an unpleasant interaction, regardless of the physical gratification.

As Laura's due date neared, they began attending a birth class. Laura had researched various birth classes—this was one of those things she talked at him about, which class to take, which hospital to have the baby in, to get an epidural or no epidural. Ted did not understand all the hoopla about birth. It was after the birth that things really started to happen, wasn't it? After the baby arrived, that's what really mattered. When he spoke this way to her, Laura would get mad, saying, "It's not your body, so you just don't care. You don't care about me, do you? You don't know how to care about me!" Then she would storm into the living room and turn on the TV. End of discussion.

The birth class met once a week in an elementary public school in the West Village. Ted hated it. The "instructor," Jane, was a beady-eyed, colorless woman in her forties who was relentlessly cheerful about birth despite an incredibly strong hostility that emanated from her person. Sometimes, one of her children attended the class and would sit in a loft in the back of the classroom playing by himself while his mother talked excitedly about vaginas, the uterus, dilation, effacement, placenta, and the like. Ted was disgusted. All the other couples seemed pleased as punch. Then came the practice sessions. Laura would lie on her side and he sat next to her, rubbing her back and talking to her in a soothing voice about oceans and forests. He just didn't get it. Couldn't she just take some drugs and put a sheet over her?

The flight attendant loomed over him suddenly. He ordered another Bloody Mary. She didn't make eye contact with him this time. Good. Maybe she did care, he thought, pouring the vodka into the tomato juice and stirring. His hand shook slightly as he banged the little plastic stirrer around. Bloody Mary. Bloody bloody. At the end of the birth class, they watched videos of births. Ted would close his eyes. Instructor Jane, and sometimes some of the other women, cried and exclaimed, "Isn't it beautiful?" Ted ran off to the bathroom, thinking he might throw up.

He tried to talk to Laura about it. It's not that he didn't want children, he just didn't want to watch them come out of her. Was that so wrong? He admitted, bravely he thought, that he was scared. Laura argued that he would be sad and feel left out if he wasn't there watching.

"What if you don't bond with our son because you're too chicken to see him come into the world?" She'd been sniffly and angry, with only weeks to go before the birth.

"I can't wait to meet this baby," he'd said. "I'm not worried about loving this baby or not. I just am nervous about the whole birth thing. You are too, admit it. You're not so sure it's going to be so beautiful."

"I don't want to be alone, Ted. And I think the immediate bonding thing is real. I want you there in the room with me, helping to deliver this child."

"Instructor Jane is brainwashing you! My dad loved us! He wasn't in the room watching us slither out of my mother's crotch!" He hadn't meant to yell. Laura burst into tears. That was it. He apologized and said he'd do his best. And he did. At the hospital, he held her hand, gave her ice chips, and told her stories of mountains and trickling rain until she screamed at him to shut the fuck up. Jake's head appeared and his wife, huffing, deranged, and drug free, touched Jake's head. The midwife told Ted to touch Jake's head too, and he did. A wet, hairy little head, stuck in the pelvic bone of his wife. He didn't like it. The room smelled of feces and some weird, thick metallic smell; the smell of fear, the smell of blood and earth. His wife's vagina expanded into something entirely unrecognizable as his son's body emerged. Her vagina was all blood and ooze, as wide as a house, and beet red except for the places where it was a dark, bruised purple; looking at it just made Ted hurt all over. Laura's eyes bulged from her face, black-green veins glistened all over her round stomach and breasts. Dark streaks of shit, poorly wiped off by the nurse, lay smeared on her buttocks, and her once tiny pink rosebud of an asshole was swollen to the size of a small melon. She moaned as if she were dying. He began to fear that she was dying. He had weird thoughts wishing that she would die, just so the damn thing would be over with, and so that he never had to look her in the face again. The midwife yelled, "Take a picture, take a picture!" He had been given a camera by his wife. He didn't want to take a picture. He wanted to curl up in a ball and disappear. Everybody was screaming. Laura was no longer Laura. Her voice came from a place he'd never known was in her. He couldn't stand it. He couldn't stand looking at anyone anymore, and he began backing out of the room, the bitter taste of vomit on the back of his throat. His wife began screaming, "I'm dying! I'm dying! Pull! Pull him out of me!" Minutes later, he held his newborn son. The midwife asked him to take off his shirt first, for some "skin-on-skin contact." He ignored her. Jake, their little boy, their perfect, tiny boy, squeaked and cried. Holding him was, undoubtedly, the most profound experience of his life. Nothing could touch that. But the birth itself rattled him. He had been afraid and now he was, well, traumatized.

The constant whir of the airplane reminded Ted of the computers at work. A soothing, white noise. He was fifteen the first time he touched pussy. A Saturday night, in the graveyard behind Hotchkiss. His first year of boarding school. She was a lovely, bulimic, Greenwich, Connecticut girl named Mary Todd. They had been drinking vodka mixed with Seven-Up. After fumbling around for a while, Ted, so nervously, put a finger into her panties, searching for it. It was warmer than he thought it would be. No one had told him it would be warm in there. Slippery yes, but with invisible, superfine grains of sand. He let his finger linger there as Mary Todd sighed underneath him. His erection waned as his hand explored, but his curiosity was sated. Like a blind man, he saw with his fingers.

In the year that followed Jake's birth, they went to a marriage counselor, a sex therapist, and finally, a doe-eyed, extremely short woman in Times Square who specialized in post-birth, male sexual trauma. She reminded Ted of Dr. Ruth and he often had to stop himself from breaking into nervous laughter during their sessions with her. He did this by thinking about death. Death, Ted would think, frowning in concentration. We all will die, we all will die, was his mantra. Laura and he spent a lot of time there watching explicit, touchy-feely, sexual-technique videos, while the therapist pointed to a close-up of a penis thrusting in and out of a vagina and said stuff like, "See? It's not a bad thing, the vagina. It's friendly!" Indeed, the vagina had once been his friend. And to a certain extent, the vagina became his friend again. Only on occasion now did he become erectally challenged, so to speak. Only on occasion was he haunted with the specter of Jake's birth. Henry, the new baby, was born while he waited outside. His wife had an epidural and read magazines throughout the labor. The Dr. Ruth look-alike had convinced Laura that Ted needed some boundaries, and that this did not mean he was a bad husband, nor did it mean he was an unloving father. Ted was so thankful for this, so thankful for the support he didn't even know he needed, so thankful that someone had articulated what he felt, that she became a powerful goddess in his dreams. He dreamt of her often, even though he couldn't remember her name. In his dreams, she stroked his head and her voice was the soothing voice of his mother.

The white-gray nothing outside of the tiny window was changing. Bits of land and water became discernible. Ted looked down at his drink. It was gone. At some point, the flight attendant had put a little box with a sandwich, an apple, and a cookie on the tray next to him. Where had he been? He rubbed his eyes. Had he slept? San Francisco was approaching. Suddenly, he felt drunk and sad. He missed Jake, he missed the drooly, gurgly new Henry. And in a lesser way he missed his bossy, aging, somewhat boring wife. She was, after all, the mother of his children. She was a decent, hardworking mother. He picked up the sandwich and started to eat it. He would catch up on sleep in his eco-sensitive hotel. He would drink maybe a little too much at the parties, but not enough to behave inappropriately. He would not get laid, this he knew for certain, because he truly wasn't interested in acquainting himself with the vagina of some strange person. And when he returned home, what to do with Laura's straightforward longings directed toward him? Her foot on his crotch at night, while they lounged on the couch, watching TV? Said or unsaid, he had grown to love this woman. He did not always like her, this was true. He had stared deep into her, watched her produce life, and it had changed him. He knew, like never before, that he would die, Laura too would die, and that even his children were temporary beasts of the Earth themselves. His job, their house, basketball, preschool, and shopping—it was all just waiting, killing time. And while he waited? He would do his best. That's all he could do.

The flight attendant came down the aisle, picking up people's food boxes and accompanying trash. Ted, after wiping up the little drips of boozy tomato juice from the tray, neatly stuck the napkin and the tiny vodka bottle into the empty cup. He was trying to be helpful. He lifted his arms to her with his garbage, to save her the trouble of reaching over for everything. "Thank you," he said, his eyes wet with vodka, and the plane continued to descend.

Virgin Snow

Jill Bialosky

It happened, not as we had hoped,
underneath the stars, or along the banks
of a lake, or in an empty pasture,
but shut in amidst a virgin
snowstorm. It was among the coats and cast-offs
on the bed in one of our parents' bedrooms,
having vacated the premise for some exotic island
just, we naïvely imagined, so we might have our tryst.
The sensation, if I had to describe it,
was like stepping over the edge
of a cliff into water and not quite knowing
how deep the fall or whether we'd surface again.
I wish I could say it was sublime,
but here is what I remember:
the smoke and liquor like a halo
over the room, the scratch
of his rough jeans on my thighs,
and the parting, swift as an axe
splitting wood in half.
Downstairs the party in full
motion as if Bacchus himself were hosting
the celebration fully aware that when the ball dropped
to announce the beginning of the new year,
sailed down the long dark tunnel of Eros,
what temptation would lead to.
Mind you, there were no bells,
no feelings of enlightenment.

OPEN CITY

Later when I was alone in my bed
I thought one thing: What if it was true,
that in the end he was irrelevant?
I waited all night but not once did I hear
the nightingale fill the sky with reason,
or glimpse the sun muscle through the sky
to announce the birth of the miraculous.

Landscape with Child

Jill Bialosky

Here I am for once on the other side.
Let me tell you what it's like.
There is barely a ripple on the lake.
Rain, yes, but we crave it, the temperate sound of water
on glass, on the wooden beams of our roof
and the sound of trucks on the road beyond the farm
breaking the perfect silence.
Our child sleeps now mostly through the night,
and when he comes into our bed we don't mind.
The horses in the barn have all quieted,
allayed by having endured last evening's storm.
We wake to the riot of birds
and we have vowed that we will learn their names
and families. It won't do to say the red bird,
or the blue one.
It is the same with these trees:
white pine, spruce, hemlock.
Yesterday a deer and her fawn crept behind a stand of them,
the fawn nursed, and the deer watched ahead,
on the lookout for danger so they might not come to harm.
Still we live in fear, but it is this field
of black-eyed Susans and bleeding hearts,
not their beauty, but how well they live without us,
we have come to depend on.
The deer and her fawn did not linger.
They shot through the open field
to the brambles and brush on the other side.

OPEN CITY

Who knew what would become of them.
We have learned to spot chicory and a spray of lavender.

Raping the Nest

Jill Bialosky

We found the blue small eggs inside the intricate nests
painstakingly made of twigs, hair, and down,

powerfully held them in the palm of our hands
like something fragile we might crush.

We were young, bored girls stealing eggs from a robin's nest.
I held one egg and shook it. There was a viable

tight little knot of life hot inside.
I wanted to crack it open to see what made it beat

so wildly in my hand. Above us in the sharp
summer air flocks swooped down making V's in the sky.

The days blended carelessly from one to the other
but on this afternoon, because there was a boy I desired

I did not care what would live or die or one day
fly into the air like the soul released from the body.

In the outline of the farthest branches I imagined his hand
on my face, the long complicated veins on his arms.

"Watch out for stray bullets," a young cop flirted, as they sidled past the saw-horses.

"Jerkoff," Marcy shouted back, "watch out for stray bricks."

(Cole, page 205)

Equivocal Landscape

Toru Hayashi

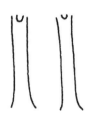

Safari Eyes

Sam Brumbaugh

KATE SAT UP, SUDDENLY AWAKE. SHE FELT A STRANGE UNEASE inside her, a sense of her past, or what she could recall, as silver, mercurial droplets falling, falling then splitting off her cupped hands and onto the ground at her feet as she watched. Slipping away like a fallen martini. She touched her mug. It was cold. Bird noises. She looked out the window. Crows, pecking the ground between quick, jerk-necked surveillances. Like those men in Nairobi, she thought. They just don't want anyone unlike them around. She looked farther out over the yellow field, rutted with tire tracks from the Fitzgerald boy's minibike, past the lone black tree, black in any light, past the tire hanging from it, to the fence at the slope of the neighbors.' She looked at their willow tree and rusting jungle gym and soundless dogs. They had dogs there that needed more room, that ran lean and pressing against the fence like caged panthers. One day she'd go cut a hole.

She could hear Ruth moving around downstairs, fixing breakfast. Same old day ahead in the ranch house. Blue outside, blue sky evacuating white clouds. Same old tray coming with the tea, juice, toast and the paper cup of pills. She felt like getting some air. She'd put on her shoes and coat and walk the yard. She'd put on her dress. She sighed, wanting to feel some kind of movement, but the sigh lingered and she felt only stress involving cash outlay.

Down the slope of the pillow she noticed her blue water cup on its side, and then the wet edge of the throw rug. She looked at the chair. It was empty. Ruth, sitting there last night, had knocked over the cup when she'd gotten up to get the novel to read aloud. Ruth hadn't noticed and Kate hadn't said anything. Kate remembered that as she'd gone to sleep, Ruth had switched to the Bible.

Kate had opened her eyes. "Please go back to the novel, Ruth."

"May I ask you a question?"

"Yes," she'd said.

"Guy, your husband, was he religious?"

"Guy was a pilot. And, well, yes. Yes he was."

Ruth had folded the Bible over her fingers. "Do you hear from him?"

"I get a postcard once in a while, aside from the checks."

Ruth had looked past her.

"He did try."

Ruth had remained silent.

"And besides that," Kate had said, "he pays for you."

"She should hate me," Kate thought. "Did I really say that?" She remembered seeing Guy the day after he'd asked her to marry him. His black hair, black brow, and razor cheeks. He was so stern, and that beautiful, lazy self-content that welled her love for him into envy. They'd gone to the theater near the college to see *McCabe and Mrs. Miller,* and she'd held Guy's hand there in the movie's strange, interior orange hue of preordained separations between people who might even want to be a little in love. But she'd been confused by the plot. McCabe's slow, oddly determined movement through trees and deep snow, and then Julie Christie's opium jar. What had made her go to that? Where was the voice-over with all that had happened to her? She'd asked him these questions afterward and he'd just said he didn't think that it was a good Western.

The light of day felt long already. The tray had still not arrived and Kate was already tired from the brief, waking considerations. A bath? It was time to wash her hair, but the red soap gave the bath water a tan color as if her skin itself was dyeing it. And she needed to buy stamps and to buy stamps she needed to dress right, not in her nightshirt and ratty slippers. And then to buy stamps she had to face the lady with the sad, fat face who chewed her up with politeness within the thirty-second purchase exchange. Above all she had to wait for the will to move, to dress. Did she have money in the drawer? It was the third and Guy's check would come by the fifth. On the fifth she could do all the big errands. She could do the small ones today. The stamps.

"Ruth," she yelled.

"Right Sweetie," came Ruth's voice from downstairs. "Now I've just got your tray going, all right?"

"Of course. Of course that's all right."

The tray came and she swallowed the pills and lay back. She remembered the itchiness of her wedding dress, of the brown August grass. It had been so hot in Ohio, so flat. The town park Guy had chosen for the ceremony had felt as mysterious as a newly mown lawn. He'd been there in his military whites. Going to be a pilot. "Oh his clean, careful motion." His hand around her waist as they'd stood greeting the guests. A brass band in the park rotunda sending them off to a safari honeymoon.

She did miss him. What had she done? It was all right that day. Too hot but all right.

Kate pulled herself up against the headboard and looked around the room. The day had grayed the white walls. She took the sweater from the chair and put it on. It had been her grandmother's and its tight weave was constructed with a patience not usually available anymore. It was a good, bedridden sweater, it made her feel older, done with more of life's comings and goings, and this relaxed her. On the bedside table was a lamp covered by a red silk scarf. She took the scarf and tied it snugly over her hair. She tried to read, but as usual, the words wouldn't settle still on the page, and she lay back. She felt the shape of the pillows around her head and the rough outline of the knit birds on the quilt, felt where she was in bed without opening her eyes. Kate wanted to remember Africa by feel, more than just sight. Sight hadn't been trustworthy there. But nothing, not even Guy, had been trustworthy there. If he had been, she thought, then maybe she wouldn't have brought the illness back with her. But then again, as the admitting doctor had abruptly concluded after listening to her, "It's not the sort of illness you just pick up in Africa. You carry it with you everywhere," he'd said, "like a bad heart."

And then Guy had left without asking the doctor any other questions, and she'd been in that ward for three weeks and had been incapable of asking about herself, or Guy, in any way.

She remembered how it had started, waking up on the plane as the captain announced that they'd just come over the African continent and suddenly feeling, weeks early, as if she were about to have her period. She rested her hands on the coarse stubble of the seat. Her palms were moist and she could feel the upraised black dots in the economy-class material stir, as though they might break off from under her palms. She stood as their descent was announced, and walked down the aisle to the bathroom. She locked herself in. Despite the pounding of the stewardess and Guy, she hid in the small bathroom as the plane touched down and, with its human tube, locked onto the Nairobi terminal.

In their hotel room in Nairobi there was a framed photo of a butchered rhino. Or Kate guessed it was a rhino. It could have been an antelope or a warthog, for that matter. It was a mess of an animal on the dirt around a watering hole. Split, cavernous insides with a curved dome of ribs protruding like the opera house in Sydney. Something kept the vultures at bay, they only stared. Kate was tired from the wedding, the flights, and tried to take a nap, but the photo loomed. A maid came in. Kate pretended to be asleep so that the maid would leave. The maid bustled around a bit, speaking softly to herself. Then the maid was quiet, and she could feel her undulating breath close by. A whiff of rose hand cream and Kate thought she felt a hair being plucked off her head.

The next morning they were heading out of Nairobi on a day safari to a private hunting ranch. The Land Rover driver bobbed hard under his walkman, harder than any possible rhythm. The city outside seemed silent and unchanging. People walked looking straight ahead. Everything ahead seemed unmapped and it gave her an intimation of fear in the air. She'd initially mistook it for malaise. There was a faint tang of sewage underneath the smells of smoke and exhaust. There were dogs, concrete huts, and muddy slashes of footpath. The ashtray on her side was jammed full with a dark-green gum. Guy was reading from the green Michelin guidebook. As the car stopped for pedestrians, Kate glanced out the window. There were two men at a café table who seemed identical. Everybody around them was black, but to her they had no color in their skin, in their clothes. No color at all. It seemed that they weren't really there, and she looked away. She looked at the driver as he inched the car through the crowd. She looked back at the café. One of the men was looking at her, surprised. She was scared and turned to Guy, who was smoking and flipping the guidebook pages. The car began to speed up and she glanced back again. The man was now staring at her openmouthed. He held a palm out as if he wanted to stop her. As she turned around to Guy the man seemed to evaporate in the corner of her eye. "Oh my God, oh my God. Please turn around."

The Land Rover stopped. Guy stared at her. "What is it?"

"Those men."

"Which men?" he asked.

She looked back again. They were there. "At the café, the ones staring at me."

"There's nobody staring at you," Guy said.

"There," she pointed, and began to bang her fists against the window.

"You're making a scene."

"But you see them?" she turned and insisted to Guy.

"The men at the café?"

"Yes. Yes Guy, those two men." But she did not look back.

"There are a lot of men there," he said. "They are all staring at you now because you are making a scene."

Kate asked to go back to the hotel. On the way back she asked the driver to stop again. "I need air," she said. "I need water." And she stepped out of the Land Rover and into the crowd. As she made her way into a crowded market, her head began whizzing, her mouth dry with dust and the market's sudden, choking smells of smoke, manure, and cloves. She saw the African sunlight stretching like caramel, hardening suddenly, and then snapping dizzily into thousands of bright, sharp bits. Then the air cleared and she noticed a man in a tin and plywood stall full of tourist knickknacks looking at her. He wore a purple wrap and a dirty, collared, white oxford. Then, across the street, she saw a group of young men on a roof. They stood around a thin plume of smoke. She walked up to the man in the stall, pointed and asked, "Why? Why does that happen?"

They looked at each other across a counter lined with dozens of wood carved animals. He said a few words in Swahili, paused when there was no response, then asked politely if she was American.

"Yes."

He adjusted his wool, Rasta-colored cap. "I will go to school there when I finish school here."

"You are a student?"

"I am halfway learning English, but have no more money to study."

"Oh," she said distantly, her eyes looking past him, "I don't have much of that either."

"Please I do not ask that." He said, and went on to tell her it would be a great help to his English studies if he could begin a correspondence with her.

But her eyes were fixed on the plywood wall behind him. Next to some sort of framed manifesto was the photo of the rhino corpse. She stared at the photo, then at him. She told him about the two men in the café as she pulled her eyelids shut with her forefingers.

"I can help you," he said with a quiet seriousness, "I can help you understand these things only African people should see."

She opened her eyes and looked at him. He handed her a pen and two pieces of paper, one with his name and address already written out, and one blank. She scribbled her name and address on the blank one and handed both back to him.

He laughed, and again handed her his address. She took it. He pocketed hers and then, in a sudden, business-like manner, bounced a finger along the heads of the carved animals. "This is the best teak," he said in a bright pitch. "Lion? Zebra? Boar?"

"So you know I saw those two men?" she insisted.

"Kate?" Guy said, coming up behind her.

"Lion? Elephant? Boar? Bird?"

"Kate, where did you go?"

"Fish? Crocodile? Boar? Bird?"

"You know I saw them." She stared at the man, ignoring Guy. "What do they want? What about that photo behind you? I've seen that, too."

Without looking at the photo, he said to her, "That's just another dead rhino." And then he turned his back to her and left the booth. Another man stepped in and took his place.

"Wait," she said, and began to pull bills out of her passport wallet.

Guy's hard blue eyes focused on her with a sudden, confounded suspicion. "Kate," he said.

The man walked swiftly away down a dirt alley. She followed, bills in hand. Guy tugged at her arm as she turned into the dirt alley. The man went up a flight of stairs and into a square, cinder-block building. "Let's stop this right now," Guy said.

She shook her head, shook free of him, and her hair came loose across her eyes as she rushed up the stairs. At the top, she pulled open the door. The man from the stall sat on a low stool between two large, Ethiopian-looking women. He halted their conversation and looked up at her and Guy. The floor was concrete and the room hot and menacingly airless. The wall was lined with stacks of plywood wrapped in wire, plastic bags of charcoal, a shovel, and a large pile of red swaths. The man stood and angrily pointed at her. "You gonna put somebody in big trouble!"

Then he took a step forward and accidentally knocked something metallic across the floor. Looking down, Kate saw that it was a stack of crushed tin cups and spoons which had been tied together with string. The man ripped off his cap and approached her as his dreadlocks tumbled out like snakes. Guy took her arm. Still clenching the bills, Kate looked at the man and began to moan. "Why are you angry? You're angry? You said you'd help me."

He shook his head. "Not supposed to come in here, not supposed to come in."

She wiped tears from her face. "But the men at the café, you said you'd help me."

He reached down to take her hand, unfolded her fingers, and took her money.

Guy grabbed her roughly around the shoulders and pulled her back down the steps. He held her elbow so hard that her arm went numb to the shoulder. He pushed her ahead, back up the alley toward the market square. She felt heavy-legged and drugged, as if she were running on lizards, on snakes, mashing them under her shoes. They pushed through the slow-moving throng. Someone dug a finger into her ear. She wrenched her head free, ducking lower. She felt faint. She could smell the vapid, pine odor of Lysol. It exaggerated the open air stench of sweat and dung. They stopped at a broken fountain in the square's center. Guy looked around. The Land Rover was gone. He grabbed her shoulders. "You just almost got the both of us killed," he said, with more menace than anything she'd seen or heard that day.

"One of those women was holding a gun under her dress."

He held her shoulders and stared at her. "What's wrong with you?" Then he looked around again. "Give me that piece of paper he gave you. Where's that piece of paper?"

Guy saw that there were faces in the periphery, watching. Plans were stoking within the slouches of some of the onlookers. "Give me the paper," he repeated.

She shook her head, tucked it in her waistband. "Why did he say he'd help me?"

He turned her to face him. "What are you talking about? What on Earth are you talking about? You went up to him."

"He knew something."

"He knew he had something when he saw you."

"They have a hair of mine, Guy."

"Oh come on."

She stared at him, hair matted on her cheek.

"Look," he said, his voice suddenly low, sensing the crowd receding and an empty space growing around the two of them, "Something's up. Let's get out of here, let's get a taxi back. You need sleep."

"Sleep!" she cried, and stepped back out of his grip. "Sleep's a horse! A goddamned running horse! My hands are full of its hair now." She knelt and scrubbed her palms with the camel-colored dirt. Then she casually lay down on her side in the crowded marketplace, like a local curled up for a nap in the bustle.

Two men, one big and thick-necked with a hand deep in his pocket, stepped forward from the ring around her. Guy stepped back. The crowd was quiet now. The thick-necked man went down on a knee and reached into Kate's waistband for the piece of paper. He knew right where it was. As he withdrew it, she jerked awake and slapped his hand. He stood up, dumbly rubbing his hand, then pocketed the paper. He looked down at her and took a step, over her now.

"Wait," she said.

He stepped forward, straddling her. She brushed her hair away from her face, pulled herself back along the ground. "Wait," she was saying. "Just wait."

There is the smell of Lysol and Kate heard Ruth moving around the room. The Lysol is temporarily shielding all the more durable smells. Despite Ruth, there are still the faint smells of Guy: talc, sweet onion, and wet wool.

She opened her eyes.

Ruth looked up from her dusting. "I let you sleep. No need pushing you if you want to sleep."

"I don't want to sleep anymore," she said. "I didn't want to sleep."

"I'm sorry dear. Do you want some tea?"

"I can't *feel* like doing anything else. It's immoral the amount of time I sleep."

"You need it," Ruth said. "It's the most important thing now. It gives you peace of mind."

"I need a piece for my mind."

Ruth collected her rags and sprays and put them into her pail. "I'll just go and make the tea."

"Oh Ruth, it's a joke." Kate said, breaking into a wide smile. She pushed aside the covers, slid into her slippers, and crossed the room to where Ruth stood, one hand on the broom handle, the other going in small cartwheels in the air between them. Kate put a hand on Ruth's shoulder and gave her a kiss on the cheek.

Flanked by the two men, Guy and she were pressed into a small car, which sped out of the downtown and the tourist zones. They pulled up to a low, white building on a contagiously rowdy slum block. They were led upstairs where there was a bar and two windows with down-turned slots letting dusty rectangles of light onto the floor. The driver stayed at the door. A small, bald, walnut of a man stood behind the bar, watching her. His forehead was large, his eyes messily red and tense, and he seemed to have been waiting for some time. He scared her. The thick-necked man from the square sat in a dark-wood, semicircle booth. He was dressed in a skinny black tie and frayed black suit, the material cheap enough to let the light rest faint and oily on his shoulders. Kate and Guy sat down across from him. His eyes were buttons of tar in yellowed milk. He did not look at Kate.

"Here," he said brightly to Guy. "Here we have a problem."

She looked at the man. "Don't you smile like that."

Surprised, and with a flash of annoyance, the man said to Guy. "You might consider telling your young wife—" And then he stopped, caught himself, and smiled grandly, sympathetically at Guy.

Kate continued to stare at the man. "You're just a big bowl of porridge. Your mouth is full of porridge."

The man laughed, looked at Guy as if appreciative "Here we call it 'ugali.'"

"Your mouth is full of ugali, ugali mush."

He turned and rolled his wrist back toward the bartender. "Let us have some tea and some other items and start again." He looked back at Guy. "Or some beer. Would you like some beer?"

Guy was staring nervously at the tabletop, pinching his bottom lip between his forefinger and thumb as if he couldn't quite catch up to what was happening.

The man looked back again and asked the red-eyed bartender for peanuts. The bartender came over, and without glancing up, set them down, red and shelled. The big man smiled and took a few. For a long moment they all stared at the bowl.

Kate leaned toward him. "You have that smile. Big as can be. What's your mouth really full of? You smile as if you're not a problem for us."

The big man unfolded his thick, gold-ringed fingers and pulled out the piece of paper. "The problem?" he said, still chewing slightly and narrowing a glutinous stare on Guy. "The problem, we think, is hers."

Kate looked past the man. The bartender's eyes were fixed on her. She looked back down at the bowl of red peanuts, withdrew back into the booth.

"What does your wife want with Somali man?" the man said to Guy.

"What Somali man? What are you talking about?"

"My friend, we have fragile borders here in Kenya." He held up the paper he'd found in her waistband, read out loud the name. "Jecko Dube, he a Somali man. His people, with the red bands, those are dangerous people who are your friends and who you are giving the money to."

"Wait, what?" Guy stammered. "We're tourists here."

"Tourists? Yes?"

"Yes."

He pulled out another piece of paper. Held it up for Guy to see. "This your wife's name, yes? Your wife's writing?"

Guy leaned over and looked at it. "Yes."

"Well, they go right to jail now, your friends, and we talk to them in jail so we know soon." He scooped up peanuts, sifted some of the red rind off with his fat fingers, and tossed them into his mouth. "We find this address, see, on Somali man."

He leaned back and smiled at Guy with a hard, cool glee. "You a military man?"

"Are you?"

"You know about jail here? You go to the jail here and people, no matter what your embassy, they don't know where you are."

"Look, we're on a honeymoon. On a safari. You know that."

"Maybe you Agency man."

Guy shook his head. "This is unbelievable."

"What does your wife want with Somali man?"

"What are you selling here? What do you want?"

"What does your wife want with Somali man?"

"What do you want with us?"

The man looked at Kate, then back at Guy. "We sell insulation."

He reached for more peanuts and said in a severe but polite voice, "I cannot ask you to ignore our customs when you go looking for things only African people should see."

"You're not scaring me," she said right back to him. "The red bands are for processions, the tins and spoons are people's things, for their funerals. I saw that in the English newspaper at the hotel." She looked at Guy. "They weren't Somali, those people. He's not police. Don't you see, Guy?"

Suddenly calm, she studied him for a moment. "What is it you see, Guy?" His face possessed an emotional—moral even—ambivalence that bordered on retardation. Would he still, after all this, see an animal, harbor bland hopes of walking up to an animal and shooting it in the head?

She reached across the table to take Guy's hand but the man took her hand before she could pull back. He pressed his hands around hers. She felt his callused skin, the warm sweat between the wide creases in his palms. "A funeral," he said, gripping her hand, "passes right before your eyes," and his hands burst open and fluttered upwards for mystical emphasis.

Guy leaned over to her and took her hand. "It does not matter," he whispered, "if they are police, secret police, or plain criminals. It's a setup. From the market. It doesn't matter, you understand? The guy in the market stall marked you soon as he saw you."

Guy reached for his wallet.

"But not the two men at the café, not them," she said. "That was different. That was something else."

The man was rubbing his hands together. "We merely want to insulate you," he said.

Guy drew out a travelers check.

He shook his head. "No, not that."

"It's all I have," Guy said.

"No," he said grimly. "You come with me to the bank now."

"Guy," Kate said, "do not leave me here."

"She has to come too."

"No, " the man said. "She stays."

"Then take the travelers checks." Guy offered.

The man laughed. "She stays. You don't run off. When we withdraw, she can go as she please."

"She comes to the bank."

The bartender had moved around to the front of the bar and was leaning against it. The man reached into his pocket and lay a gun on the table. "Are you ready, military man?"

"Guy," she pleaded, "don't you leave me here. Guy!"

The dinner tray sat on the nightstand; tea, the pills for sleep, a small can of grapefruit juice and a bacon and tomato sandwich. Kate did not hear Ruth downstairs. It was dark outside. Ruth had gone home. It was difficult to keep her eyes open. She'd close them and again the dreams would come. A train leaving a besieged city, a train she could have made if she'd ran. But the airplanes had been criss-crossing the sky all night, nose-diving into the city, just ahead of her in big concussion booms and slow-motion balls of fire. Hearty kamikazes, Guy and those young pilots. Going out with the yahoos, the trusted noise. Guy had always talked so loud, the more volume the more truth. Kate opened her eyes but against her will they closed again, closed back into the false heaviness in her veins. Against the dreams that came she said to herself: "These aren't my dreams; these aren't my dreams."

Lying there alone in their newlywed bedroom, the memory of her last day with Guy rose up out of her as if it were a ghost. She watched herself as a ghost go downstairs, her ghost in her cocktail dress. She made herself a drink and walked the halls of their brick ranch house, listening to its sourceless creaks and knocks. She sat on the arm of the sofa with her untouched drink and stared out the front window, down the wide lawn sloping to the road. Across the road was a lawn that sloped up to an exact same brick ranch house. It was a mirror-image specter that made her go cold with an instant of unutterable images: a canopy of stretched flesh strewn with chicken bones, clumps of gelatinous blood, and the sucked-clean, white knob of a joint.

She went to the garage, sat in the car with the drink in her hand. She turned on the engine. She was scared, felt as if inside, her determined spirit of solitude had frozen into a blue-nothing sea. The car engine was running but she was waiting, the first push of exhaust coming through the vents. She couldn't bear the McLellons' party, the African honeymoon pictures Guy was no doubt showing despite everything that had happened there. She was scared but she didn't need her drink. If she was at the McLellons' she would need a drink. The engine seemed to rev itself and for an instant the headlights brightened. They were fixed on the lawn mower, the cases of ginger ale and beer, a hoe, and the wedding presents that they hadn't even bothered to open when they'd gotten back. She looked into her glass. What was it, she thought, that made it so she didn't want her drink?

The Key Lounge nagged at her. She'd passed it once a few days before on one of the time-emptying drives she'd been taking every day since Africa. It was familiar, or at least it seemed a place she was supposed to go to. A visit she had overlooked. But it was just a shabby bar in the tumbleweed and trash-strewn part of town and she'd definitely never been in. She should go there now. The exhaust was getting thick, as if a dark, vaporous part of her had escaped and was trying to take her along. Kate rolled down the window. She'd been dreaming up a man at that lounge, a bluesman and a barber, dreaming of running with him under the ice where the water was black and the animals translucent.

When she'd been balled up under that booth after Guy had gone to the bank with the man, her skin outraged and burning where the bartender with the messy red eyes had been groping her, she'd felt that push through something, felt that bluesman's sudden presence there. His judicial, staring presence. "You're there!" she'd said aloud. She thought this must have saved her.

Why else had that bartender, with all his shuddering weight onto her, suddenly stopped and looked into her eyes? Why else had he gotten up looking startled, buckled his pants and left? Why else had she not been raped? She coughed in the exhaust. She felt an odd, uncomfortable rush pass through her. Her eyes burned. That man was at that lounge, she should go there now. She leaned out and pressed the garage door button on the wall. She rolled the window back up and backed out into a velvety orange, suburban dusk. She passed the McLellons'. She stopped, reversed. The McLellon's was a white stucco and glass house on stilts with water nowhere to be found nearby. In the large, central window she could see—the gold and ruby sloped backs of the cocktail guests shifting among bobbing faces like a liquid Klimt painting. She leaned across the passenger seat and tried to spot Guy in the window. A man saw her and waved. She accelerated away, but took a right turn and came back around the block. She parked where Guy could see. She sat in the car and waited.

Guy came out a few minutes later. He paused at the door, the McLellons' patting him on the back, looking at her and then back to him. Then they got on the highway and headed downtown. They exited in the black part of town and she drove around until they'd found the Key Lounge. He'd agreed to go with her but hadn't believed it existed.

They sat in a red booth up front by the window, drinking powdery, acidic whiskey sours. The bar was empty. Guy was talking. "Don't think that it's certain you can trust me about helping you, whatever it is that has been happening to you. I can't understand it, but I want to help you, and I do have an idea."

Kate tried to tell him some of what had happened to her, but the words wouldn't come right and she got flustered. She looked out the window, studying the tattered, piano-key awning, broken and yellowed like teeth.

"Look," he said hesitantly. "Kate. There's a place the McLellon's know of. A charter hospital. It's a good place, they say. It has military coverage. I want to take you there, now maybe, to talk to someone."

She thought she saw a movement outside. "Look," she pointed haltingly.

He looked out the window to the motionless street. He took a deep breath. "Are you all right?" He asked.

She shook her head.

"Are you not all right?"

She shook her head.

He laughed a little, to himself, and looked into his drink. "All right," he said to himself.

They sat there for a moment, silent. Then, reaching down into his briefcase, Guy said with a forced smile, "I want to show you something, it might cheer you up."

She covered her eyes with her hands and smiled. She heard him shuffling through his papers. She slid her hands down off her eyes. The honeymoon photos and various African postcards were fanned out across the table. Amidst photos of the two of them, there was the postcard of the animal corpse.

"Look," he said when he got to it, "of all the things in Africa, the long bones of what's left, the long ears, it looks like a kangaroo."

"It's a rhino," she said. "Don't you even remember?"

"Well it doesn't say anything on the back."

The bluesman, the barber, she knew, was not there. "Guy," she said. "Would you ask for the check please?"

"You want to go?"

Kate nodded, looking out the window to the moon.

"Good. I don't much like this place. Don't know why on Earth . . ." He shook his head, and then signaled to the bar.

"Look," she said, pointing out the window. The moon was gone.

"There's nothing there," he said without looking up, counting dollars and laying down a tip.

He led her out of the lounge and back to the car. They drove out of the neighborhood, and as the car momentarily glided on one of the last pieces of exposed trolley rail, Kate saw the neighborhood below, the pawn shops, Goodwills, churches, and liquor stores mutate into orange, octagonal lights.

Before his sole hit the pavement a half dozen times
The world had ended
    (Samton, page 191)

Directions to My House

Evie McKenna

And all night a low voice chides me
(Wetzsteon, page 285)

Poem to Beer

David Starkey

Like a bee on the tip of my tongue,
its tiny wings buzz.
Already my lids languish,
my inner anvil's muffled in velvet.
The sour smell finds its way
to my throat, cold aluminum
tingles my fingertips.
I taste the Elgar on the radio.

Gerald Locklin, you and I drank warm beer
in the public houses of Hull at noon.
Language, too, hummed
in The Star and Garter,
The Spurn Head Arms. The bitter
filled our mouths with words.
"Right, all right?" the bartender asked
as we stumbled into the bright
fist of afternoon closing time.
But rather than take a dive
we rose like martyrs above the streets.

Beer was our parachute.

Today, I awake from my nap queasy,
dreaming of dishwater.
Securus judicat orbis terrarum,
said St. Augustine as he conquered

OPEN CITY

the world with chatter, pious
and sober, the hem
of his robe winking the gold of lager.

Casseroles

Heather Larimer

CLAIRE HAD NEVER NOTICED THE PROLIFERATION OF BLACK-berries along her carpool route. They were everywhere, snaking through white fences, loops and tangles among the orderly planes of pavement and gates and boxy wooden houses. In the backseat, her son Max, the eldest and therefore the resident sage, corrected his sister Tessa about the politics of Sunnyslope Elementary while the other two children sat in silence, lulled by the gentle dips and peaks of the road. Claire watched her passengers in the rearview mirror.

"Mrs. Cairns is not the meanest teacher. Everyone knows it's Mrs. Kroeger. I can hear her yelling at her class all the way down the hall. She wears really pointy shoes, too," Max said.

Tessa opened her mouth as if to say something, but instead grabbed her foot and placed it on the seat. Claire could see that her braids were uneven and one of her hair ribbons frayed and untied. How could she have missed that this morning, especially when last week her husband had gently noted that the children were looking a bit unkempt? After checking the road, Claire noticed that the quiet kindergartner, who was looking particularly dazed—or was that car-sick?—had something blue smeared around his mouth. She hoped it wasn't ink, but didn't really want to ask. He belonged to some-one else.

The minivan approached Harding's Horse Stables and Tessa gasped "Horsies." A wide vista appeared on the right: horses, green rolling hills, and a large stable with a corrugated metal roof. As they sped past, an enormous patch of blackberries pressed against a split-log fence obscured the field.

"You say that everyday," Max said. "Horsies," he imitated.

Tessa replied, "So what?"

The blackberries ended at a gravel driveway, and briefly the hills peeked through until a long, manicured hedge, leaves blurred by speed, sprang up to block the view again. All this parallel motion, things popping up and dropping away, and then, an unexpected movement. A small, brown animal shot from beneath the hedge and straight toward the car. Claire stomped on her brakes, flinging her arm instinctively in front of the empty passenger's seat. The brakes squealed, then there was a hollow thud against the right tire. Claire shifted into park and climbed out of the driver's seat. She crossed in front of the van and saw that several feet ahead, on the road's gravel shoulder, lay a beagle. Blood oozed from the mouth of the convulsing dog, and stained the white fuzz on its chin. Its dark eyes were locked on the cuff of Claire's khaki pants.

"Oh Jesus," she said. A wail came from the van. Tessa and Max were crowded together, hanging their heads out the passenger's window. Behind them, the other two children squirmed to see what was happening outside. Tessa screamed again. Her face was flushed and wet with tears. She opened the door and lowered herself onto the road.

Claire kneeled on the asphalt and placed a hand on the beagle's side, in the little hollow behind its small rib cage. The russet fur was surprisingly warm as it twitched beneath her palm. The sun glinted off her diamond ring and tiny spangles of light moved across the dying animal.

Tessa sobbed and leaned over the dog. Clear mucus dribbled from her nose. She wiped it on her sleeve.

Max sat in the passenger's seat staring straight ahead, the door still wide open. He turned to Claire and said, "It's dead, isn't it Mom?"

Claire peered beyond his head and saw the other children sitting rigidly in their seats. "Shut the door," she said to Max. "Tessa, get in the van." They got into the car and Claire backed it onto the shoulder. She said, "Max, watch them. All of you need to stay in the van."

Claire walked back to the gravel driveway before the hedge. The pink farmhouse it led to looked so tidy, she decided not to disturb it.

Instead, she followed the road to the neighboring horse farm and headed for the covered stables. She passed several dark horses before she spotted a person crouched beside a stately Arabian. As she moved closer to the horse, she watched a woman in dusty jeans brush its haunches, smoothing its shiny coat with her free hand after each brush stroke.

She noticed Claire and stood up. "Can I help you?" she said.

"Yes, I just hit a dog. With my car."

"Oh my," she said, holding her palm as if to keep the news at a safe distance.

"It was a beagle. I'm pretty sure it's dead."

"A beagle? You mean little Jenny? Oh, God." She twisted a large, football-shaped turquoise ring on her middle finger.

"Do you know the dog?"

"Yeah, she's from up the hill. She likes our black Lab, Butch." Deep vertical lines ran down either side of her mouth. She shook her head.

"Do you know the owner's name or phone number or anything?"

"Her dad's name is Brad. His number's 842-5051."

Claire pulled her cellular phone from her purse and dialed. When the phone rang, she felt faint and leaned against a wooden beam. She closed her eyes and saw the beagle's slightly open mouth again, the blood on its white chin. An answering machine picked up and a voice said, "Hi, this is Brad. Leave a message." Claire listened to the faint static of the line for a moment before shutting off the phone. She looked at the woman, whose eyes focused somewhere around Claire's right shoulder, as if she couldn't bring herself to look at her face.

"He's not home," Claire said. She clutched the phone and lowered her head. She pinched the bridge of her nose between her thumb and forefinger.

"I can talk to him," the horsewoman said. "I'll wait till he gets home." She twisted her ring. "He knows me."

Claire left her phone number with the woman. "Please have him call," she said. She turned to leave, but then spun around, adding, "What about the dog?"

"I can carry her into the stable. I'll keep her until Brad gets here."

Late that night, Tessa slipped into Claire's bedroom and wiggled between her father and Claire. "Mom," she whispered, "are you going to hell for killing that dog?"

"No, Tessa," Steve said through his teeth.

Claire rolled over with her back to them both and stared at the spherical light fixture in the hallway. She pretended it was a hidden camera and that she could see her own face lit demonically. She knew that by now the horsewoman had told the man his dog was dead, that a woman named Claire had killed it. Was he lying awake, paralyzed by the news? Was he wishing Claire would die instead? Her heart beat faster and she tried to think of something else, something ordinary and businesslike, but the voice that normally recited to-do lists in her head just hissed like radio static.

The next day, when the children were at school, Claire ignored the half-finished baby blanket she was knitting for Tessa's former day-care supervisor and skipped the monthly Junior League luncheon to begin a new project. She consulted the casserole section of her favorite cookbook, a classic, a bridal-shower gift from Steve's mother. After Claire's father's death when she was fourteen, casseroles had appeared en masse. Some were accompanied by women who shook their heads and cupped her cheeks, others magically appeared on the front steps as if made by elves. After several days of continued deliveries, the mostly uneaten pans of layered sauces, vegetables, and starches had been transferred to the Deepfreeze. They languished there until those nights of her mother's disabling migraines, when Claire and her brother would pick a casserole at random from the freezer and pop it in the oven. After reading several recipes, Claire decided that lasagna was safe for a complete stranger. Who didn't like lasagna?

The process of layering cheese, white sauce, red sauce, and noodles into a disposable aluminum pan (why waste good Pyrex?) seemed endless. Spreading the sauces always broke the noodles or caused gaps between layers. Finally, the layers approached the top. Claire sprinkled some extra cheese and fresh parsley on top and covered the heavy rectangle with foil. She reached for her monogrammed stationery in the paper drawer and sat at the kitchen table to contemplate what to write, how to present her offering. "Sorry?" "My condolences?" "I feel your loss?" She settled on "In Sympathy," writing in long elegant strokes with her favorite pen. Below it, she printed her name and phone number. She affixed the card to the foil with a dainty tab of clear tape.

The only road that could access the property behind the horse stables was framed by logs, like an old ranch entrance, but with no sign. A battered metal mailbox stood to the left. She turned the van down a gravel driveway and wound through dense trees, ferns, and rotting logs. A small wooden house peeked through the tree trunks. As she drove closer, she saw it had a metal smokestack, like the hobo houses in cartoons. She stopped the van. To the right of the porch, a rusting Weber grill lay on its side. A weather-beaten, ripped bag of charcoal slumped against one of its legs. A small gust of wind came up, and then the air was still. The dense woods made the house feel as though it was perpetually in shadow. A blue enamel dog bowl, half full of water, sat in front of the house. Claire set the casserole on the front porch and walked quickly back to her van.

At home she found herself staring at the phone like a smitten sixteen-year-old or a shut-in. Whenever it rang, she sucked in her breath. Could it be him? Would he be furious? Grief-stricken? Accusing? It was never the dog owner. It was Marilyn from the Hospital Foundation or Jim, her husband's golf partner, or her mother-in-law, or telemarketers. Three days later, the image she had constructed of Brad followed her everywhere, like a ghostly twin. She found herself flipping through the pages of her cookbook, trying to see with his eyes and pick something he would like. Maybe he hadn't liked the tomatoes, she thought, settling on a green-bean casserole. This particular recipe belonged to the genre she dubbed "Catholic food," for its prominence in neighborhood weddings and funerals when she was growing up. Maybe Brad was Catholic.

She was writing her phone number again on the monogrammed stationery when Steve sat down at the kitchen table with his beer.

"What's that?" he asked.

"Green-bean casserole," she said.

"I thought we were having pork roast."

"We are. This is for someone else."

"Who?"

"The man whose dog I hit. I thought he could use a casserole."

"What?" Steve squinted and looked away, like a bright light was aimed at his eyes. "Why now? That was almost a week ago."

"Well, he didn't respond to the first one."

"You've already done this?"

"Yes," she said. "I was thinking I should try again. Maybe he's just shy."

"Don't you think you should leave the poor guy alone? I mean, his dog's dead. He probably wants some space."

"But, I'm not sure if he lives with anyone. He might need to be taken care of a little. Anyway, I'm just trying to extend some human kindness. What do you suggest? I just mail him a note: 'Sorry I killed your dog?' Good idea."

Steve rolled the bottleneck back and forth between his thumb and forefinger, calming himself with the repetitive motion. Claire recognized this gesture; it was part of his repertoire. Steve raised his eyes and said, "Accidents happen, Claire. People don't send flowers to the guy they rear-ended. It's just understood—the world is a random, dangerous place. Casseroles don't change that."

The blue dog bowl, still sitting by the front door of the house, was becoming polluted. Two tiny leaves, edges curled up like cupped hands, swirled slowly across the water's surface. Claire placed the casserole next to the bowl.

She approached the nearest window and peered in, half expecting to see a face looking back at her. No lights were on. She could barely see a couch with a patterned cloth draped over it, maybe a tapestry, and what looked like newspapers strewn across a coffee table.

Two nights passed and he didn't call. Saturday morning, she did her usual errands. In the grocery store, at the post office, at an intersection, she began to wonder if one of the men surrounding her was Brad. She scanned her surroundings for forlorn faces, unshaven men with mournful eyes. What does a man who lives in a wood cabin look like? Do beagle owners share any common characteristics? Was it possible that she and Brad already knew each other? He could be the fish guy at the market, the one who always coughed when she asked how fresh the "fresh halibut" was. He could have pumped her gas this morning, while she sat oblivious in the driver's seat, scrawling in her day planner. Maybe he was that handsome cable guy who visited last month, on the one day, out of hundreds of well-dressed days, when she had worn a grubby sweat suit.

In the kitchen, Steve tapped his pen against a crossword puzzle.

"Did I get any calls?" Claire asked, pouring herself iced tea.

"Yes. Judy Walker called about the Halloween party at school. She wants you to think of some games or something."

"Was that it? Just Judy?"

"Were you expecting someone else?"

"I guess not."

Steve put the paper down. "What do you want from him?"

"Who? It's not about him. I'm—" she clutched her pant leg and inhaled, "waiting for something from the tailor."

"Oh." Steve eyed her pants. "No. No tailor."

Claire thought of the woman from the stables, of going to ask her for Brad's number again. In the chaos, she had forgotten to write it down. But something about the woman's demeanor the day of the accident had felt accusing. Maybe she and Brad were having an affair. Who knew in these small communities? Clearly, contacting her wasn't a good idea.

By early evening, Claire decided to take control of the situation. She sneaked the phone book into the laundry room and began scanning the gray pages for Brad's name. The town phone book was thin—how many could there be? Each time she found a Brad, she tabbed the page with a Post-it note. So far, in the Fs, she had collected eight Brads, one Bradford, and three Bradleys, however, none were on the right road. You couldn't call information to ask for "Brad," even in Greenville. Finally, in the Js, her search ended: Bradley Joyner, 2134 Mill Creek Road. She held the page with one finger and pulled her cellular phone from her purse. Claire listened to the bodies crossing the floor upstairs, waiting for them to stop. She dialed slowly, pausing for three full breaths before hitting the "Send" button.

"Hello," a male voice answered, kind of low, with a hint of texture, like a person who smoked or who had just woken up.

She froze for a second, like a small animal, and then pressed "End."

She replayed his greeting in her head several times, analyzing the tone. Did he sound depressed?

Claire walked upstairs with an armful of folded towels. The thick smell of fabric softener wafted into her nostrils. She found Steve in the living room in front of the television, and said, "You know, I completely forgot about this planning meeting at Lily Strauss's. They're going to kill me. I'm supposed to have the pledge list typed up. I'm really sorry. Will you be okay for dinner?"

He looked utterly helpless. "Well, what should I make?"

"I don't know, I think there are some TV dinners in the bottom of the Deepfreeze."

"You want your children to eat TV dinners?"

"I'm sorry." She tried to think of some conciliatory words to add, but was too distracted, already imagining the walk up to Brad's front door.

"How could you forget a meeting? I think you've been a little overextended lately."

"Hmm." She pretended to contemplate his diagnosis. "I'll go to yoga on Tuesday. That always helps. Anyway, I'll be back by eight, okay?" She jangled her keys and left.

Halfway down the gravel road to Brad's house, Claire pulled the van to a stop and switched off the headlights. Through the trees she could see several lit rooms in the house. A figure moved through one room to the next and sat down. A flutter began in Claire's chest and then became a strange tingling sensation on her scalp, like having wet hair on a breezy day.

"Brad." She said his name, trying to rehearse a speech, but after that word, none followed. All the words she had learned in her lifetime cowered in the trees, watching in pity. She picked at lint on her slacks.

Claire let the van coast closer to the house. Gravel crunched under the wheels and the figure inside the house stood up. He was wearing a red shirt. She pulled up the brake and opened the car door, slowly swinging each leg to the ground. Her right foot landed in a small puddle. The Weber grill still lay on its side. To the left, a stone frog the size of a basketball squatted in a patch of long grass, an item she had missed on her first visit. Clearly, the frog was not moved for mowing. It seemed out of place, a bit knickknacky for this otherwise spartan arrangement.

Claire swallowed hard and knocked twice on the unfinished wood door, focusing her energy on staying upright and conscious. The face that appeared in the opened door was cautious, then quickly contorted into bewilderment. The man wore a flannel shirt and several days' worth of stubble. His hair stuck up in the back, like the grass around the frog.

"Hello," Claire said, with a little too much emphasis on the H. Then, calmer, "I'm Claire Waters." He stared right through her, as if she was pushing propagandistic literature. She shifted her weight forward to the balls of her feet and added, "I've been leaving you casseroles."

The man wrinkled his brow for a second and then his mouth slackened a little, as if he had just been told something utterly bizarre, which, Claire realized almost immediately, he had.

Exhaustion spread across his face. He leaned against the doorjamb and hung his head. He worked his jaws back and forth, as if trying to grind a sentence into manageable units. Finally he said, "I'm Brad." Without extending his hand he added, "Joyner."

Claire wanted to fly away. "I," she paused, "just wanted to apologize . . ."

"Do you want to come in?" Brad said. He looked as if he was about to yawn.

This possibility had not occurred to Claire. Now she couldn't remember exactly what she had expected from this encounter. Or from the casserole campaign. "Sure, that would be nice," she said, as a polite reflex. She sat on the rumpled, tapestry-covered couch.

Brad walked into the kitchen space, an extension of the living room, and grabbed a bottle. "Port?" he asked.

"Ah. Sure. Why not?" Claire said. The purple tapestry was littered with white dog hairs. She was sitting on them, the cast-off hairs of the dead beagle.

Brad walked around the kitchen counter and presented Claire with a smudgy glass filled halfway with port.

Claire sipped hesitantly and her throat constricted. She had forgotten how sweet port was, how viscous.

Brad sat down in an overstuffed chair covered with a white sheet. "Cheers," he said flatly, and drank.

Neither of them said anything for a while. Claire dipped her head to the glass repeatedly, like a bird, and licked the thick residue from her lips. She scrutinized what she could see of the house; would it be rude to ask for a tour? The newspapers still lay across the table, the same ones from days earlier—or was this strewing thing a habit?

Several dead flowers stood in a vase on the countertop. A pair of tall rubber galoshes leaned against the wall by the door, one of them bent over like a drooping plant.

Brad crossed his legs and looked at her breasts, two slight mounds shielded by crisp cotton. He lowered his eyes and said, as if to his glass, "So Claire. What is it that you do for a living?"

Claire took a long swig of her port and said, "Well, I'm a home-maker. I volunteer a lot."

"Family?"

"Yes. I have two children, Tessa and Max."

"Mmm-hmm," he said, looking at the wall above her head. His eyes snapped back to her and stayed there until suddenly he rose and pointed at her glass. "You finished with that, Claire?" he asked. She shook her head and he said, "Well, drink up."

It had been a long time since someone had told her to "drink up," decades, and she was so shocked by his forcefulness that she tossed the remnants of the port into her throat. Fearing the liquid would come back up, she placed two fingertips to her lips and handed him the glass.

"I'm tired of port. How 'bout some scotch, Claire?"

"Oh, that's okay. I'm . . ."

"You do drink scotch, right? Or are you partial to white zinfan-del?" Brad walked to the cupboard again and smirked to himself.

Claire felt her face flush. "Scotch is fine," she said.

Brad handed her the same glass, rinsed and filled with warm scotch. The outside surface was wet. She wiped one hand stealthily on the couch and several dog hairs stuck to her palm. She brought her hand to her thigh to wipe off the hairs, but saw that her navy slacks were covered with the tiny white strands. She balled the dirty hand into a fist and wedged it under her leg. Using her free hand she tipped her glass to her lips and swallowed. The burning sensation spread across her throat and then subsided.

Her whole body was feeling warmer, especially her toes, and she said, "Brad, what about you? Are you married? Do you have a family?"

"Yep, huge," Brad said.

Claire was taken aback. The place was too small for more than one person.

"Goddamn Catholics," he continued, smiling wryly. He was quite handsome, once you got past the poor hygiene.

"What do you mean?" Claire asked.

"Five sisters. Used to burn me with their curling irons." He laughed and raised his glass. His eyes narrowed. "Savages."

Claire sipped her scotch. "Where do they live?"

"All over. My parents live in Michigan."

"Do you have anyone here?" Even Claire wasn't sure what she meant by "here." This house, this town, this state?

Brad's body became rigid. He leaned forward. "I had a dog."

Claire's cheeks burned, and then her chest followed, as if tiny heating coils lined the inside of her lungs. She watched the blotchy shimmer that floated across the amber-colored liquid in the glass, like oil on water puddles. She said softly, "Yes, I know." She squeezed the glass between both palms. "I'm so sorry." She took another sip, felt its warmth travel the length of her throat, and sighed. "I guess that's what I came here to say." She felt noticeably lighter as those words left her sticky lips.

Brad stared at her.

Claire thought, he's not going to say anything. When someone says they're sorry, you're supposed to say, "It's okay." That's how the world works. She felt dizzy with desperation. She closed her eyes, hoping that when she opened them again she would be in her bed, next to someone predictable who believed she was incapable of destruction. Under the darkness of her eyelids, she pretended she was on a gently rocking boat. She could almost hear the water splashing the sides. A beatific smile crept across her face. She rested like that for a few moments and then she opened her eyes. Brad was still watching her, as if she was inanimate.

She racked her brain for words and none came. Then, as if from another mouth, "I just thought that after you didn't call me I should . . ." she stopped and bumped the back of her hand against her lips, just to make sure they belonged to her. She could smell her rose perfume.

"Usually," Brad said, "when people don't call, it means they don't want to talk to you." His voice was laced with contempt, but artificially steady and monotone, as if he was teaching a child a bitter truth of human existence: Things die, honey.

Because of his strange tone, and the scotch, it took a minute for this sentence to register. When it finally settled in her brain, Claire realized that her face had been stretched into a vacuous grin, waiting for absolution. She noticed for the first time a deep crease above Brad's left eyebrow, the result, she imagined, of years of asymmetrical scrunching of the forehead, an expression she had come to recognize through a lifetime of formal socializing, as "judgmental."

"Well, I more," she said, "just, you know, wanted to make sure that my contribution was received."

"Excuse me?" The edge was gone from Brad's voice. He really didn't know what she was talking about.

"My contribution," Claire said, not sure how that particular word had found its way into this context. It was a word for the silver dish at church. For dividing spousal workload.

"You mean the food?"

"Yes."

"Yeah." Brad's lips were pursed. He worked his first finger against the side of his thumb, as if looking for something to catch on, begging for a hangnail. "You want those pans back or something? I certainly don't have any use for them."

"No. No," Claire shook her head as Brad stood up and turned toward the kitchen, "they're disposable. You can throw them away."

Brad propped one arm on the back of his chair. Claire wasn't sure which she feared most: that he would sit again or that he would stay standing like that. He sat.

She examined the brownish film on the bottom of her drained glass and felt acid eating at her stomach. Claire placed her glass on the pile of newspapers. She realized it would leave a wet ring and the paper would never be the same, but she left it there anyway.

"Yes, well, thanks for the drinks Mr. Joyner. I should be getting back."

As Claire walked out of his house, Brad sat utterly motionless in his chair. He reminded Claire of the Lincoln Monument. Just outside the doorway, as she fished for her keys, Claire heard him mumble, "Drive safe."

The drive home seemed thrillingly fast, although the speedometer hovered around thirty. Claire felt that she and the van had a special symbiosis; it read her mind and responded to every maneuvering whim with minimal effort. She felt like she was in a driving commercial. Maybe she should pursue an acting career. "Let Plymouth set you free," she practiced, although she had never heard that particular slogan. It sounded good to her, though. Maybe she should write commercial slogans *and* act.

"Oops." Claire snorted a laugh to herself in the driveway, when the minivan's front bumper rocked Steve's car. She followed the walkway to the front door and turned her keys in the latch.

Steve met her in the front hall. "How was the meeting? You smell like booze."

"Oh yes, Louise Barnett's daughter just got engaged so we had a toast." This, in fact, had happened weeks ago, without the toast. Claire was pleased with her ability to think on her feet.

"Oh," Steve said. "You okay?"

"Yes, fine, thanks. Are the kids in bed?"

"Yeah. I'm going to work down in my office for a while. See you in bed?"

"Yes, sounds good."

In the kitchen, Claire stared at her favorite pen. "Nice things are nice to have," she said, noticing a lack of crispness in her consonants. Claire rummaged in the paper drawer for her recipe cards. She pulled the cookbook from a shelf and flipped to "Lasagna." Carefully, she copied the recipe on a small card, leaving the line that read "From the kitchen of:" blank. She opened the phone book, copied Brad's address on an envelope, and placed the recipe inside. After sealing and stamping the envelope, she began to write her return address. Abruptly, she stopped and chewed the end of the pen. Claire scribbled over her name, leaving a large black spot in its place. *Out of respect,* she thought to herself, blowing the ink dry.

"I'm not a very
well-read man.
Someone once
said, 'If there
had not been
any God we
should have
had to invent
one.' Who was it?"
　　　　(Ford, page 305)

Incomplete Proposals 1999-

Henrik Håkansson

chickenscratch in chickenscratch in chickenscratch
(Doyle, page 203)

December 24, 1999–January 1, 2000

Tim Staffel

LARS   I hate this day. Jesus day. The gas explosion a block away is like an earthquake. The ice in the canal splits open. The entire house is a torch, and it doesn't look like anybody will get out. The kids on their skates are surprised by the bursting ice. A red wool cap breaks through, and the others try their lot as ice fishers. The entire street starts to churn and plays the part of rescuers. I light a cigarette, enjoy the live spectacle, and try to make a plan for this fucked-up day. The mail is already taken care of. I consider whether it makes sense to bring structure into the manifestos. Some kind of serial story. I declare myself crazy. Words no longer have any value for me. There is no reason to organize the matter. It runs on its own. I run on my own. A full-scale fake that has no rules. I write a new manifesto that I will place under Hakan's tree. I gradually get myself into the mood. The firefighters synchronize their rescue efforts with my music. I discover a crack in my window that doesn't belong there. I take this to be a warning. I will warn everyone who crosses my path. A few charred corpses are carried out of the house that is collapsing very slowly. Slow motion. The red wool cap doesn't make it ashore. The ice has already wiped away every trace of it. The rescue kids stand around on the banks of the Lincke bawling. They probably imagined Christmas somehow differently. Jesus is born, and here people croak. Everything totally normal. I draw a bath, crack open a bottle of bubbly, put the telephone next to the tub, and climb into the water. I dial the customer-service number of Berlin Public Transportation. I impart to them that a package bomb is possibly stuck on the rails of the Wannsee streetcar stop. I clink my glass with the telephone receiver and hang up. The idea of a rail bomb fascinates me. I imagine the rail workers and the bomb squad in their fluorescent outfits as they test the track inch by inch with their Geiger counters and then, disappointed, wander home to their Christmas sparklers. It is time to install a few cameras in order to collect souvenirs. I don't want to remember. What should I remember.

THE ONE THING THAT LASTS IS LOSS. LOSS COUPLED WITH OMISSION. LOSS AND OMISSION. LOSS/OMISSION/TIME. THE ESSENTIAL CONSTANTS. THE DETERMINANTS. CHEERS. I CREATE LOSS BY REDUCING OMISSION. I HAVE ALL THE TIME IN THE WORLD, AND THIS WORLD SHALL BURST.

I call Hakan and ask what's going on. He seems to be in high spirits. I'm surprised that he doesn't uninvite me. I pull the plug out of the drain, rinse away the foam, embalm myself with cream, and pull my tuxedo out of the closet. The fire is having a hard time against the cold; only the attic of the neighboring house burns down. I tie a ribbon around the letter and paint an angel on the envelope. The other gift for Hakan is already wrapped. I refuse to think about what it is. A mild nausea overcomes me because I am playing along with this Christmas crap. It is worth making a play for Hakan. Especially his back. I snort a line, drain the rest of the bubbly, and hit the road. I head in the direction of Südstern traffic circle and count the Christmas lights behind the windowpanes. Every light a burning sailor. The masses of snow on the sidewalks mutate into icebergs. I give Jan a hickey. He twists his ring with an eagle's head into my heart. Dogs lick up the road salt and puke their guts out. Starry heaven. In it a moon dying of laughter. The Milky Way celebrates a completely different feast. The fucked son of God has no business there. The father of the Jesus child was in reality a Roman captain. Jesus is therefore only a half Jew. The stars know that, and we know it too. The masters of repression. I lose my innocence at your heavenly gates. A comet is underway toward Earth. I calculate the time of place and impact. My coordinate system is flawless. An ambulance with red lights flashing and sirens wailing cuts off my path. They refuse to take me along. The comet crashes on the Urban Hospital. I approach Bergmannstraße and try to pump the blood back into my head. The sounds of a zither emit from the Austria bar. The employees strike up "Silent Night, Holy Night." A pagan feast, and all the Christian assholes are totally into it. I put the Austria on my list. I walk up to Chamissoplatz, only a few meters left to Hakan's. I sense a renewed desire for Turkish fruits and decide to forget the rest. In the entrance way, a few jerks pretend it's New Years Eve and tie poppers on their cat's tail. A small, earthly comet. Hakan opens the door. He's dressed almost like me. He kisses me on the mouth. I get a taste of the festive mood and regret not having snorted more coke. Hakan put up a tree in front of the television. Approximately thirty ball-shaped, metallic-blue ornaments, silver lametta, white angels' hair, and seven hundred blue candles. I can't believe it and say:

—Wow.

—I'll get the bubbly.

I am still afraid that I'm not the only one on the guest list. Something isn't right here. A different smell than usual. A different Hakan.

—What is wrong with you, Hakan? Are you on speed?

—Something like it.

—Something like it?

—Yeah, exactly.

He opens the oven and bastes the turkey with the juice flowing out of it. I ask him what the title of the movie is that we're in right now. He tells me something about caramelized potatoes. The Long Fin Killies sing about the dead surfers' heads. I go into the bathroom to fill up my nose. I am certain it's a mistake. I see my mug in the mirror and make faces. I wonder if that's me. If Hakan will at any time understand anything.

—Lars!

—Fuck you.

—Lars?

—I'm coming.

There's still no one there except me. I count the seconds until the miracle explodes. Hakan folds the napkins. Two of them. The miracle explodes. I open a bottle of Chardonnay, pour two glasses, and suggest to Hakan that we address each other with our first names. He no longer notices me, for he is engaged in a battle with the turkey and the poultry shears. I have to take care of the caramelized potatoes and the Kenyan beans, refill my glass to be on the safe side, and fail nonetheless. At least I imagine that. I ask Hakan if it turned him on to put his fist through the turkey's opening to get rid of its stuffing. He grins at me and raises his glass. I am absolutely certain that something is wrong here. I tell him that I'll probably stop loving him. He says:

—Good.

I draw his attention to the fact that I only said "probably." He blots his mouth with the napkin and asks me if I enjoyed my meal. I haven't even started eating. At least I think so. He lights a cigar. I feel sick. He is still grinning. I have already lost the game but try to keep on my feet to at least protect my chances as an underdog. I say to him that it is truly a goddamn beautiful Christmas. He lights the candles on the tree.

—Every light a burning sailor.

He doesn't register me. He's on his own trip. I refrain from depositing the letter and turn the television on. Hakan screams:

—Asshole!

and pulls out the plug. He cracks open the next bottle of Chardonnay. I have cleaned out my kidneys enough for now. I roll a joint and hope that it puts me in a better mood. I ask Hakan how positive he is now. He says:

—Number 1359 is absolutely negative. The test result confirms this.

That the crap sits and breeds on the mucous membranes of the tonsils and therefore is not immediately detectable doesn't seem to interest him. Nor that the tests are by now faked by the health fuckers. I wonder whether it interests me. In which form I should offer myself to him. I didn't put on this tuxedo in order to keep it on the whole evening. Hakan hands me his gift. I hand him mine. I still can't believe it. The dope at least brings me down a bit. I go to grab a beer from the refrigerator while Hakan tries to unravel the strings from his present. He asks if I want to unwrap mine, but I really don't feel like it. I am still holding his package under my arm, drinking my beer, and waiting for his reaction. Long Fin Killies sing: "Don't call me nigger." This gay Christmas gets on my nerves. Hakan holds an urn in his hands that has our names engraved on it. I claim to have made the thing myself. He drains the bottle of Chardonnay in one gulp, looks at me angrily, and I make the sound

—Uuuhh!

because I am fucking scared of his evil gaze. He cocks his arm and aims the urn at my head. I take cover in time, and the thing smashes on the wall. He wants to know why I don't unwrap my gift. I ask him what I am supposed to do with a sack full of ashes when the urn is already broken. Only now does the fucker notice that the tree behind him is on fire. He rips open the balcony door, grabs the burning tree, and dumps it on the street down below. I think it is time to break off the celebration because I have no desire for the epilogue. I make my way out without him noticing. The turkey is sitting heavy in my stomach. I regret not having taken beer along. Outside the tree is still flickering to itself. No trace of Hakan. At least he didn't jump out after it. I convince myself that I didn't really have a chance tonight. I bury the envelope with the angel in a garbage can and start searching for a taxi. I want to see how the evening is going at Tom's.

FELIX   Anna fiddles around in the kitchen with a kitchen maid. She's wearing a long, sleeveless, silver sequin dress. I go to get some chips and the kitchen maid gawks at me stupidly. Tom is sitting in the living room with uncle Nico and acts as if he is engrossed in a book. Nico stares out the window. He holds his hands pressed between his knees. I lay down with the chips in front of the television and turn on MTV.

—Felix, what's up with that?

I don't know what's up with that. The whole circus is probably put on for my sake, and nobody knows what's up with that. Michael Jackson stomps on the Earth and sings the "Earth Song." Nico says:

—I know that.

Tom rips the remote control from my hand, snatches the bag of chips, and disappears into the kitchen. Perhaps to beat Anna, perhaps to show his thing to the kitchen help. I get ill at the thought that he made me. I sit down next to Nico because Tom forbid me to go to my room. I ask Nico what's going on. He says that he would like to be at home now.

—Then why don't you simply go?

—Because Tom said it's Christmas.

I somehow like my uncle even though he's totally fucking crazy. We light cigarettes and try to blow smoke rings. Nico manages to maneuver his smoke rings through mine. Anna shouts from the kitchen that I shouldn't smoke. I'm surprised that she hasn't fallen asleep yet. Nico likes the thing with the smoke rings. He lights another smoke and begins to cough. I pat him on the back. He drops the cigarette and it burns a small hole in the Berber carpet.

—What's going on, Nico, can't you be careful, or what?

Tom is standing with his whiskey glass on the staircase, playing the king. I wish I were with Button right now, playing pool with his brother at the Nansen-Eck bar. Nico asks me why I go to school.

—No clue.

—That's what I thought.

—What the fuck, Nico, do you want to make the boy crazy?

—He's already crazy.

—Don't judge others by your own standards, Nico.

—School is no problem for me.

Nico thinks it's okay, but Tom draws fodder from it.

—School is no problem for you is it? Perhaps my dear son can then explain to me . . .

—Tom! Dinner's ready.

Anna looks great in her dress. Tom, the king, battles with the poultry shears. Nico tries to put the napkin around his neck. Anna fills herself with wine. The kitchen help dishes out kale and dumplings. Because I am the child I get a drumstick. The fat still blubbers through the brown skin. I ponder whether I should vomit now or later. Tom raises his glass to a successful Christmas feast, and Nico splashes his wine across the tablecloth. I wonder what the kitchen maid is up to in the kitchen and think that her job can't be any shittier than the dinner here. Anna asks Nico if the job at the museum is fun.

—It depends who you ask. Something is not right in the museum.

He sorts out the little pieces of bacon from the kale.

—Something is always not right for you. You should be happy that I got you that job. As far as I've been told, you're not earning too badly for doing nothing. Or is it too strenuous for you?

—My dear brother got this job for me but he was never there. He doesn't know what kind of people are there. He doesn't know the dangers that lurk there.

—I don't know what you expect with your qualifications.

—I can observe.

—Well great. You can observe the paintings. As I said. An ideal job for you.

—I don't observe any paintings.

—Do you want more dumplings, Nico?

Anna tries to change the topic. Nico takes a dumpling and mashes it in the sauce.

—As far as I know my dear son, he will certainly also end up a museum guard. Then I will at least know what I slaved for all these years.

—Something our father used to say. Tom is only repeating it, explains Nico.

—Tom, please, not tonight.

Anna remains amazingly calm. She must have tried a new downer. I ask Tom what kind of slave work that is when you hold your masked mug in the camera and babble shit. Nico snickers and drops a piece of goose breast from his fork onto his lap. Anna quickly pours herself another glass of wine.

—Do you want to fight?

I don't want to fight. I gave that up years ago. You can't fight with Tom. Not with a royal asshole. I understood that early on.

—I asked, if you want to fight?

—Is everything to your satisfaction?

The kitchen maid is standing behind Tom and smiles. He says that he'd call for her if he needed her. I want her to make a curtsy, but she simply withdraws from the room. I think she staggers a bit. I uncover the layer of fat beneath the skin and maintain that maggots are crawling around in it. Tom reaches over the table and slaps me in the face. Nico says that he also thinks that something is living in his food. He is certain that somebody wants to poison him. Anna tries to calm him down although her eyes are already totally humid. Tom tells Nico that he should pull himself together. But Nico throws his knife and fork on his plate and waves his arms in the air:

—I don't want to pull myself together. You were never there. It is dangerous. They want to poison me. Because I know everything. I know everything. They want to kill me because I know everything. But I'm a professional. I'm really a professional. You have no clue, Tom, no clue at all.

I tell Nico that I think he is really cool. Tom calls the kitchen maid and orders her to finally clear the table. She is irritated and doesn't know what she should do with her dessert. Tom explains to her that no one asked her for her opinion, that she should simply clear the table and shut up. Anna excuses herself for a moment and withdraws upstairs to replenish her supply. Tom says:

—Well great, Nico. Are you happy now?

Tom loosens his tie, knocks back his whiskey, and says:

—Merry Christmas.

I knock my knee against Nico's as if I were an accomplice, but he has stepped into another dimension and no longer notices anything. I ask if I may leave the table. Tom offers to make peace:

—Everything is in order, Nico. Everything in order. Nothing has happened, do you hear? I'm sorry. Everything okay? I apologized to you, Nico.

We are sitting again in the living room, Anna with glassy eyes. The kitchen maid brings mocha coffee and almond pastries. Tom lights the tree. Every light a burning sailor. The kitchen maid says good night. I wait for Tom to offer to fuck her home. I unwrap my presents and everyone stares at me. The child rejoices the most beautifully. A Discman, a modem for the Internet, new threads, computer games, a subscription to the *Basket*, Nike Air NDESTRUKT, a check for five hundred marks for CDs. I kiss Anna on the cheek. She strokes my head. I look at Tom and say:

—Thanks.

Nico stares out the window. Tom presents him with a gift certificate for a new bike. Nico fixes his gaze on the voucher and says:

—But I would rather have a Ford Mustang.

—A what?

—A Ford Mustang.

—You don't want a new bike?

—I want a Ford Mustang.

—A Ford Mustang?

—Yes. Ford Mustang.

Tom takes the gift certificate out of Nico's hands and tears it up.

—What about you, Felix, are you also dissatisfied?

I say:

—Everything's okay with me.

—Fine. That reassures me. Really.

Anna receives an emerald ring that doesn't fit. I give Tom Ray-Ban sunglasses that I stole from some fucker and Tom can't believe it. He opens an envelope with an angel painted on it and pulls out a note with a red ribbon around it. He reads the scrap of paper, and I think it is yet again a gift certificate from Anna for who knows what. Nico tries to puzzle together his gift certificate. Tom kind of turns pale and his hands shake. He sticks the note back into the envelope and throws it into the fireplace. Anna doesn't react. Tom says to Nico:

—You shall have your Ford Mustang.

Nico stops putting together the pieces of the puzzle. I think I'm not hearing right, but Tom repeats it once more:

—Everything is okay, Nico. You will get your Ford Mustang. We will take care of it the day after tomorrow.

Nico smiles at Tom and can't say a word. Anna is on the verge of falling asleep, a burning cigarette between her fingers. Tom goes into the kitchen to get more ice. I fish the envelope out of the fireplace. It is only singed. I read the piece of paper:

THE FAMILY IS THE NUCLEUS OF SOCIALISM. THUS THE FAMILY MUST BE DESTROYED.   V

I have no idea what's up with the socialism shit but the stuff about the destruction of the family is all right. I think it's cool. I put the piece of paper in my pocket and ask Anna if it's too late to go to the Nansen-Eck. Anna says I should show consideration for Tom. I plop down in an easy chair and know that I will not survive this evening. Nico is staring out the window again and suddenly jumps as if something scared him to death.

LARS   I plunge into the darkness beyond the streetlight and have a very good view. The big window front is as inviting as a movie screen. The sound doesn't work. There is no rottweiler, no bullterrier. Not yet. Tom is not to be seen. Instead, the fucked-up museum madman stares out the window. The world is too small. Tom's son seems to be bored to death. I ask myself if Tom has already read the letter out loud to his family. He returns to the others with a full whiskey glass, sits down next to the woman, who is probably his wife, and doesn't utter a word. They are celebrating a death vigil. Their Jesus child is a stillbirth. I regret not having bottles of gasoline with me, so angry I could puke, because I don't know what I'm doing here, because it's a totally fucked-up evening. Hakan. My time is running out if something doesn't happen soon.

FELIX   We gradually bore ourselves into delirium. Nico says that he has to go now because Fred Faser is in trouble, because he otherwise wouldn't wait for him outside. Tom gets upset because Nico is raving. I have no idea who Fred Faser is. Tom wants Nico to spend the night because he is too drunk to drive him home. Nico refuses because he still has to take care of Fred Faser and Betsi Baller. I ask him who Betsi Baller is. Nico gets nervous, but Tom refuses to drive. Nico says that he doesn't need a bike because after all he came with his Mustang:
    —And Buddy can always drive.
    I think Nico is totally cool. He's out the door before Tom gets what's going on. I pack up my gifts and leave Mary and Joseph to themselves.

ANETTE   Calm prevails in the editorial offices. The double issue with mine, Tom's article came out before Christmas, Tom's program will not air again until the end of January, Mehnert is in the Grand Canary islands. I polish my nails and wait for Tom to return from the masseur. A text by V makes its way through the Internet:

THE VACUUM CAN BE INJURED. AN INVISIBLE LEAK HAS THE POWER OF AN ATOMIC BOMB. WE REMAIN CALM. THEY EVEN REBUILT HIROSHIMA. A MODERN CITY. NO MORE QUESTIONS. THE DEMISE OF THE QUESTION MARK. THE REFUSAL. THE LEAK.   V

    I try to imagine what V looks like. If V is a woman. Tom stinks of oil. I disconnect from the Internet. Tom asks me if I have any idea where you can get hold of good dogs. Rottweilers. I ask him if he already has plans for New Year's. He looks at me as if I were a ghost. We drink a coffee, awaiting his answer.

—New Year's?

—We're entering the year 2000, in case you forgot.

—Anna is in the Grand Canary islands.

—I know.

—What do you think of a rottweiler?

—Depends.

—On what?

—Do you want to train it?

—Sure.

Sure. He is paranoid. He is ordinary. He's good-looking.

—Shall I try to find out?

—Yeah. Why not.

I treat him to a grappa.

—What's with New Year's?

—I don't know. Do you already have plans?

He hesitates, carefully feels his way. I smile. Stroke the rim of my grappa glass with my index finger.

—I'm worried about Felix.

The devoted father of the family evades the question. He's trapped. I don't let up: I say nothing. He takes a second grappa. I hold my hand over my glass.

—I could make reservations at the Florian.

I won. I agree. He nods and can't help grinning. He peers into his glass. He can't yet face my gaze.

I'm standing in front of my closet, still undecided on which strategy I should employ. Outside the storm slowly picks up again. I count the steps I have to take outside, but the agenda for after dinner hasn't been established yet. I must remain flexible. I still have forty-five minutes to make the right choice. On the radio they report the first firework accidents. Tom is going to lock Felix up. I imagine Felix going after his father with a Swiss army knife. I forbid myself the thought, turn off the radio, and decide on the blue velvet dress. As a fragrance, anything besides Paloma Picasso is out of the question. I know it makes Tom crazy. I ask myself if I'm crazy. He is paranoid. He is ordinary. He's good-looking. I look at myself in the mirror. No defects. I am certain of it. I join him in the taxi and say:

—Hello.

—Hello.

We have a table next to the bathrooms. Tom complains and the manager apologizes. Now we're sitting at the window. The storm strikes against the glass. We clink our champagne glasses. Tom chooses the menu. I have to be looked after. I have no idea about "haute cuisine." I'm only a secretary. Tom looks after me. Visibly ashamed. He has no clue. I play my role. At first. He will be surprised. He pays me a compliment and is careful that nobody hears it. I smile thankfully and wish that his head were in a vice. I pull myself together. He smells like Biagiotti Uomo. Cheap. That reassures me. During the meal I see to it that I don't look at him. He says:

—Anette . . .

In one ear and out the other.

—Anette?

I keep him guessing.

—I'd like to make a toast.

Go to hell, you idiot! I raise my glass and wet my lips.

—I'm worried.

—About Felix?

—No. Something different. I don't know how I should begin.

He can trust me. He's drunk enough. I encourage him. I lay my hand on his:

—What's wrong, Tom?

—It is . . . I receive . . .

—What do you receive?

In front of me the little boy that I would like to give a good talking to.

—It's nothing.

—You can tell me everything, Tom.

I booked a trip in a soap opera. He's not aware of the ridiculousness. Perhaps I should cut out his tongue before he kisses me.

—I receive letters.

Letters. I try not to laugh.

—What kind of letters?

—They are . . .

The waiter pulls away our plates.

—Thanks. It was very good.

I am beginning to get tired of the matter. I could kiss the feet of the waiter. Tom orders more champagne. He smiles at me. Not really. He waits for me to ask another question. I disappoint him. I know what he's talking about. He's not the one I would like to talk to about it.

—Let's enjoy the evening, Tom.

—Yeah, sure. You're right, as always. My love . . .

He has no clue about the fantasies of his "love." He surprised me. A declaration. I didn't expect: "love." We actually keep the whole surface occupied. I order a dessert with two spoons. Cream of curd cheese. The storm threatens to push in the windowpanes. Tom looks at his watch. Our spoons click against each other. I lift my spoon to his mouth. The little boy is fed. He gladly accepts it. The gaze at the neighboring table. Nobody saw it. 11:10 P.M.

—We have to hurry up.

—Where do we want to go?

A naïve question that has its effect. He plays the man full of secrets. He gets excited. I fix myself up. He helps me with my coat. I will defend myself. If need be. The taxi driver explains to Tom the detour through the blocked-off streets. Because of the trees. The uprooted city. I sit in the back and attempt to regain my orientation. Tom actually is crude. The last hope vanishes. I have to fight in well-known territory. We stop in front of my apartment. I unlock the door. Tom whispers in my ear. He dreams of a New Year's fuck. 11:45 P.M. I don't have much time left. He opens the champagne. He embraces me from behind, holds the glass in front of my face. I ask him to open my zipper. He follows the opening with his tongue. I feel the goose bumps and withdraw from his grasp. He poses as the conqueror, follows me into the living room. He stands in front of me and doesn't know how he should go about it. I ask him to sit down next to me. He is confused. His hand runs across the inside of my thigh, under the dress. 11:55 P.M. He's still dreaming. I press his hand on my thigh and push my tongue into his mouth. He plays along. Tongue and teeth. He can't get his hand free. The storm dies down. Fireworks. I bite his tongue. He screams. His hand disappears.

—Let's raise our glasses, Tom.

He whimpers. I taste blood. Only an injury.

—What's wrong with you?

—Shit.

—Let's raise our glasses.

He doesn't get it yet. He clinks glasses with me. New Year. 2000. He wants more. I hold myself back. That's the foreplay. He's paranoid. He's ordinary. He's good-looking. I have a lot of time. The year will be long. He starts another attempt. I say:

—No.

He gives up. He didn't expect that. He grins. He thinks I'm playing hard to get. He likes it that I'm playing hard to get. I say:

—Please.

He struggles with his erection. Again the hand. He asks what I like. He thinks he has what it takes. I say:

—I'd like to look at you.

—Look at me?

—Yes.

Tom, the adventurer. He can't tolerate alcohol. The hero. I undress him. He doesn't notice it. He undresses himself. He attempts to find his rhythm. A dance. He disrobes. Clothes fall. I drink champagne. He prances before me. The erotic attraction. The brain distorted. He smiles. A pale body. Wiry. Sinewy. Untouched. He doesn't know his body. He dances. Only the ridiculous underwear remaining. I laugh. He beckons me to him. Convinced of his rhythm. I remain seated. He pulls back the veil. Proud of his erection. He no longer dances. He offers himself. Lost. Every second that I hesitate damages his virility. I say:

—You misunderstood me.

—What?

—I wanted to look at you. Your face. I wanted us to look each other in the eyes. You misunderstood me. I'm sorry.

I wake the animal in him. He is no animal. He draws in his horns. I place my trust in him and smile at him. Openly. He collects himself. Quietly. I burn in him. Because I am so calm. So open. I offer him a glass of champagne. He drinks. Hastily. He's still standing tall.

—I better go now.

—As you like.

And outside it's also burning. I accompany him to the door. He says:

—Thanks, anyway.

I grab him on the pants and twist my tongue into his throat. He hesitates.

—I'm the one who should say thanks, Tom.

I let him go.

—Well then, Anette. I'll see you.

—Sure.

I close the door. He is mine.

FELIX   I hang around with Button at a party that does nothing for me. I drink Red Bull with vodka. I tell Button I want to go outside. He thinks it's a good idea. I take the bottle of vodka; he takes the fireworks, and we're off. Just about every goddamn tree is now lying across the road, but the wind is letting up. No danger for Button's missile base in Viktoria Park. We're at the memorial. It's fucking cold but the people are in a good mood. I am quite turned on. Button installs the artillery. Some freak flings his arms around my neck and smooches my forehead. I don't get upset because I am more than turned on. We drink vodka. A Goth girl comes on to Button. He curses because he has better things to do. The first things go up. I stare into the sky. The absolute outer space. Button brings me down and gives me instructions. We light the fuses. I'm too slow because my hand is frozen stiff, because I would prefer to watch. The freak is again hanging on my neck. Button is bugging me, asking what I want from the fag. He wants to make a statement. He makes his statements in the sky. The ground swims beneath me. No longer any wind. Only waves. Button howls. 2000. I take Button in my arms. He pushes me away and asks if I'm losing it. The sky is burning. Cannon blasts. Button, the master. I get dizzy. The freak goes with his buddies to a rave on the "Island." He asks us if we want to come along. The explosives expert is skeptical. I finally show Button the E and he agrees. "Island of Youth." Goa trance. Button goes to get beer and we swallow the E. Rave. We take off. I no longer see anything. We sweat. I dissolve. Button disappears. My body takes off on its own. I replenish fluids. Trance. Trance. Megatrance. I'm lying in the chill-out zone. Button has disappeared. I feel like some physical contact but don't know how I should go about it. Outside it's getting light. I'm at the back of beyond. No trace of Button. I make my way out. The river Spree the Arctic Ocean. No idea where I am. Fuck the year 2000.

LARS   Fuck 2000. The idiots detonate their statements in the sky
and nothing happens. I drag my Molotovs around and don't know
what to do with them. I enter the Ankerklause bar, but no trace of
Hakan. Easy Listening. The joint is bursting with people. Paper
streamers. They don't believe it themselves. Brain amputation.
Lobotomy. They perform the operation on themselves. A bottle of
gasoline on the deejay table. That would be a beginning. It is so full I
can't raise my arm. Happy New Year. First of all, unconsciousness. I
am morality. Fuck morality. Hakan won't come anymore. The mob
pushes me through. I wait for it to wash me back out. A couple of
Turks hold flags out of their moving cars, yell a lot. A couple of Turks
fall out of their moving cars and break their bones. I walk along the
Maybachufer and play peace. A whore lost her way and wants a light.
I light her wig and wish her a Happy New Year. She tears the torch
from her head and screams:
    —Fucking asshole! Goddamn fucking asshole.
    She's right. On the Maybachufer, between Pannierstraße and
Lohmühlenplatz, car wrecks on the side of the street. Mattresses and
refrigerators. Funeral pyres for burning witches. Between them
Romanians who sing without freezing solid. The women hold apples
in the fire. The children sleep in their laps. Very romantic. I say:
    —Love and peace!
    and count the knives being stabbed in my back. But instead of that
I drink homemade schnapps with the Romanians. How romantic.
They stop singing. Now it is really deathly silent. Happy New Year.
They let me go. Lars, the cop for the people, paces out the streets. It
is time for a plan. I hate New Year's. A pink-colored Mustang turns
into the Karl-Kunger-Straße. In the leftist mobile homes on
Lohmühlenstraße they celebrate their own feast and grill their dogs,
because they no longer have anything else. Everything is peaceful.
Today's dead don't matter. I cross the canal bridge into Görlitzer Park
and hope to at least be raped. But it's already getting light. It wasn't
my night. I sit down on a bench in front of the soccer field and decide
to die a martyr's death. Alone and abandoned, frozen to death on a
park bench. I first smoke my last cigarette. A kid surfaces from
nowhere and wants to bum a smoke. I tell him that I have already seen
him somewhere. He asks:

—Really?
I say:
—Yes.
And ask him what's his name.
—Felix.
—I'm Lars.
—Hi.
He sits down next to me and we smoke. He's at most fifteen.
—Did you have a good night, Felix?
—Fuck 2000.
—*D'accord.*
He asks what I'm doing here, and I say that I'm waiting for the end of the world. He thinks that's cool. I think it's cool to sit next to Tom's son.
—Do you feel like breakfast?
He has nothing against it. I show him the bottles of gasoline and ask him if he has an idea what we can do with them.
—No clue. Why?
—Should we try them out?
—I don't know.
—Come on. To hell with 2000.
We head for the small-animal zoo. Felix plays the flame-thrower. I imitate him. The goats bleat from the burning shed.
—Cool, man.
—Not bad for a beginning.
He looks at me inquiringly. We go to my house. Felix turns on the television and plops down in an easy chair. MTV. He asks how old I am.
—Twenty-four.
—I am fifteen.
—What about your 'rents?
—No clue.
—Aren't they mad?
—Tom thinks that I am sleeping at Button's.
I wonder if I should try to get into the boy's pants. He says:
—That was pretty crazy with the Molotovs. Do you do stuff like that often?
—No.

—Some guy says that the family should be destroyed.

—With Molotovs?

—No. Because of socialism, or shit like that. No idea. I'd have nothing against it.

—Everybody's got to know why he does what he does.

—And what kind of stuff do you do?

—All kinds of stuff. I blow my lotto winnings. Do you want coffee?

—Yes.

I am careful. Felix trusts me. He is okay.

NICO   Buddy steers his Ford Mustang through the New Year's fireworks. His nerves are stretched to breaking point. This is the night in which Buddy will free Betsi Baller and Fred Faser from the grasp of MISS MEGATRANCE and THE RAVEMAN. The night in which he will reveal himself. Buddy checks over his Beretta. He rolls his Ford Mustang into the Sredzkistraße. Music is pumping from the courtyard. MISS MEGATRANCE and THE RAVEMAN are having a party. Buddy is ready for it. TEMPLE OF LOVE. Buddy's admission ticket: a black leather vest on his naked torso and a studded band around his right upper arm. Ray-Bans and boots. That's enough. Buddy passes through the bouncers. The Beretta in his waistband. Buddy checks the location. A labyrinth of rooms. Latex bodies and leather mugs. Sweat. Buddy moves confidently. Buddy is wide awake. He presses himself past the twitching bodies. A few hands, but Buddy tolerates it. He has a mission. Buddy reaches the last room. Strobe light. MISS MEGATRANCE is dancing on the gallery. THE RAVEMAN directs. Buddy discovers the platform under the gallery. On the pedestal Fred Faser and Betsi Baller strapped to chairs. Betsi Baller talks insistently to Fred Faser. Buddy can't read her lips. Because of the strobe light. MISS MEGATRANCE swings a whip. THE RAVEMAN lowers himself by rope from the gallery to the platform. Betsi Baller screams. A spotlight on the platform. Buddy pushes his way forward. Every muscle in his body is vibrating. MISS MEGATRANCE follows THE RAVEMAN. The whip flickers across Fred's face. THE RAVEMAN kneels panting in front of Betsi Baller. Buddy springs onto the platform. MISS MEGATRANCE is confused, because Buddy grabs the leather strap with his fist and pulls MISS MEGATRANCE toward him. Buddy sinks his tongue into the stunned mouth of MISS MEGATRANCE. MISS MEGATRANCE puts her tender hands around Buddy's strong neck and presses on his Adam's apple. THE RAVEMAN is sitting on Betsi Baller's lap. Rusty razorblades rotate between his bony fingers. Betsi Baller faints. Buddy's resolute head flies against MISS MEGATRANCE's high forehead. MISS MEGA-TRANCE sinks to the floor. Buddy unties the stunned Fred Faser while THE RAVEMAN slashes open Betsi Baller's dress. Buddy draws his Beretta but THE RAVEMAN shamelessly grins at Buddy. Buddy instantly releases the safety catch of his Beretta which makes THE RAVEMAN carefully move away from Betsi Baller. Buddy aims at his left kneecap. Fred Faser attempts to free Betsi Baller, but THE RAVE-MAN kicks her chair. Buddy gets out of the way. Fred Faser loses his balance. THE RAVEMAN dives into the mass surging below him, and Buddy loses sight of THE RAVEMAN. That doesn't belong to his plan. Buddy throws Betsi Baller over his shoulder, the Beretta still cocked. He indicates to Fred Faser that he should follow him, but MISS MEGATRANCE wakes up. She gets hold of Fred Faser's leg at the moment he jumps from the platform. Fred Faser crashes and hits his nose against the edge of the platform while MISS MEGATRANCE sinks her teeth into his hairy calf. Buddy can no longer help him. Betsi Baller has priority, and Buddy fights his way with her through the receding mob. Betsi Baller wakes up. Screaming in despair she hammers Buddy with her fists. Buddy is about to lose the ground beneath his feet. Betsi Baller slides down his wide back, but Buddy grabs her by the wrist and drags her along behind him. Two enor-mous dudes plant themselves in front of Buddy. Through their nipples, silver rings that are bound together by a chain. Buddy aims his Beretta between the blazing eyes of one of them. The other says:

—That's enough now, little man.

Buddy senses that he's trapped. Before he can pull the trigger a brass knuckle lands in his face. I tumble. My hand lets go of her wrist. They grab me under my arms and drag me outside. No trace of Betsi Baller. I drag myself to the car. Around me cannon blasts. Tomorrow or on another day they will drop again like flies. My left eye swells shut. I start the Ford Mustang and retreat. Buddy swears eternal revenge. Nobody puts their hands on Buddy and goes unpunished. It is already getting light as Buddy finally finds his way home. Nobody can feel safe. That is Buddy's trump card. He decides to play it.

It's the first of January 2000, and since 2 P.M. I've been guarding the pictures again. It must be easy to get a picture out of here. They are not secured. Not one of them. Not even the Chagall. I ponder how I can get the pictures out of here. Jan turns his eagle-head ring next to me. I stare at Adolf Hitler. On wood. On a horse. The flag bearer. I bet the picture is from Monty Python. A fake. And under the eye the injury. A wound. A visitor asks me when and how the picture was damaged. I tell him that an American soldier saw the picture in 1945 and became enraged. Then he rammed his bayonet into the picture. I got to get the pictures out of here. I have to get THAT picture out of here: *Stalin After the Rain.* I ask Jan about his friend. Jan grins at me. I should piss off. I give Jan a "hunny." Jan will let his friend know.

LARS   Jan calls and gets me out of my coma. Felix has disappeared. I don't immediately get what's going on. It's the first of January, 8 P.M., and Jan says I have three hours, they close at midnight. I say it'll be okay; that he should leave a ticket for me. The forecast promises better weather. I don't believe the fuckers. My friend Roman Herzog holds his New Year's speech. He appeals to the citizens. On this point we agree. He reads a letter out loud that he received. His New Year's greeting. I can't believe it:

THE FAMILY IS THE NUCLEUS OF SOCIALISM. THUS THE FAMILY MUST BE DESTROYED.

The asshole forgets to say who the letter is from. He says that something was misunderstood here. A plea for the family, the bearer of the democratic and constitutional state, based on rights. He emphasizes: RIGHT. The great conviviality. I call the station and complain. The idiot says that it is a recording, that you can't correct anything anymore. I add him to my list. No news from Hakan. I'll have to talk to him. I go out. Traces of last night's accidents everywhere on the streets. In the subway station Kottbusser Tor a twelve-year-old junkie shoots up for the last time. The security service throws him out because he can't croak down here. I get out at Hallesches Tor and head along Stresemannstraße, toward Potsdamer Platz. A few creeps occupy an Adria-Grill fast-food place, which triggers turmoil. The owner of the Adria-Grill doesn't want the creeps in his joint and tries to throw them out. The creeps smash the joint to pieces. My gaze falls upon the Telecom high-rise. A potential target. I make a note. In the Gropius museum building I have to pass by the fag and the Turk again, who can barely keep on their feet. The Turk is in the process of giving a television interview. He babbles some shit about genuine exertion that brings in good money, and that in a week everything will be over anyway. He misses the chance of his lifetime. I add him to my list. Jan works in the room where Hitler gives a speech accompanied by the Horst-Wessel song. We give each other five and I ask him what's up. We go to the next room to Nico and I'm afraid that he will start his Fred and Betsi shit again. The guy begins to shake and refuses to look at me. Jan says that we should get some sun, that he'll take care of the rooms. I have no idea what he's talking about. Nico leads me up to the next floor, through some closed-off section, through a thousand doors and hallways, and then up another floor onto a type of lower roof that from the ground you could believe is the actual roof: the glass dome of the inner courtyard, over which the spotlights are installed. The sun. Nico is obviously paranoid, because he can't keep still for a second. He asks me if I have seen the picture *I.O. Stalin and K.E. Woroschilov in the Kremlin After the Rain* by Alexander Gerassimov. I ask him if that's the monstrous thing and he says:

—Yes. We have to get the picture out of here.

He's totally fucked-up. I do him a favor and ask him why.

—It's a fake. The second half of the formula is concealed beneath the paint.

I play along:

—Right, the formula. Where's the other half?

—You already know: Betsi Baller.

This guy is crazy. I like him. Nico doesn't stop:

—The problem is, if the picture disappears Moscow will declare war on us. Even the officials don't know that it's a fake. For them the painting is a relic. They can't just give it up for lost.

—Got it.

I don't get anything. The matter begins to interest me:

—How do you want to get the picture out of here? I mean, it's the goddamn biggest picture in here.

—The picture is not secured.

Nico is a serious case.

—I mean that the thing is really fucking big. And what should I do with it if it is a fake and won't bring in any money?

Nico stares at me and I'm afraid that he's beginning to bawl.

—Jan has all the keys.

—How did that fuck get all the keys?

—He has them.

—Then why don't we simply take the Chagall?

Nico despairs. I promise him I'll think it over.

—It's a matter of life and death, you know.

I pat him on the shoulder and tell him I know. Jan is standing in front of the photo of an Armenian cultural delegation from 1930. You can see the backs of two Armenian folk dancers on the Red Square. I think of Hakan and I feel ill because it is simply too much at once. Jan asks if everything is okay. I have no idea if he knows at all what it's all about. Whether Nico already got him to buy into it. We set a time with Nico. Nico is still shaking. I make my way out, hail a taxi, and drive to Hakan's. Telecom or Stalin in the Rain. I have to decide, because obviously I've gone crazy.

HAKAN   It is the first of January, shortly before 11 P.M. I've made a few resolutions for 2000. I want to stick with them. I'm into principles. I unlock the door for Lars, because I have to make that clear to him. He has a right to know. Or so I imagine.

—Hi, Hakan.

—Hi.

—How is it going?

—I'm okay.

Lars is in a strange mood. I haven't seen him like this yet. It makes me sick. He makes me insecure. He can do that well. But I have to talk to him. I don't feel like this shit anymore. He begins:

—Done with Christmas?

—Don't mention it.

—Okay.

Pause. He wants something, but plays the mute. That's annoying. I don't know how I should begin.

—Hakan?

—What is it?

—I think I'm fucking in love with you.

—I know.

—No one can endure that.

—What do you want from me?

—What do I want from you?

—Yes, what do you want?

—Shit, man.

I'm an idiot. I don't dare open my mouth.

—Listen, Lars . . .

—"Listen, Lars . . ." Are you talking with a handicapped or what?

—I can't do it.

—What can't you do?

I'd like to punch him in the kisser.

—I'm not into this fag shit, understand?

—No.

I don't understand why the asshole stays so calm.

—I'm a bit slow on the uptake, you have to explain it to me. Come on, Hakan, explain it to me.

I'll kill him.

—I don't want to fuck you, and even if I were crazy about every cock in the city, even if you were the only human being on the whole planet—not you! Is that clear enough? We have nothing, absolutely nothing in common. You make me sick with your fatalism shit, your entire fucked-up babble. I still have an idea about my life here and I believe in it. In principles and, kill me if you want, in rights and democracy. I'm living quite well, and I don't plan to change anything about it. I don't plan to stage my demise with you. As far as I'm concerned you can get smashed, puke your guts out all over the place, and piss on people, but leave me out of it. And goddamn it I'm not gay!

—Now that really impresses me, did you learn it by heart?

—Fuck you.

—I mean, you have no clue. What's up with all this crap? Since when am I a fatalist? You know nothing, you know absolutely nothing about me.

—Because I don't want to know.

—You mean then that the upright Mister Lawyer no longer wants to know anything about Mister Loser.

—Bingo.

He doesn't go after me; he doesn't wreck the apartment; he just sits there totally calm. I feel sick. I want him to finally go but I don't say anything.

—Do you know that you actually have the most beautiful back in the world?

—Forget it.

—You can't forget a back like that.

He stands up, kisses me on the cheek without touching me anywhere else, and goes. I have to throw up.

Translated from German by Elke Siegel and Paul Fleming.

Show #7

Benjamin v. Stuckrad-Barre

IF ALL OF THE READINGS WENT THAT WELL OR EVEN MORE SO, I thought, the industry could kiss my ass. Of course I couldn't tell them to quite yet, but the main thing was not to lose sight of what's important. My public? Quite right, Roland Kaiser.

Joy! Fun, rock, I'd even say—Punk rock. The prospects for that were excellent, despite my post-TV-appearance delirium which the health insurances are bound to add to their list of refundable treatments over the next few years. For scheduled that evening was a double reading with my friend Kracht.

We were both huge admirers of the George Michael video in which he offers a stadium his version of an Elton John song and, in the middle of it, takes the masses to the screaming limit when he proudly presents:

— *Ladies and Gentlemen, Mister Elton John!*

Upon which the man himself enters the stage, they sing a duet, and the stadium flips out. That was sort of our concept.

The travel information desk of the Deutsche Bahn had provided us with some top research, so we arrived nearly simultaneously and were able to give each other a blissful hug. We called the promoter and invited him to an organizational meeting at our hotel. He sounded very professional and asked whether he should bring his technical assistant. Of course we insisted he do that, although we had no idea what exactly the jurisdiction of a technical assistant might be. But the fact that he existed was good, since we were convinced that this was the right place and the right cast to finally expand into musical dimensions. Lights, sound, effects! Smoke grenades, dry ice, hydraulic stages, a catwalk into the audience, merchandising booths! Our promoter had booked a theater no less, and on the phone he had spoken of a "full house." A full house was one thing. Full, that is to say, fully-tanked authors was the other. I was in a bizarre mood and flung the two pills that I hadn't popped with Katja Riemann on the smoked-glass table in the hotel room, which I had since renamed the "Strategic Planning and Artist Prep Room." Well, if it's going to be like that, said Kracht, and placed next to them a Vizir environmental globe filled to the brim with cocaine. This left us with just one question: WHEN were we to begin our intake?

— Hmhmhm, I said, and began to spread out two lines. Maybe relatively soon?

— Certainly, granted Herr Kracht. It tasted excellent. I was still a little dazed from that morning's raisin-roll disaster, but now it was clear that I wouldn't want or be able to eat anything else for the rest of the day, so everything was back in order. It worked, burned, smashed. We stowed our provisions and waited for the promoter. By turns we jumped up to do sketches of various hard-rock scenarios. We would require a catwalk into the audience, a video-projection screen, and Steven Tyler scarves on the microphone stands. And, no matter what, a deafening overture. We cracked open several bottles of a regional premium pilsner, as the cocaine was just getting ready to corrode our pharyngeal cavities with the hundredfold power of legal Ahoy pop; we had to put a stop to that. Whereupon entered the promoter with his technical assistant. By means of several none-too-hurried expositions and a few carefully placed inquiries, we attempted to leave an impression of passable responsibility, despite all the beer bottles. The promoter was somewhat reserved, but he was probably thinking exactly what was just then shooting through our heads along with the drugs: artists!

The technical assistant said that if we were indeed planning to walk all across the stage during the reading, we would need clip-on microphones, which he could provide. We praised his expertise and flexibility. A fog machine, though, wasn't something he had on hand, and he was also skeptical about being able to arrange for video projections. We were crestfallen. In any case, he promised to light our way to the stage—which was to remain dark until the first sounds of reading—with powerful pocket flashlights, all to the accompaniment of rousing instrumental music. He touched his nose like a conspirator and asked whether the Chemical Brothers would be appropriate for this purpose. The technical assistant was a truly humorous man.

In the afternoon we chilled on rubber lounge chairs next to the twelve-square-meter basement pool and felt ambivalent about our conclusive appraisal of the situation. Due to the high humidity in the basement, the Vizir environmental globe was stored in the Strategic Planning and Artist Prep Room so, from time to time, whenever doubt got the better of us, we ran upstairs to tank up and, after a few minutes, renew the drooling euphoria with which we faced the evening. Based on my own good experience, we urgently needed a set list. This quickly grew into a four-hour program, which was to be tailored according to the external circumstances. Then we tried to rehearse and read aloud from our books, unsuccessfully. We couldn't help laughing or slipping up in the lines. Our audience had a right to coherent sentences, we agreed, but the words on the paper were slow and stood around stupidly while our eyes rushed on, wanted to leaf through the book, get it over with, change the channel. We dunked our heads under the far-too-hot water. When we resurfaced, we had lots of chlorine in our eyes and blinked dully, but everything else seemed to have improved. We quickly set out to find a Thai restaurant, as the well-spiced, nutritious diet of the Asians would be just the thing to get us back on track. Though we had no appetite at all, we gobbled down an extra-spicy soup.

The Asian restaurant offered a take-out menu for people in a hurry and for that purpose provided a manifold assortment of paper plates, as Kracht discovered on one of his nervous jaunts through the restaurant. We helped ourselves to several of them and inscribed them in the name of the masses of spectators we were expecting, because just then the drugs were working so well.

TICKETS WANTED

we wrote—and

AT ANY PRICE.

These signs, which we would somehow have to press into the hands of a few people longingly gazing about, would be the world's best advertisement. We might hire two Jehova's Witnesses somewhere. Anyway, with these signs we hurried back to the main camp, picked up our medications and books, and bought some sunflowers to be thrown into the audience after the regular part of the show (Encore! En-core!) with gratitude. On the way to the theater we snorted a fingertip of coke in front of each announcement poster. The promoter had put up a lot of posters.

Still a good hour to kill before the reading. Lots of people were standing in front of the theater, but for sheer excitement we forgot to distribute the signs and hastened through the back entrance, and got a chance to do wonderful entertainer things:

Testing, testing—voices, lights, sound, music louder, at the beginning please have ONLY the exit signs lit, everything else dark, thanks, no, please don't open the doors yet, so, you enter stage right, I enter stage left, then a gleaming spotlight, stop the music and take a bow. Yes, by all means pour the wine into water bottles, that's urgent, otherwise it'll seem too forced, exactly, OK, aha, they're from the bookstore, good evening first of all, we hope so too, of course we'll do book signings after, let's have the fee up front, yeah, why not, photographs, sure, as far as I'm concerned during the reading too, or wait, no, just for the first ten minutes, that's a good rule the photographers will be aware of, but of course, the interview might be better to do after, after is no problem at all, we'd just like to have a moment now, good, you can open the doors, that will be all, see you later.

Backstage! We had really been very careful to behave as abnormally as possible. Sort of like it is said of Richard Gere or Whitney Houston, when they arrive in a helicopter five minutes before show time for *Wetten daß* and get on everybody's NERVES. Now this was a backstage room, for once: velvet chairs in front of a big wall of mirrors, exactly as if, only a few minutes ago, the last touchups had been administered to Marlene Dietrich's hair and makeup. A basket with fruit, champagne and sesame breadrings was sitting on top of a Biedermeier dresser. Post-It notes on the mirror wished us "Success," brushes, creams, powder, and Kleenex were available in such quantities that you'd think they were expecting a Russian ballet troupe, and the make-up table's marble top was apparently intended just for preparing coke.

In theater they still really know how to treat entertainment artists properly! we wrote enthusiastically into the guest book. Before us

Wolf Biermann had signed in and, next to some well-chosen words of thanks, he had, unaccountably, drawn two copulating Ottifants. There's no accounting for the effects of adrenaline. Thank God our salaries had been paid in bills that didn't come from the evening's cash register, but straight from the bank—flat, crisp, easy to roll. Ready, steady, coke. We plopped into the hairdressing chairs and cried YEA! Ten minutes more and we would grow tattoos and denim shirts. The door opened slowly, and the promoter looked in questioningly:

—You've been taken care of?

Indeed we were. He looked at his exact-to-the-second, everything-under-control diver's watch and said that in exactly six minutes the lights would go out and the music on, and he was excited to see what would happen then. The technical assistant would come by to pick us up. Followed by an intermezzo of we're-so-sorrys typical of coke:

—Hey, anything the matter?

—No, everything OK. Same with you guys?

—Are you mad or something?

—Why would I be mad?

—You think we're drunk!

—Come on, nonsense!

—No, you're annoyed.

—Naw, it's nothing, what's to be annoyed about.

—You ARE annoyed. Shuh-uh!

—Well. Do you guys have anything?

—Hm?

—You know—drugs?

—Oh OK, sure, want some?

—All right, since it's Sunday. Are you guys even going to be able, um, that was strong, thanks, that was your banknote, wasn't it?

The technical assistant came in with the requisite pocket flashlight and asked *now* what was up, sheeez, NOW what?

The promoter threw his head back and said nothing was up. The hierarchical gap between them did not appear insignificant. We asked for another minute and shoved the two now rather importunate men out of the dressing room. It was time now, but the time for the intermission that we had planned during our afternoon delirium was far away, two hours into it. In two hours we didn't even want to be here.

What was keeping us from NOT taking off right now? There was a loud knock on the door, and we heard the familiar strains pleasantly droning

The brothers gonna work it out/The brothers gonna work it out/The brothers gonna work it out/The brothers gonna work it out/The brothers gonna work it out

That they did, big time.

It would be exaggerated to say that our respect for Jon Bon Jovi increased significantly that evening, but being brought onstage with a flashlight was really pretty cool. Maybe we'd get lucky and they would at least think us self-ironic. But then maybe we'd get unlucky and stumble and fail to get one word out.

We took a bow, the lights flickered on, and the people began to clap. Somebody also whistled extensively, but that didn't necessarily HAVE to be meant in a mean way. Besides, we had the light, the microphones, the drinks, and oh, our books, we had forgotten our books! The technical assistant had gone into our dressing room, probably to look for drugs, and brought our books just in time, no one had noticed a thing, everything appeared casual and even planned. Then Kracht said

—*I am the god of hellfire—and I bring you*

And I completed

—*. . . fire!*

With that we got at least our breath back. We read and talked. Magically, so did the audience. Then Kracht grew ever quieter, while I rambled on. I glanced over at him encouragingly, but he was snoozing and smoking, the very picture of a Buddhist bronze sculpture. And on I talked. My jaw was starting to list noticeably, but I just had to rescue us. I thought of those black-and-white photos of the Berlin Waldbühne, an outdoor stage that was ripped into handy pieces by outraged rock-music fans in 1960-something. Kracht got up and started pacing back and forth behind me, returned to his seat, and chewed on a sunflower. When I addressed him he didn't answer, at best started reading at random, to stop again abruptly and smoke some more. People probably thought we had figured out this charming division of labor and didn't turn on us. In the newspaper two days later Kracht was described as an introverted, charming, distinguished author based in Hamburg (interesting, considering he is living in Bangkok);I, however, was merely a loudmouthed something or other. But then another newspaper said there was good chemistry between us. It was in this spirit that we had scheduled the intermission, the technical assistant switched the lights, let music strike, and people stood up, went to smoke in front of the door and bought our books. We went into Marlene Dietrich's dressing room, also to smoke, and said nothing. Then we cracked up and said Oh God, for five minutes in turns.

I fished out the pills, we had no more thinking to do, just swallow them, our glands were already going crazy, which we noticed when the pills started dissolving in our hands, down the hatch, and then back up—up on the stage. To our relief the people had stayed and were eager to see what we might come up with in the second half. We were fairly curious ourselves, but mostly about the effect of the pills.

On his own initiative, Herr Kracht fired off what we had originally, within our dramaturgical scheme, elaborated as our prop-killer encore. He hung around his neck a singer-songwriter's harmonica rack purchased at a Malayan music store, the by-product of some educational trip. We then quite noticeably lost control, but according to our set list still had two hours to go. We plugged away slavishly, it never occurred to us to be flexible and put an end to it. Cocaine, it is true, is not generally known for bringing out one's sensitive side. I got up to go backstage to smash some cold water on my forehead. There I ran into the by-now heavily intoxicated promoter carrying a bottle of Kirsch. Ten-mark bills were spilling out of his pants pockets, and he said that we didn't have to keep going, if we couldn't. Oh really? Aaah! Yesss! Full of joy I jumped back onto the stage to let Kracht also taste of the sweet fruit of knowledge, but there I was confronted with the spectacle of an unbelievably silly auditorium. My travel companion was standing on the edge of the stage, throwing sunflowers into the standing, clapping, jacket-buttoning, departing crowd. The promoter's suggestion to end soon had reached the audience through my clip-on microphone in stereo, at a moment when Kracht was probably smoking or sleeping. During the book-signing that followed we garnered a lot of praise for that closing gesture in particular, so very surprising and funny.

Because all this had to end—no: had to GO ON in a rock-star-esque way—the technical assistant drove us to the hotel. Back in the room, a short nap to clear our heads. Oh no, no, not at all, let's clear our heads as far from now as possible. A minute later, we were awake and highly so—and, as we met in the corridor, clearly, we had to keep going. Next door was a neighborhood center. One of those renovated town houses with colorful walls, a counter made of pine, and a football table. The blue defensive row was, as always, graced with a red replacement man, since the blue one had broken and there were no more blue replacement men, plus some joker had drawn willies on the pants. On the way to the can, stacks of boxes containing Rainbow Tour brochures, guitar-workshop applications and schedules for movie theaters that did not care about the works of Roland Emmerich or Steven Spielberg. The level indicators on the tape deck only rarely made it into the red zone because the heads needed cleaning. But with One World percussion music that doesn't really matter. In the basement, a library based on trust. Control would be better.

In the sanitary zone, conditions for taking drugs were not exactly optimal: The door couldn't be locked, and there was no clean surface in sight. We went into the library and misused a laminated edition of the bestseller

Gaby Hauptmann—The Complete Poems and Ballads.

Back at the pine counter the tape deck was yowling peacefully, but at least our own level indicators were clearly back in the red zone. In the meantime a game had begun; unfortunately we had missed the announcement of the rules. It was an auction, but without money. Everybody had brought an object and was auctioning it, we now learnt, for a good idea or everyday help. The proposals strove for originality, and we applauded appreciatively. On offer were a decorative printer's case, a coffee grinder with the word "Coffee" on it, a Red Hot Chili Peppers CD and one by Franz Josef-Degenhart (you had to take both), a wok, a travel typewriter with two replacement ribbons, one pair of beige sailing shoes with the felt-pen inscription "Hey Ho Let's Go!," a World Savings Day desk blotter, a juice press, a standing lamp, and much more that would have created a sensation out on the curb, and then it was raining offers:

—a breakfast at Vitamini

—six rainbow candles

—one bicycle repair

—a haircut

—a music tape for driving
—assistance with tax returns
—translation of a text of your choice into Spanish, up to 4 pages
—carry your Saturday shopping up the stairs
—help with dowels, percussion drill on hand
—lawn mowing
—installation of a pirate copy of favorite word-processing software
—as many piano lessons as it takes to be halfway able to play the melody to the Mariacron ad.

We also called out several hot offers, and I ended up with a toy car, without having given a thing for it, which was a success in itself.

Then some drunks came in and screamed when they saw us. They asked us to come with them to a disco. Why the hell not. The disco was called Discotheque, and we drank several trays of one-mark-fifty schnapps, and I didn't have the impression that the evening WASN'T a hit.

Fortunately we couldn't talk because the music was too loud. Now and then someone from the scream gang stood next to my ear and roared something, and each time I just nodded and laughed and sort of moved my lips. Kracht had put up the hood of his raincoat and was smoking into the screamers' faces. They laughed their heads off and thought it was great. Then the seldom-sober Hamburger requested the ethnic hit "*I've been watching you—alalalalalong*" and drove the screamers to the dance floor. *Sweater, you can't sweat no more.* Words to live by. Perhaps get out of here. Right. But where to. True enough. Maybe stay a little longer. But how much longer. And what are we waiting for. Maybe a touch more, good idea, the can's over there.

When we came back, one of the bawlers had removed the shelves of an empty Afri Cola refrigerator, had sat down in it with wedged knees, and was now licking the condensed water from inside the glass door and wanted to be considered exciting. But somebody else was going to take care of that for us, we had things to do. Whenever on such evenings everything slips away from you, your handle on things, time, your jaw, the end of a sentence and the like, things become basic, and people look for a moment of human understanding—while exposing issues of international politics. Monstrous monologues disguised as discussion: One guy wants to save Prince's career, no really, it's not all over for him yet, it could be really easy, another guy has a pretty precise idea of how the Borussia Mönchengladbach soccer team might once again rise to the top, a third makes confessions and demands to rescue a friendship demoted to acquaintanceship. Another guy just ran to the phone to call his ex-girlfriend (not at home, just the answering machine, the invention of which will be profusely cursed the next morning). Nods everywhere. Another schnapps, OK, one more. You too? Two for everybody? Nods.

After hours more of this, the revelation: Go NOW. Not another five minutes, not two more songs, not another beer, or cigarette, no more schnapps, of all things. RIGHT NOW. Jacket, door, air, whew.

In the Strategic Planning and Artist Prep Room we ate some headache tablets. It was altogether too late, within this too-lateness however still relatively early. Maybe we WOULD be able to sleep this time. Haha. Protestations, regrets, sympathies. And accountings: How was it, how much did it cost, and what's left over (of money, coke, of the evening, of our lives). One thing had run out for sure: euphoria. Always the sad part. But suddenly—and I attributed this to the mystery pills—I could do a half-decent imitation of Falco.

—I just got nuzzin' ina middle! Eizza reeeee-ly baad. Oh-or dammmmmmn good za' guy, Fallllco. Betweeeen, nuzzin.'

—Yeah. Or else ab-so-LOOT-ly nuzzin.'

—I'm going to the bathroom.

—Hm?

—I'm going to the bathroom.

—Go ahead. Sure, go ahead.

—Uh oh!

—Whassit?

—I've got blood in my eyes. What's up with that? Hey, take a look at this, what's going on?

—What, what, turn the light off, it's bright enough outside already, oh, you've burst a blood vessel.

—How did that happen? Is that from the pills? How long have I had it, how do you make it go away, is it serious? Man, that looks just brutal.

—It'll go away on its own. Maybe I have some eyedrops. No, I don't.

Finally some VISIBLE damage, so I didn't feel like such a sissy any-more, for my ill humor had a reason: I had blood in my eyes! I—or was it John Wayne?—tried to project an image of composure and thoughtfully tidied up the junkie things, because I wanted to spare the cleaning staff, who surely would come knocking soon, this bleak spectacle. And so I wiped the white dust off the marble with Kracht's damp tie, unrolled the banknotes, and even cleaned the phone cards.

Most hotel-room TVs display the time. Four digits jumping at you in red. Still time. But no more sleep. No point. We needed entertain-ment, direction, discipline. That is to say, a third person. We wan-dered about the corridors, toward the light, to where we could hear a clatter, that's how afraid of the quiet we were. In the breakfast room Dietrich Schwanitz, who had also given a reading in this city last night, was sitting with an elderly woman, perhaps it was even his mother, or a fan, as it would be disrespectful to refer to someone of her age as a groupie. Hard to say, since Dietrich Schwanitz is ageless himself. He could be forty, but just as easily sixty. Schwanitz was eat-ing a lot. He had gathered a considerable assortment from the buffet, and had an unconventional way of eating it: his right hand guided toward his mouth a Gouda roll adorned with jam, while his left hand spooned in some muesli. And his muesli spoon also took turns with a bit of scrambled egg. Everything ends up in the same place, he thought to himself. Did Schwanitz end up kneeling over the toilets of pastry shops when he was on tour? The woman only drank coffee and tried to restrain the heartily chewing professor:

—We have time.

It probably was his mother after all. Because with no sense of embarrassment he allowed her to take a napkin, spit on it, and start rubbing various quark stains off his dark-green merino-wool sweater. Schwanitz wasn't in the best of moods, perhaps he had shaved around his obscene little goatee a tad too cavalierly. The best-selling author was bleeding profusely, and then, too, everyone, even a professor, is in a poor mood at breakfast. Who could understand that better than I, with my bleeding eyes. At the buffet I had the opportu-nity to catch, in the silver lid of the scrambled-eggs pan, the distort-ed reflection of a pale, red-eyed, Darkwave reactionary—and yet it was only me. Kracht ate seventeen kiwis, drank a Bloody Mary, even poured Tabasco into his coffee, and conjured up the salubrious effect of this arrangement. He had deep faith in such matters.

Translated from German by Sara Ogger.

Schmetterlinge und Butterblumen (Buttercups and Butterflies)

Thomas Hauser

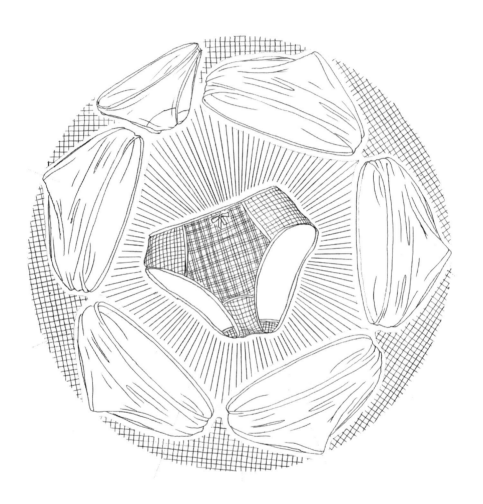

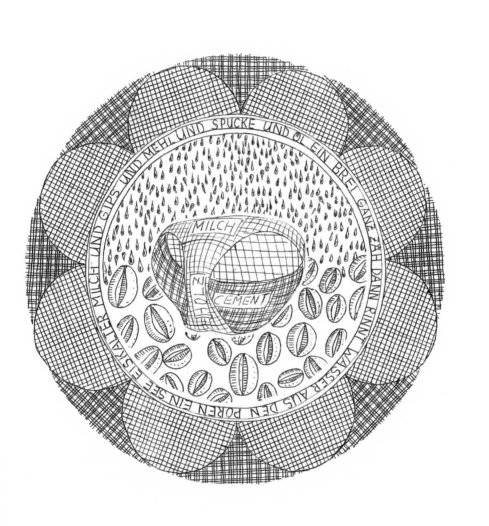

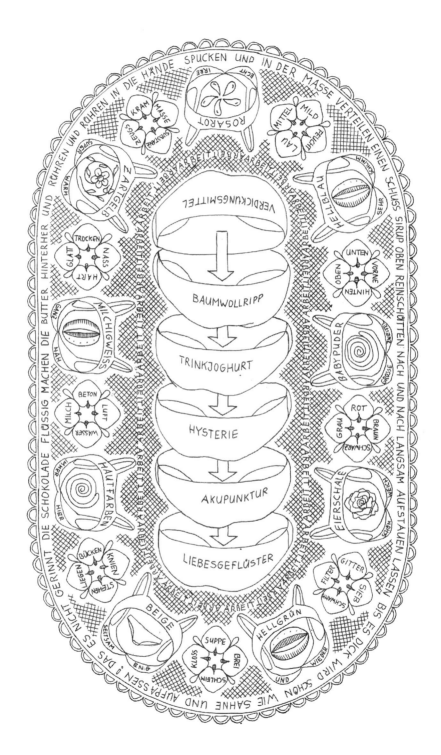

Kitty Hawk

Hunter Kennedy

DEWITT TOOK ONE LAST TUG OF BEER THROUGH THE PARTY straw and walked out back to practice some archery. He hunted through the weeds until he found the rusty compound bow under the big bay window. DeWitt was surprised it still worked. Through the window, he watched his buddy Jedson pace deliberate figure eights with a cordless phone to his ear as he worked the sorority switchboards. Jedson was trying to "seal the deal," as he so often liked to say, and DeWitt knew exactly who he was dialing—a couple of Theta sisters who were hard up for weed, these little stoner jockettes who'd been kicked off the field hockey team. Ambling to their makeshift firing range across the overgrown yard, DeWitt notched an arrow in the bowstring and considered exactly why this deal needed sealing. Jedson had just lost his license for driving under various influences and, without DeWitt, had no ride down to Kitty Hawk this summer. So Jedson was setting up a cash guarantee that things were going to work smoothly at the Outer Banks, and *that* DeWitt could relate to. He balanced the compound bow in his left hand, drew across his chest, and sighted on the square black target. He lacerated the damn thing.

He and Jedson never bought what they could appropriate, and occasionally bragged about being psychic assassins. They made targets from random Polaroids shoplifted from Salvation Army scrapbooks. The firing range was roped off by sawhorses that they'd stolen from a construction site after getting wasted one night on someone else's wine coolers. They had permanently borrowed the quiver and bow from a sporting-goods store run by a couple of fellow stoners, and had amassed so many arrows that when they missed the stack of hay bales they usually didn't bother looking for them in the woods. DeWitt was spooked by the dark acre of oaks behind the firing range, a dead zone littered with the ant-hollowed remains of crucified squirrels and impaled blue jays that was unfit for even growing dope. One day these small creatures would avenge themselves upon him, he was certain. But like his other regrets, he quickly pushed this thought from his mind. He checked the Polaroid target and saw he had scored a bull's-eye, knocking it right through an unassuming fat girl's mouth. The uncanny placement made him suddenly laugh out loud, and crows thrashed out of the branches at the sound of his rude voice. He was starting to feel slightly better.

The night before, DeWitt and old-man Jeffers had been positioning the school's cannon-sized telescope when the astronomy professor had wounded his pride. As old-man Jeffers focused the lens, the finishing touches on thirty minutes of hard calculations, DeWitt had started grinning uncontrollably. His mind was elsewhere, lingering on all his summer plans far away from the department, but Jeffers mistook the smile for one of camaraderie.

The wrinkled professor cleared his throat to signal he wanted to offer some man-to-man advice. DeWitt knew what to expect, as it usually involved something vaguely scandalous, and encouraged the old man with an even broader grin. The more Jeffers confided in him, the sooner DeWitt would have enough dirt on the old codge to neutralize whatever discoveries his professor might later make.

"You've got big plans for the summer, don't you, DeWitt?"

"Yessir. Fair to middling."

"Goodness, I remember those days well, and lemme tell you what. If you ever get out to McDonald Observatory, DeWitt, you should bring a lady friend. I did when I was your age, and there's nothing like getting head under that spread of stars."

Jeffers, a man with baggy, ashen skin and liver spots, chuckled at the thought. His pure level of enjoyment made DeWitt recoil in irritation and embarrassment. It just wasn't goddamn fair. And if he didn't change the subject, the old man would drone on about it all night. Faking a sneeze, DeWitt jacked the telescope several degrees off course. He couldn't resist sneezing again to really fuck things up, bumping the thing two hairs' sideways. His apology was surprisingly convincing. Old-man Jeffers cursed the outdated equipment and shook out a fresh Camel from his soft pack. "Nothing works in this department," he griped, "not even the lights." Then he began the required steps to reposition the scope while DeWitt slipped out to the back steps to burn a joint and reestablish equilibrium. It would take Jeffers twenty minutes just to get the knobs aligned.

Now DeWitt had never told anybody this, but he hadn't ever had a blowjob. The fact that he was a pot dealer made the whole thing that much more embarrassing. He had kept Jedson and the rest of their friends completely in the dark about the situation, but he wondered if the old man had somehow figured this out. For the past few years, Jeffers had lived vicariously through the tamer stories of DeWitt's nightlife while spending his own evenings watching out for a new comet. DeWitt admired him for standing guard over the heavens while the rest of the town screwed and slept, and he always had a good tidbit from the night's activities for old-man Jeffers to ponder. Maybe he had given himself away with his own big mouth.

"This crusty monk got blown in bumfuck West Texas, and I can't even get head in Charlottesville!" cursed DeWitt as he strung another arrow.

He was ambivalent about his next target, the same kind of indifference that had led him into dealing dope. He briefly sighted on his friend Jedson, who was slowly moving back and forth behind the plate-glass window like a duck at a sideshow, then on somebody's dog trotting in the gravel road past the house, then a chicken hawk on a power line which he completely missed.

The sliding door slammed shut, and Jedson was laughing at him. "Nice shot, Jack. Har har. You ought to borrow my Visionware sometime," he hollered. Jedson wore prescription tinted glasses and with his severe part, resembled a televangelist. "I got you lined up to make some serious denominations. Can you give those girls a tour?"

"Which Thetas you call?" scowled DeWitt.

"The goalie and what's-her-name. They're bringing some friend who sounds cool. How about let me drive the Cherokee?"

"Fat fucking chance. You navigate."

"But I got your keys. Jingle, jingle."

The meeting was at dusk by the Balz Observatory air conditioners. DeWitt let Jedson drive after his friend sighted a loophole in the open-container law about how the passengers could drink. Nobody had ever adequately explained the law to DeWitt, and he figured Jedson to be somewhat of an authority on the subject since they'd stripped him of his license. DeWitt sipped cold beer through a party straw and directed Jedson this way and that down the desolate collegiate streets. The guy was a terrible driver, and when they pulled up to the observatory's turquoise AC units, he hit the brights, then cut the ignition with a screech that raised the hair on the back of DeWitt's neck. Three women crept sniggling out from behind the hedges with their hands in front of their eyes. They obviously thought all this transaction business was very funny. DeWitt wasn't going to show them any mercy.

"Charge them an extra ten a bag, okay?" he told Jedson, the money man.

"Yeah, we'll fleece them."

The Thetas were exactly as DeWitt had pictured them, jolly broad-shouldered girls with calves the size of pineapples and breasts like mosquito bites. He hadn't seen either of them sober since January. The third was a skinny redhead in jeans and a hunting jacket. Standing between the chunky deadheads, she looked slightly exotic, her pale face framing light-green eyes, her snaggletooth tucked slightly over the edge of her full bottom lip. While Jedson swaggered around with the introductions, she stared steadily at DeWitt with a quizzical look. The other two were in hysterics.

"I can't believe you're a dealer now," said one of them.

"You better believe it, lady," replied DeWitt.

"You look so J. Crew," tittered the other. "Shouldn't you be in like a down parka?"

"Hey, I didn't pay for the clothes."

"Your mom did."

"Watch your mouth."

"All right, separate," said Jedson, stepping between them. "Let's get you ladies a look at the crime lab, and you can stay up here with— what did you say your name is?"

The redhead didn't blink. DeWitt wondered if she spoke the language. Or maybe she was just looking right through him, the dealer who'd never been blown.

"I'm Audrey. Nice to meet you, mister dealer," she said, extending a hand.

While Jedson took the jockettes for the tour, DeWitt and Audrey smoked cigarettes on the back steps. She claimed she was a chain-smoker, but she didn't have a voice like one. It had a slight lilt to it, no gravel, and DeWitt guessed it was Shenandoah. It turned out he was right—she was from Roanoke and headed cross-country for a month. She needed weed for the road. Audrey also added she had just dumped her boyfriend. He knew that was a gratuitous comment. She wanted some extras.

"How long you in town for."

"I don't know, whenever I decide to split."

DeWitt was trying to think of a reply when one of the old janitors came walking around the building and gave him the nod.

"Heyya, Mistuh DeWitt. Nice evening, ain't it."

"How's it going, Luth. Your TV working now?"

"Yeah, but I mostly listen to that little radio."

"Say hey to your old lady for me."

"Shih, I'm headed there right now." He walked on down the hill.

After a minute, Audrey looked at him, blowing smoke out her nose. "How do you know that guy?"

"I know all the janitors. I give him weed so he can go to sleep at night. His wife's a motormouth and a total insomniac. Luth tells me funny stories."

"What, you give all the janitors dope?"

"All the ones I know. They pretty much got a handle on what's going down anyway, and they don't mess with me."

"Damn," muttered Audrey. "Not bad."

After twenty minutes, Jedson swaggered out with the bloodshot hockey chicks, and the Thetas both stuffed fifty dollars in his belt, giggling like they were tipping a dancer. They went and sat under the oak trees to watch the traffic zip by on Jefferson Parkway, and DeWitt stood up and dusted off. Audrey pursed her lips, pulled out her wallet, and slowly folded two twenties inside a ten. She wiped a red lock of hair out of her eyes.

"Where do you want it?"

"Try my pants pocket."

She tucked the cash down into the bottom of his pocket, right over his erection. She let her fingers slide over it on the way up, and his stomach muscles went into contractions, not that she noticed. She was already waltzing off toward the door.

DeWitt was the star pupil, so to speak, of the Astronomy Department, and old-man Jeffers had given him keys to the observatory. Nobody questioned why he would be around at night because he did research and he also had a little office with a desk propped on bricks and a star chart behind the chair. He knew seven different zodiacs and could work a calculator like nobody's business, but he had been pushing it lately, not showing up for lectures, showing up high at night, and was generally on a short leash with the rest of the academics. Jeffers couldn't give a shit because he liked hearing about his hijinks, but if Jeffers knew about the crime lab, he would lead the lynching party. Dope lab equaled funding cut. So it was with some trepidation that DeWitt led Audrey into the building. He guided her down the moldy basement stairs and under the heating pipes to the end of the hall. As part of his purchased janitorial neglect, the lights that had burnt out in this part of the building had not been replaced. The hallway was as dark as a planetarium, and they had to go by feel. DeWitt guided Audrey into a pitch-black doorway, but she halted, leaning back into him. She complained that she couldn't see, but she had caught his erection hard between her ass cheeks, a calculated move of appraisal.

"I can't go in there. Where's your flashlight?"

"You're leaning on it."

"Then show me something."

He gave her a push, and she shrieked as she stumbled through the black velvet curtains into the glare of the grow lights. Audrey wheeled around, coyly staring at DeWitt as the curtains flapped behind him.

"Where the hell is my bag?"

"I don't know. Maybe it's in my front pocket."

"You want me to check?"

"Well, you paid for it, didn't you?"

Audrey didn't respond, drifting around the room of young dope plants. There was a thousand dollars' worth of marijuana sorted and bagged in a plain shopping bag under the makeshift lab table. This picked bud would leave a Carolina surfer paralyzed from the eyes down. DeWitt's name wasn't anywhere in the place, but it wouldn't be hard to figure out. Even these small-town cops knew how to dust for fingerprints. She ran a finger through the sticky buds, then held her hand up to the lighting.

"I can see my bones."

DeWitt stepped up beside her and took her small, glowing hand, examining the pink skin at the edges of her fingers. Audrey gave him a sidelong glance.

"You want me to strip-search you?"

"I'm not asking," replied DeWitt.

She leaned into him, patting down his thighs and crotch as she looked him in the eye.

"Nothing here," she giggled.

His voice cracked. "I don't know about that, lady. Better call in the dogs."

"Maybe I'll give it a closer look."

DeWitt kissed her and her tongue tasted sweet like tobacco leaves. He ran a hand under her shirt and felt around. The freckles dusted across her collarbone turned him on even more. They made out in their original awkward position, almost sideways to each other, until she thought to pull him over to the counter. Every move he made, she immediately met and upped him one. He went for the breast, and she went for the two-handed ass grab. He palmed her crotch and she undid his belt in two swift jerks and had his cock in her hand before he could say "cat's meow." Not to be outdone, he ran a hand down her smooth belly into the furry crook of her jeans. They stood lip-locked and almost motionless as they exchanged exhaust. Then she edged away.

"You're going to have to give me another bag."

"Sure," he muttered.

"You're sure you're sure, cause I'm sure."

"It's all good."

Audrey dipped down on one knee and just kind of stared at his dick. She leaned on one arm and blew on his purple tip.

"This doesn't look like a flashlight to me."

"You put your mouth on it, and it'll shine right out my ass."

The pressure was building in his prostate. This had usually been as far as he'd ever gotten with the blowjob scenario. Then it was sky-loads on her shirt or even her pretty nose. Premature ejaculation blues—it had never been a problem with sex for some reason, just this, the long stare. How long was she going to look at it before they just got it over with, he wondered? And the worst part was he couldn't say a word or it was definitely off.

"Take me to the movies tonight," she asked.

"Talk into the mike, I can't hear you."

Audrey leaned closer and in a deeper voice demanded, "Take me to see something Italian."

DeWitt's mind was racing. He had to pretend like this wasn't happening or he'd get too excited. Yet it was definitely in motion, and Jedson would probably be in here any minute with one of those Thetas. Or Jeffers would come bumping in here looking for his map of west Texas. He groped for something else to say to her. It was as though she had cut out his frontal lobe.

"You got it," he stammered.

"Wash my feet."

"I got the tub."

"And wash my car."

"What?"

"You heard me. Wash my goddamn car."

"Fine, fine, fine."

Just as she was going to go down on him, a scruffy-looking cat slipped between the velvet blackout sheets and started yowling beside them. Then they heard heavy footsteps at the end of the hall. Audrey quickly stood up, brushing off, and DeWitt hastily folded his erection into his boxers and zipped up. The cat darted into the corner.

"Who the hell is that?" hissed DeWitt. "Cut the lights out for a second. Over there."

He ran to the curtain, and when the room went black, peeked down the hall. It was a fucking janitor. He had never seen the guy before, and he was cradling a shotgun.

"Here kitty kitty kitty," the janitor whistled.

DeWitt slid the curtains shut and hissed again. Audrey cut on the lights.

"What's the deal? Is that a cop or something?"

"Give me your hunting jacket. Quick, goddamn it. We got to shut this cat up."

She threw the jacket to him and he stalked the tomcat, which ran in circles around them looking for the door it had come in from. DeWitt dove and pinned it to the ground. He tied the sleeves tight around its legs so it couldn't claw him, then clamped his hand over the cat's mouth. The tabby struggled but was wrapped too tight to move. It hissed through its teeth like a viper, then bit him on the wrist. It drew blood and hurt like a mother. Only then did DeWitt notice the foam at the corners of its mouth. Suddenly the scenario with gun and cat clicked, but it was too late to do anything about it. The cat was rabid and he couldn't let go.

Audrey cut off the lights and listened by the curtains. DeWitt stood in the opposite corner of the room. They could hear the man muttering in the hallway as he flicked the light switch. She cracked open the curtains, then whispered back to DeWitt, "He doesn't have a flashlight." The janitor walked the length of the hall anyway, feeling his way under the pipes until they could hear his breathing on the other side of the curtain. "Goddamn feline," cussed the man, a white man's voice. He spat and then stamped hard with his boot, accentuating his irritation. The cat squirmed violently at the sound, but DeWitt didn't flinch. His dope, his diploma, and the blowjob were down the shitter if he did. Steps faded down the hall. Audrey whispered, "He's walking up the stairs." The cat started gnawing into the web of DeWitt's thumb.

"Don't cut on the lights yet."

"Why not?"

"Don't move. Just don't move."

He grabbed the cat firmly by the neck and swung it over his head. The neck snapped with a grinding pop, but he wrung it ten more times. When he cut on the lights, Audrey was crying.

"You're fucking evil!"

"I was too scared to let go. Look at my hand. It's goddamn rabid. Jesus, let's get the car."

He tossed her two quarter bags from under the counter.

"Can you roll me a joint?"

They smoked it then and there. His arm felt better; she stopped crying. He didn't know what to do with the cat so he put it in a trash bag. They walked outside and the Cherokee was gone. It took a moment to register, but then made perfect sense.

"Is your friend coming back?"

"Nah, I think he took the car down to Kitty Hawk."

"Is it his car?"

"No. Fucking coward. I know he split."

They started walking down the hill toward the emergency room. Neither talked, though what was there to say? Her friends had left her too. The hospital was a few miles across town. Suddenly, DeWitt remembered Luth was home and he pulled Audrey down the gravel road that pinched off the observatory's drive. After a minute they came upon a gray sedan snug up on the embankment in front of an old shotgun shack. Luth was smoking a cigarette in the tattered front seat and staring at the city lights below.

"What's he doing in the car?" asked Audrey.

"It's the only place he can get any privacy. Don't ask."

The hillside two-room house loomed above them on weathered stilts like a spider about to leap. Luth rolled down the window and ashed his cigarette.

"Whatchoo doing over here with this creature. Need a best man?"

"Nah. I do need a ride to the hospital. Cat bite." DeWitt held up the plastic bag, but Luth waved it away.

"I believe you, I believe you."

Luth cranked the ignition, flooring the gas before he let her settle. A door to the house slammed and a small woman hollered "Luther!" but the driver ignored the voice completely. They slid into the backseat and rolled down the windows. After a moment, the door slammed again, the small woman gone. The vehicle smelled like a clothes hamper used as an ashtray.

"That new Shifflett been looking for a rabid kitty! How'd you catch him?"

"He ran into my office. Oh yeah, this here is Audrey by the way."

"Howdee doo."

"Nice to meet you, mister Luth."

Luth eased the sedan over the embankment, over a sapling, and down the slope into town. At the emergency-room doors, DeWitt and Audrey scrambled out with the cat in the bag and blinked in the bright lights.

"Do you want me to come in?" asked Audrey.

"Yeah, if you don't mind. Luth," DeWitt added, leaning in the window, "thanks for the ride. Take a little something."

He dropped a ten on the seat. Luth shook his head like it would kill him to touch it, but DeWitt backed away from the window, effectively ending the discussion. Luth slowly pulled away. He heard Audrey talking to a nurse but stared out at the red taillights dwindling to pinpricks up the road. Somebody took him by the shoulder, like it was time to turn around and face some music, bad stuff with a long solo on an organ.

After he filled out a ream of paperwork and handed over the cat, an orderly led him behind a curtain and told him to take off his shirt. He lay on the cold examination table and listened to nurses shuffle past. Somebody spilled some coffee. A guy was moaning. A girl who was screaming as her mother explained that her face had been pecked by a parrot. He looked at his wrist, which was slightly swollen, and said to himself, "I'm rabid."

A balding, ponytailed doctor named Dr. Faigle took care of his situation. With cold, rubber hands, the doctor examined DeWitt's wrist, which began to ache more and more as the man turned it in his gloves.

"This is the rabid young man, nurse? Get me thirty cc's of so-and-so." Checking DeWitt's pulse, he asked, "Where did you get that tattoo?"

"It's Orion, a constellation."

"Well, we're going to have to give you a quite painful series of shots in the lower abdomen to offset the rabies virus," he said, poking the bottom of his connect-the-dots tattoo. "We also have to, um, shave your pubic area in the process."

"You've got to be kidding me."

Dr. Faigle paused, sizing up the victim.

"Yes, Mr. DeWitt, I am kidding. I only wanted to give you something to be happy about."

When DeWitt hobbled out of the examination area, Audrey was still waiting for him, slumped against a chair. He shook her awake, unsure why she was still here. The shots had numbed his body even more, and he just wanted to go lie down somewhere.

"Your friend was here."

"What friend?" asked DeWitt.

"That guy, what's his name, Jetson? He showed up full of arrows claiming he'd been attacked by Indians. I think he'd glued them onto his suit, but it caused a big ruckus in the ER. He was waving his arms around, screaming bloody murder. Then he tossed me the keys to your Cherokee and ran out the door. Last I saw, the security guards were chasing him. That guy is a total freak."

"Holy shit, that's his San Sebastian routine. We did that for Halloween."

There was only one place Jedson could have gone without a vehicle. At the jockettes' house, they found him sitting on the porch in his arrow suit drinking a bottle of wine. The chunky girls were passed out in the hammock.

"Dare me to walk through town again? Har har. I heard you were rabid. You still going down to the beach, or is the water going to be an issue?"

"No, and who the hell told you—Luth?"

"Audrey did at the ER. I didn't know y'all were there. I didn't know where the fuck you two went."

"Thanks for sticking around."

"That guy had a twenty-gauge. You got the keys back, right? Chill the fuck out."

Audrey grabbed DeWitt by the arm. "Let's lie down in the backyard, mister dealer. I've got some sleeping bags in my car." Then she turned to Jedson. "Get your ass off my porch, clown."

Jedson threw his wine bottle in the neighbor's yard.

"You don't live here," he yelled as he trotted down the sidewalk in the martyr suit. "So don't pretend to!"

They lay in the backyard and DeWitt showed her the constellations he knew. He made up names for most of them: car trip, praying mantis, the bra and girdle, the dog leg. Audrey toyed with the hair Dr. Faigle had threatened to shear while he demonstrated their alignment on her abdomen. He couldn't see her face when she talked to him, and after a while he couldn't summon any of her details save her skeptical eyes. Before they could have sex in the backyard's chamber of trees, DeWitt dozed off, and he dreamt she peeked from behind a curtain foaming at the mouth. When he shook awake, she was giving him head.

DeWitt came like a rocket bursting in two stages and descended back to earth with a thud. He stroked her hair, barely able to speak. The whole big fucking deal came down to these seconds of strange clarity and a pathetic notch on the belt. As she studied him, he muttered thanks and kissed her on the mouth. At some point in the night, he felt her get up and throw a sheet over him. Next thing he knew, he was alone in the bright backyard, a neighbor chuckling at his candy-striped boxers while he wiped his eyes. It felt like he'd been abducted and dropped in a strange place. It took a moment to place the surroundings, the dogwoods and tangled magnolia shaking hands with each other. He limped up the hill, but her car was gone. The house was empty so he walked into the strange kitchen and ate a bowl of cereal standing up.

Her absence settled into him by degrees. He searched for a snapshot of her with her jock friends, and if he had found one on a shelf, he would have stolen it. What he did find was an empty garbage bag over the Cherokee's steering wheel and his last quarter bag tossed next to his car keys on the front seat. So much for killing time—she had already split town with his cash crop. He picked up the compound bow and dug up a couple of unbroken arrows from the back. Jedson was going to wish he had never seen an arrow suit by the time he got through with him.

Claire noticed that the quiet kindergartner, who was looking particularly dazed—or was that carsick?—had something blue smeared around his mouth. She hoped it wasn't ink, but didn't really want to ask. He belonged to someone else.

(Larimer, page 75)

Lonely

Mary Donnelly

Oh Bigfoot Oh Yeti
Correct me if I'm wrong
but it must be rather lonely.
Only the occasional naturalist
running away in fright,
heading back to camp
for the camcorder.
Perhaps you could move
to the Bermuda Triangle or Loch Ness,
someplace with mystery, someplace
where you wouldn't outfreak the freaks.

Oh Yeti Oh Sasquatch
Don't come down.
They'd only accost you in bars,
want to stand next to you
while their friends snapped a picture.
None of this bounding past casually,
your arms still swinging
as you turn and pause
like a runway model
You'd have to cooperate,
shake hands. They'd want you
to bathe, wear shoes.

Oh Sasquatch Oh Bigfoot
you're a natural comedian,

and they can't take that away from you.
On weekend afternoons you starred
in a TV movie, *The Legend of Boggy Creek*,
complete with reenactments
and sinister voice-over.
Your finest scene was the one
when you put your fist
through a bathroom window
while some guy was on the toilet,
and he went fleeing down the hall
with his pants around his ankles.

Oh Yeti Oh Yeti Oh Yeti
You can't relive that moment.
And anyway they wouldn't
understand. The world needs
more important things
than monster men, flying saucers,
telephone psychics.
But everyone loves a mystery.
And when it's solved,
maybe they'll stop to wave at your cage
before heading on to the next.

In Zenoburg

Guiseppe O. Longo

I WAS SHAKING LIKE A LEAF FROM THE INFLUENZA WHICH HAD struck me the previous day, I should never have undertaken a journey with influenza, I deluded myself that the relative well-being I felt after a night's rest meant that I was cured, so I took the train, but even during the journey, especially during the stops in that freezing mountainous region, the fever came back and after my arrival at Zenoburg it had risen a lot, infantile obstinacy made me not want to know my temperature, I didn't ask my hosts for a thermometer due to one of those childish stubbornnesses which take me from time to time, on the contrary, I hadn't said anything to my friends about the fever, not wanting them to worry about my health on any account or to feel remorse for inviting me so insistently to spend Christmas with them at Zenoburg, so I tried to be relaxed and during the supper I'd even told some funny stories, excusing my hoarse voice, a frighteningly rough voice, but they liked the stories, most of all Signora Gutgasteiger liked the stories and laughed till she cried, with that coral mouth and white teeth of hers, and before supper I even had to sing a couple of Schubert's lieder, I certainly couldn't disappoint my friends by refusing to sing, Max and Valentino had waited for months to hear me sing *Heidenröslein* and *Das Fishermädchen*, Carlotta had accompanied me at the piano in anxious trepidation and everyone applauded even though the voice wasn't there, the voice wasn't there at all but I had felt that same profound emotion which Schubert always gives me, and I had even spoken of Joyce and of his habit of going 'round the inns of Trieste singing with his fine tenor voice, going from one tavern to another and singing with the dock laborers and the sailors, I told them, and so the evening concluded in the best possible way, everyone was happy, we exchanged good wishes and gifts, and I too received my ration of wishes and gifts and was really happy that I had decided to come up here to Zenoburg, it was such a good idea, I told myself again, but later, going up the stairs which led up here, to the top floor of this fourteenth-century tower, I had begun to tremble like a leaf and now, seated on the lavatory bowl in my pajamas, I trembled and moaned from cold and fever, the cold came out of the stones of the tower and I could feel it in my bones, my body gave off the typical smell of fever, wherever I touched my skin it hurt, I felt in a pitiful state, I could do nothing but tremble and moan, moaning in synchrony with the tremor, accompanying the trembling with moans and groans, hoping to warm myself a little, at least enough to allow me to leave the lavatory and get into bed, I told myself that the trembling served to increase body temperature in cold environments, that was what trembling was for, I told myself, but then I told myself that having a fever, the body had no need whatsoever to raise its own temperature, and I grappled helplessly with this sort of contradiction, but the fact remained that I trembled violently and that continuous trembling even prevented me from passing water, which I had soon to do anyway in order not to get out of bed and return to the bathroom, covering those three or four meters in the freezing air of the fourteenth-century tower, and meanwhile my eyes fell on an Italian translation of a medical handbook from the Karolinska Institute in Stockholm, which lay there on the stool and which Margareta certainly made use of, or had used when she studied medicine, and opening it at random I found there the therapeutic indications for an unlimited number of diseases, syndromes, pathologies, imbalances, and insufficiencies, from podagra to cerebral stroke, but there was nothing about my problem, no mention of these uncontrollable shiverings of influenzal fever, increased out of all proportion in intensity after the train journey, after the Schubert lieder and after the Christmas dinner and the presents, the handbook made absolutely no mention of my case, perhaps only a hot bath would have worked, a very hot bath and then a vigorous massage accompanied by a last dose of grappa, over and above those taken many times during the evening, this was the treatment of choice for my illness, but there at the top of the fourteenth-century tower this therapy was unthinkable, there was no grappa, there were no expert physiotherapist's hands, the most I could do was take a bath, the tub was close by, and I could hear the hum of the water heater, but the idea of making myself take a bath at that hour of night, whilst from the window I could make out the widespread whiteness of the snow-covered mountains, the mere idea of taking off my flannel pajamas and getting into the water and above all the idea of having sooner or later to get out of it, all these ideas appalled me and I rejected them energetically, and meanwhile in the handbook I had found the techniques and therapies to be used in cases of frostbite, treatment which seemed to me most suitable for my present situation, and I went through them with a certain relief, since my tremor seemed to be decreasing, and I repeated in a low voice, hot dressings, mustard plasters, camphorated oil, friction rubs, poultices, and all this appeared to work, since I had even succeeded in passing water, and I was asking myself if it wasn't time to set out toward the bed when I started to cough a dry cough, stony and malign, which gave me a violent pain in the middle of my back and in the middle of my chest, a pain to take your breath away, which by now I didn't have much of, and I remembered that imbecile of a doctor who years before I had found myself sitting next to at a charity dinner and having looked at me sideways the whole evening, having stared at my hands, particularly at the nails for the whole evening, sitting next to me he had fixed his gaze on my fingers and nails for hours, and finally, having consulted under his breath with his wife, she too a doctor darting incessant curious glances at my hands and especially my nails, stretching her neck for a better look at my nails around the voluminous mass of her doctor husband, who eventually, after a great many observations, hesitations, and consultations had made up his mind and communicated to me, with a regretful look but to tell the truth with the diagnostic satisfaction typical of doctors in such cases, that I had watch-glass nails and I replied with a smile that this should allow me to tell the time effortlessly, but he didn't smile, he didn't smile at all, the doctor, faced with my unawareness took on an even more worried expression, it really seemed as if my total unawareness and irresponsibility in the face of his announcement pained him, so he took up

again this business of the watch-glass nails, he repeated with a lu-
gubrious air that my nails were in fact typically watch-glass, perhaps
he was so insistent on this business of the watch-glass nails to press
me to ask him some questions instead of laughing in his face as I was
doing, but to tell the truth I laughed because I had known the story
of the watch-glass nails for a long time, I used to go to bed with a
female medical student who screwed well but studied little, and
amongst other things, I had even helped her prepare for the examination in medical pathology, I've always had a weakness for medical
pathology, not for surgical pathology though, and this story of the
watch-glass nails and the clubbed fingers made me laugh a lot with
my student lover, but now my fellow diner doctor did not laugh at all,
the wife laughed even less, having observed me and so to speak measured my nails the whole evening now hid herself behind her husband and left to him all the disagreeable—or agreeable—tasks of
acquainting me, as her doctor husband was now doing, after all that
apparent discreteness, after all that hypocritical pantomime and
medical po-facedness, the doctor was now revealing my frightful
condition, that is to say that I suffered from a terrible lung condition,
indeed that I was in the final stage of this terrible lung condition, as
was revealed, without any shadow of doubt, by the peculiar round-
ness and convexity and sheen of my nails, which had so struck him
from the moment he sat down at table beside me, and even his wife,
he added sanctimoniously, even she was aware of that unequivocal
sign, but I did not allow myself to be affected, I hadn't been at all
affected by the pious medical intonation that my neighbor assumed,
while his wife immersed her large apoplectic face in a goblet of peach
melba pretending to ignore our conversation, whilst in reality she
didn't miss a syllable, because she flinched as from a blow when, in a
low but distinct voice, which drew the attention of other diners too,
I said that this was the first time I had been diagnosed as having
Pierre-Marie syndrome, and the most amusing thing was that the
diagnosis should have been made at a charity dinner in aid of cancer
research, and what's more free of charge, for God's sake, and here my
voice took on a questioning tone, so much so that the sanctimonious
doctor nodded in assent, that the diagnosis he had made of my terminal condition was entirely free, and it certainly had surprised him
that I knew the name of the syndrome and many of its symptoms

and effects, which I was now rattling off to him, while his lady doctor wife, more and more embarrassed, toyed with her peach melba,
turning it 'round in the goblet with the teaspoon without making up
her mind to eat it, and my exhibition of medical science, entirely
unexpected in a singer, had much impressed my doctor neighbor,
who was now looking at me with pity and admiration, with great pity
but also with a certain admiration, but I had been magnanimous, I
hadn't rubbed it in, I had resumed my light tone, and smilingly said
that my final stage must have lasted for at least forty years, because as
far back as I could remember I had always had watch-glass nails,
something which the medical student and I had noted as soon as we
had arrived at that chapter in medical pathology, and was borne out
by numerous sketches which I had made over the years of my right
hand, including the nails, fingers and nails exactly similar to those of
my left hand, but I am left-handed, so I used the left to portray the
fingers of my right hand, I had always had a real passion for drawing
my right hand, and several of these portraits of fingers and nails I
had actually drawn here, in Zenoburg, and these were the most successful, because Elizabeth Hanna, friend and fine portrait artist that
she was, had been generous with advice, in sum precisely here were
born some of the proofs which disproved the final stage diagnosis of
my neighbor at table, and after this long tour of memory I returned
da capo, I was back here again, in the freezing bathroom at the top of
the fourteenth-century tower, I had put down the Karolinska manu-
al, I had blown my nose on lavatory paper and coughing and wheez-
ing I'd left the bathroom, pressing my painful chest, my back I
couldn't manage to press at all, but, I thought, that very bad pain in
the spine could corroborate what the doctor and his lady doctor wife
had said, at the end of the day the doctor and the lady doctor of ill
omen might even have anticipated by years, with infallible instinct, a
diagnosis which at that time no one except them, with the unerring
clinical eye of the birds of ill omen that they were, would have been
capable of making, that acute pain in the back confirmed with cer-
tainty their early diagnosis which I had incautiously hastened to dis-
miss with a shrug of the shoulders and a few jokes, meanwhile I
dragged myself through the fourteenth-century freeze toward the
bed, lost, deep in space, surrounded by the eternally frozen pack ice,
with the strength of a polar explorer in extremis I sought to reach the

gelid splendor of that petrified pile, that lifeless whitened expanse, and the fact is that having at last touched the side of the immense bed in which I was to spend a few nights, I felt a strange dismay, most of all I was dismayed by the vastness of that bed and the fact that from there, even more than from the bathroom, through an immense mullioned window excavated through the enormous thickness of the wall of the tower, immediately in front of the bed, I could see the snow-covered mountains and the air, misty from the snow which continued to fall, and all that snow made me deeply melancholy, but the melancholy perhaps came rather from the vastness of the bed, where for the first time I would sleep alone, in my many Christmas visits to Zenoburg I had always slept in that bed and I had always shared it with my successive partners and girlfriends, the teacher of jurisprudence, the student and later doctor of medicine, the nursery-school teacher, the physiotherapist, the biologist, the violinist, with all these women I had shared this bed at the top of the tower, this bed which you reached up increasingly steep stairs, first of stone and then of wood, I had never been alone in that bed, under the huge beams darkened by age and by pitch, in this sort of alcove facing the balcony where the mountains came into view through the enormous window, from which in the past my companions and I had watched, lying under the bedclothes, the gentle snowfall, the early dusks of December, I remembered those brief winter periods at Zenoburg as blissful intervals, warmed by the fire of love, whilst this time I was alone and what is more ill, precisely in time of illness I would need the nearness of a woman, I told myself, the company of a woman would have been beneficial, even essential, and, on the other hand, in my lonely condition I would at the very least need all my strength, only with the help of all my strength, physical and psychological, could I face the loneliness, instead I was alone and ill, I was ill and alone, I reflected, all by myself in the silence of the great fourteenth-century tower, in the depths of the night, Christmas Eve, what's more, when no one should be alone and deserted, there were my friends, it's true, sleeping on the various floors of the tower, several meters below, but I felt the lack of a woman, of one of those women who had shared with me that huge bed, on the edge of which I now sat in my flannel pajamas, reflecting on the successive and inexorable loss of all those women, all those women had left me, and since the last one had left me I hadn't managed to find another, as had always happened before, until that moment, when a woman left me, another would come forward at once and everything fell out in the best possible way, when the dentist disappeared, the gym mistress presented herself, when the contemporary history researcher disappeared I found the wholesale stationer, but after the director of the nursing home disappeared no one came forward, and I remained alone, as was demonstrated by the fact that I was sitting all by myself on the edge of the bed in my heavy flannel pajamas, uncertain whether to keep my socks on to face the medieval icy cold of the bedclothes, and meantime I watched two distant lights halfway up the snow-covered mountain, the sadness of solitude mixed with the sadness of the snow-covered mountain and those lights halfway up and I asked myself if I would ever manage to sleep in that lonely bed, at the top of the tower, almost balanced on those flights of stairs, squeezed by the looming mountain, with its ghostly lights, but all these questions and reflections did not warm me up, and I actually started to sneeze and shiver again, and with an abrupt decision I slipped, pajamas, socks, and all, under the covers, which were in fact warm and dry as all winter covers should be, especially on the top of towers in the mountains, especially when one must sleep alone because one has seen not a single sign of a woman who wanted to stay with him, especially after a long train journey facing up to discomforts and stations full of freezing draughts, especially when he has influenza and the cough brings unbearable stabs in the back and chest such as only the accursed Pierre-Marie syndrome could give rise to, such a sweet name, almost Christmassy, for such a horrible disease, but with these thoughts I began to feel sleepy, and while I nodded I murmured Zenoburg, watch-glass, Pierre-Marie, panettone and then the names of my past companions and I even tried to hum *Röslein, Röslein roth, Röslein auf der Heiden,* trying to remember the tune which Schubert had given it and which in the afternoon I too had given it in spite of the horrible voice I found myself with, and all strangely mixed up with the snow which continued to fall, thick as thick on the mountain, on Zenoburg, on the square roof of the tower just above my head, whilst underneath me I knew that my friends slept, my dear friends were asleep in the small rooms and alcoves and upon the cornices and corbels of the great tower, and I saw the tower, as it were, from the outside, about halfway up, the thick walls as transparent as crystal, and each of my friends curled up in a small bed, tall and narrow, with fists clenched and eyes closed, a slight smile on their lips, shining snub noses, feet sticking out from under the duvet, and they were really models from a crib with tow-colored hair and walrus moustaches and nightcaps with tassels, they seemed so many Father Christmases and Mother Christmases in their cots and the smaller ones were little Boy Christmases and little Girl Christmases sunk in sleep after a long day but still clinging to something solid and everyday, and in the air floated flakes of snow and the notes of Schubert and I heard my voice rise up clear and pure as it had never been, strange that there outside, in the midst of falling snow, I no longer felt cold, I was no longer tormented with shivering, I wasn't even coughing, my back didn't hurt and I told myself that the doctor was mistaken, it certainly wasn't Pierre-Marie syndrome from which I was suffering, but it was the syndrome of the lonely man, that's what I was suffering from, but now, watching those sleeping manikins and maniqueens, pink and plump with their somewhat ruffled white hair, even the loneliness melted away, everything quivered like the snowflakes and the small hours struck in the most intimate and secret heart of Christmas Eve.

Translated from Italian by David Mendel.

Premonitions

Pieter Schoolwerth

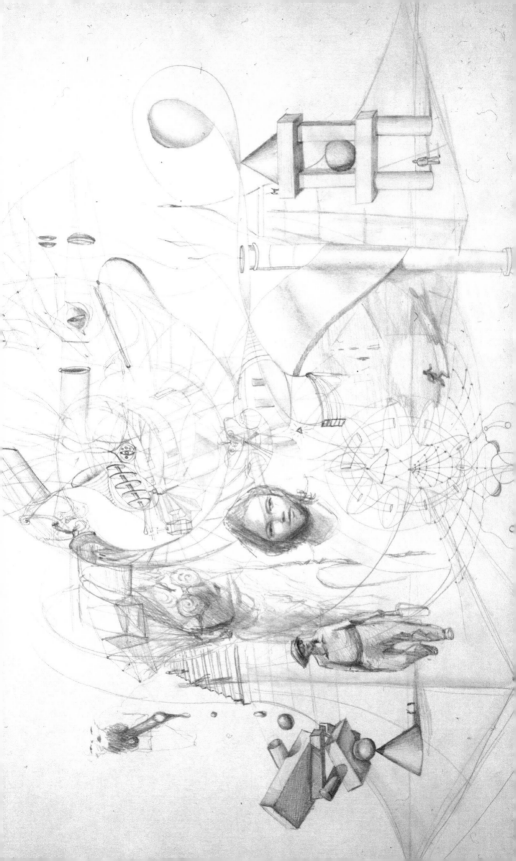

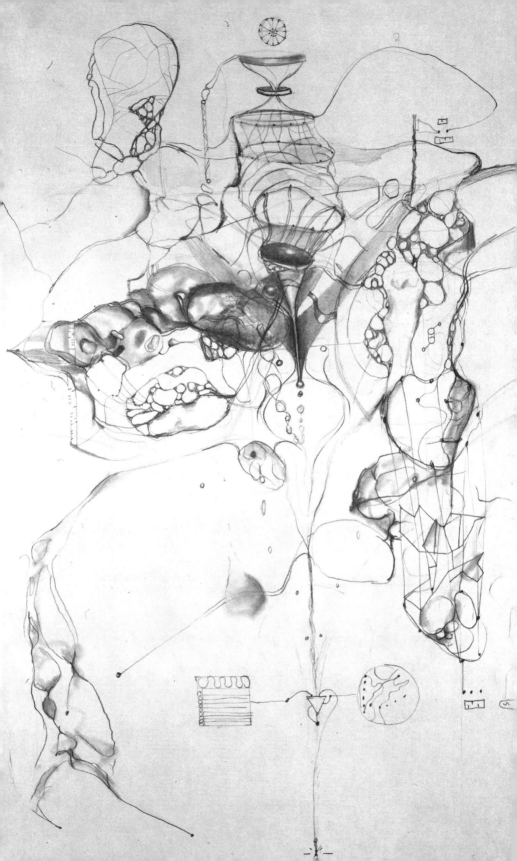

Driver

Matthew Miller

On a two-lane highway with no turnoffs
they saw it: a lost world governed by sane
forgiving laws, in which fair curly haired lads,
howling with merriment, greeted strangers
heartily at the gate. Then it receded
in the rearview mirror. Crushing the butt
in the ashtray, she reached between her legs
for the mini-cooler, felt for a cold one
& peeled it open. He admired how she looked
with a beer clutched between her thighs,
just one hand on the wheel. They were
being followed by a cormorant which,
though they couldn't see it from the car,
regarded them with small black eyes.
It was the man's turn to be in love.
His emotions made colors teem from her
like sunlight against a fine mist.
She, a wrenched rainbow, shuddered.
The cormorant wheeled overhead.
Far off, in a pool at the center
of a castle's arboretum, a bubble burst.

"Kate?" Guy said, coming up behind her.

"Lion? Elephant? Boar? Bird?"

"Kate, where did you go?"

"Fish? Crocodile? Boar? Bird?"

(Brumbaugh, page 49)

Eternal Bliss

Daphne Beal

THE TROUBLE, OR THE MOST RECENT TROUBLE I SHOULD SAY, ALL started with the dahl buckets after dinner last night—nine of them stacked up, greasy and crusted with yellow lentils. We had just eaten the evening meal, which isn't four-star grub by any stretch, but it's sustenance, and if it works for the living saints, it'll work for me. Flat bread, lentils, vegetables—chapatis, dahl, subji—it has almost a poetic ring, even if the chapati are soggy, the dahl watery, and the subji salty.

I was on cleanup detail in the pots and pans division, which I often am and don't mind, because I'm a guy with the heft for it. But unfortunately, this skinny, older rat named Richard was assigned to work with me. This guy really fries my ass. First of all, he's been here for about ten years, and he still says "ash-*ram*"—flat, nasal, straight out of Pasadena, like some kind of pornographic term. I've only been here three years, and not only have I mastered the somewhat delicate phonetics of "ashram," but I've also picked up more than the average amount of Sanskrit, if I say so myself.

But Richard, well, Richard thinks he's above it all. However he wants to pronounce things, however he wants to live, that's okay by me. He can redefine the word "ascetic" for all I care. The man doesn't even eat the main kitchen's cooking, just lives off care packages his wife still sends him after all these years (Lipton's soup, Hellmann's mayo, After Eight dinner mints, you get the picture). And now, as of two months ago, his twenty-one-year-old daughter Rachel has come to look after him and cook for him—his own fair, personal handmaid—a pert little college dropout who addles me in a whole new way. But old Richie Rich still has to do chores like the rest of us. I know this and he knows this.

So when he came back to our area, having deigned to clear a few plates for the regular dishwashers, I was already at work filling vegetable pots with hot water and setting them on the floor to soak. Folks were mopping down the main part of the dining hall, and the smell of bleach was mixing up ripely with the curried-grease smell. I watched Richard navigate the obstacle course of pots and pans and begin scrubbing his arms up to the elbows.

I wanted to be amenable—weak as he is, he can get overwhelmed, and I've seen it—so I said, "Richard, if you do four dahl buckets, I'll do five." Five's a lot. It was good, the right gesture.

But drying his hands with a fresh dish towel, he said, "I'm sorry Melvin. I'd like to, but Swamiji said I should attend all of satsanga, every night right now."

"You're not going to help?" I asked. Frankly, I was astounded.

"I'm afraid I can't," he said.

"You self-serving prick," I muttered and threw a bucket at the sink. I thought he would move, but he didn't, and a sharp end of the handle caught the back of his hand before it clattered to the floor.

He sucked in a sharp little breath and examined the skin, then showed me the red line across it, barely a scrape, no real blood.

"Melvin Kreutzer, I don't have to put up with you and your self-ishness—it's relentless," he whined.

Faucets ran, shoes squeaked, and plates were scraped all around us as Richard rewashed his hand and dried it with yet another clean towel, wrapping it up war-wound-style while I scrubbed the guilty bucket, carefully lest I wound the clod a second time. And he exited seething and silent.

Not one person stopped to help or say an encouraging word as I worked alone, doing double duty now. No one would even answer me when I asked if there was any more soap; a lady I didn't know just put a beige block of it on the counter. By the time I finished, the rest of the place was dark, and my hands were pruny and pink, except for the web of creases dyed yellow from the curry. I inspected the stacks of gleaming tin and cast iron one last time, and satisfied, I turned off the lights.

Inside the back entrance of the large, peach-colored prayer hall, I faced a computer-printed banner on the wall that advised: LOVE THY NEIGHBOR AS THYSELF. Good idea if you can, I thought. But actually, I've liked this aspect of Swamiji ever since I first heard him speak in Chicago four years ago, when things were going to hell in a hand-basket fast for me. He's never afraid to call on other religions, child-hood moralisms, and even classical philosophy to make his point. "Do good, be good," he said then, his warm, stubby hand on my head as he zapped me into clarity.

I settled into only a half-lotus because of recent knee trouble, and touched my forefinger and thumb together to keep the energy flow-ing. I closed my eyes on the wall-sized image of the bare, nut-brown head of dead Swami Ramananda in a purple flower mala, with a ban-ner beside it advising: DO NOT PUT OFF UNTIL TOMORROW WHAT YOU CAN DO TODAY.

"Hari om! Hari om! Hari hari hari om!" I sang ferociously. There's a way to get inside chanting as if it were a vibrant, cool, cushioned room, and this was all I wanted. I opened my eyes a moment and found myself staring halfway up the room at the back of Richard's knobby gray head and Rachel's springy red curls beside him. I quick-ly shut my eyes again, breathing in deeply through my nose, "o-om, o-om, o-om, om." The sound shot out like a white laser from the top of my forehead.

Soon, the chanting stopped, and I bowed all the way forward to seal in the energy called up by the vigorous singing. When I looked up, the auditorium was more than half empty. Richard and Rachel were on their way out a door farther down the room, and I slipped out the back to meet them.

"Richard," I called and he turned. The fluorescent lights inside showed the tense lines of his face. "I'm sorry if I hurt or offended you. My ego gets the better of me sometimes." The apology was easy, as easy as exhaling or peeling a banana. I waited for the angry mask to melt.

But he stiffened further and held up his right hand, wrapped in a white, sterile bandage, and spread out his long, bony fingers, shaking slightly. "Thanks to you Melvin, a tetanus shot."

"The bucket wasn't rusty," I said. Rachel pivoted her perfect ski-jump nose back and forth between us, her green-eyed gaze a spiritual poker face.

Richard snorted. "This is India, Melvin, in case you've forgotten. It doesn't take much to get a life-threatening infection." No, I thought, I haven't forgotten, you supercilious moron. The peace of chanting flew away like an uncaged bird. "Om," I breathed, turning the mala beads in my hands, and finally said, "I'm sorry. I didn't mean to hit you."

He jerked a curt nod, turned on his heel, and left, Rachel swishing away beside him in her pale pink sari. Of the people left milling around outside the prayer hall, chatting, no one came near me. News of transgression travels fast in an ashram, and I walked off toward the dorm.

At the gate, I raised a hand to Arjun and Rex, the night watchman and his mutt—a sign that I was in no mood to chat. Arjun's a friend of mine, but he can talk a blue streak if you get him going.

I lit candles around my room, turned off the lights, and organized myself to meditate. I was angry, I admit that, but I knew I could handle it. Three years in an ashram, cut off from your previous life, especially my previous life, is not nothing. Pre-Swamiji, at twenty-nine, I thought I was king of the world, or at least of Chicago: money rolling in from my own vintage car-repair business; women, young and old, in no short supply; and at the end of the day, or the night, as the case may have been, I would go home to Karen. Hot-shit, ball-busting, not unintelligent, though maybe a little clingy Karen. She was a nurse and gorgeous in a regular person's way, and she had a way of making everything about her seem good, too good maybe. I let her know I was messing around by leaving out a letter from a girl for her to find. And that was the unceremonious end. It was a relief at first, but I also expected her to come back. Instead she took up with my main competitor Benny, an event that got me so distracted he started taking my business too. She wouldn't return my calls, meet for a drink, anything. Karen never looked back except once when she sent me a ticket to see Swamiji with a note attached: "A guy like this might actually be able to help an asshole like you."

And it was times like this, pre-Swamiji, if I happened to have the presence of mind, that I would go to the garage no matter how late at night. Before Hinduism, cars were the closest thing to spirituality for me. Money was religion, the green nirvana goal, but working on cars was as close as I came to real meditation, even bliss, and staring down into the cool, dark guts of a Porsche Spider, knowing I could make her go, was like looking at a dead person knowing I could bring her back. People towed their babies from Indianapolis, Milwaukee, Iowa City, even Cleveland, to have me work my magic, to pay me too much for my own good.

Now I was using the downward-facing dog pose to bring myself to undistracted concentration, when there was a forceful rapping on the door.

"*What* Arjun?" I said more sharply than I meant.

"It's Surinder. Swamiji wants to see you."

I got up and turned on the light. "Now?"

"Yes."

"I'll be right out."

I checked the square of mirror above the sink. Unfortunately, I looked guilty, gaunt, and unremorseful. I massaged the muscles around my eye sockets, ran my hands over the brown stubble on my head, and pinched my cheeks like a girl.

"Come in," Swamiji said at Surinder's knock. He was sitting in a ratty little armchair in his receiving room. He wore an orange ski hat and was swaddled in a brown blanket over his papaya-colored robes. I prostrated, three times, forehead to floor, and sat down at his feet.

"Sit here," he said gesturing to a low stool. His sunken eyes were ringed with dark circles, and white blotches of skin showed on his jaw and wrists.

"Swamiji, I didn't mean to hurt him—"

"Silence, please," he said. I looked down, listening to the rasp and rattle of his breathing. "In my opinion, this rivalry between you and Richard has gone on long enough. The complaints and excuses from the two of you have gone on long enough. And when your fighting happens in public places such as the kitchen, it affects the whole community."

"I've tried to make peace—"

"You threw a bucket at him. I cannot have physically abusive people here."

"Swamiji, I was putting it in the sink," I said and stopped. Feet crunched on the dirt path outside. "I should have been more careful."

"Why do you insist on monitoring him?"

"I don't. I just wanted some help tonight so that I could go to satsanga too."

"And when he told you that I asked him to attend all of satsanga and had to leave immediately?"

My stool creaked as I shifted. "I didn't believe him."

He actually tsk'ed as he shook his head. "And how often, would you say, do you act in poor judgment with regard to Richard?"

I twisted the frayed end of my belt cord, making a note to fuse it later. "Maybe once a week?"

"How often does he act in poor judgment with regard to you?"

Every time he breathes, I thought. "Not that often," I said, thinking, he's always stalking off. "But Swamiji, I try very hard to act well toward Richard."

"But you fail. Because you tell yourself not to act badly instead of looking at the illusory root of your unfounded hatred, which is the idea that you and Richard are fundamentally different, separate. He is, in some ways, a more valuable teacher to you than I am." Swamiji pulled the blanket tight around himself, so that he was a compact brown and orange mound on the chair.

I smelled Richard's American deodorant in the room.

"Did he report me?" I asked.

"A disturbed witness did. I asked Richard to come so I could see his scrape. Melvin, your dishonest life before coming here hinders you now. To mistrust people all the time is not to see the humanity in them or the Brahman in them."

But I see the Brahman in you, I wanted to shout, but I was afraid it would sound like pandering. I contemplated my yellow-stained knuckles.

"Swamiji. I'm sorry. I will try harder to seek out the root of my dislike and not indulge my mistrust."

He closed his eyes and when he opened them he said, "Melvin, for now you must leave the ashram. You may come back for darshan and evening prayers. But in a daily way, I think that you and Richard could use a break from one another, the community could use a break from gossiping about you, and I could use a break from dealing with your squabbles."

"Where will I go, Swamiji? This is my home. I don't know any other."

"Melvin, the world is your home. If you consider the ashram your home, you have become too attached to it."

"Will you allow me to live here again?"

"Possibly, in a few months."

My heart sank, and I got down on the floor and put my forehead on his small, bare feet. "Swamiji, I will do anything to stay." If only I had some indispensable skill—doctoring or cooking or carpentry—but it doesn't matter how good a car mechanic I am, and I am unreasonably good, because Swamiji just doesn't use his Mercedes enough to care what I can do.

"The only way to stay is to leave," he said. "And now I must go to bed." He pulled his feet away, and my head thunked on the floor.

"When do you want me to leave?" I asked.

"Tomorrow, before breakfast. Please get up now Melvin."

"Thank you Swamiji," I said. I made it out the door and sprinted up the hill, taking the long way back along the edge of the woods so that I wouldn't run into anyone. At the top of the path, I dropped and did fifty push-ups, which killed my back but spread out some of the throbbing in my head. Sometimes yoga doesn't hurt enough.

I walked down slowly, looking out at the town lining the wide, black river, where a stripe of the moon's reflection shimmered in bands on the water. A few yellow-lit windows shone in dark ashrams across the way, the black hills rising behind them, outlined against the star-filled sky. I was a long way from Chi-town. The world is my home. Ha! For once, I thought, he was dead wrong.

Through a window in Richard's apartment, I could see Rachel sitting on the floor reading a book, as she tugged her fingers through her hair and bit her lower lip. In gray sweatpants that she'd pushed up over her knees and wearing a faded green T-shirt, braless, with her pale freckles all over, she made me think of taking a girl, any girl, to the beach on Lake Michigan late at night when everyone else was gone. I wanted to move closer, but I stayed in a tree's shadow in case anyone came by. Her eyes were sharp, changing as they scanned the page. She was lost in thought, and she wrinkled her nose. Beautiful, I thought. It made me ache.

I didn't have much to pack. A few clothes, a blanket, a hooded sweatshirt, some toiletries, incense, and a notebook—only one; I burn them when I finish them so I don't get too self-pitying.

I wanted to leave right then—no sense lingering—and I picked up my canvas pack and stared out past the flood of outdoor light into the dark. Did I see the yellow flash of animal eyes? Nothing was open at this hour, and I wasn't about to go down to the Ganges and crawl into a cave. I'm devout, but I'm not crazy. I sat down on the low bed and breathed, finally setting the pack on the floor. I got under the blanket and set my watch alarm for five. It's always easier to make changes in the morning, I thought. Not that I sailed off to slumberland. I woke up every hour or so to check the time, afraid the alarm wouldn't work and that I would have to leave in broad daylight. Finally, the square numbers said 4:29, and I got up. It was dark and chilly out. Even Arjun was asleep at his post. Rex barked.

"Come here boy," I whispered, and he trotted up to me, dropped and rolled for a belly scratch. I thought of convincing the scrawny pup to come with me—Arjun would understand—but I knew this was no time to be taking on pets. "*Nai*," I said, and he gave me a quizzical look before he ambled back to his sleeping master.

Crossing the compound, I could make out people going to old Satyananda's room for morning chants, his sitar already twanging out the window. Beggars slept on the ground outside the main gate, some curled up, knees to chest, others sprawled out as if on a bed, all waiting pathetically for a morning meal. I walked past them down the road toward the big suspension footbridge spanning the river. Ganga Maiyya has always been good to me, and I was glad to see her emerging, a fuzzy blanket of mist still on her. The water's as pure as it should be up here, direct from the Himalayas.

Following a path of white sand down between two boulders, I stepped over rubber flip-flops set in front of small cave openings—crash pads for men heartier than me. I put down my pack and walked into the cold water, sang the Gayatri Mantra, and belly-flopped in. Bang! An elixir! I swam a few strokes out before heading back—its coldness steadied me like a grip—and when I came out, I changed into a dry dhoti, wrapped a shawl around me, and sat on a flat rock to meditate and warm up in the morning sun. It was a clear, pale yellow and pink morning and the air was sweet, even pillowy, around me. And for the first time in a while, I felt lucky.

Raj and Hari, the two brothers who own the Tourist Bungalow, were drinking tea in the office when I knocked. Hari chuckled as I entered; he knew me from yoga class where we sometimes had a friendly competition on the sly in the back of the room.

"Melvinji, finally you have come to visit our humble inn. What can we do for you at this early hour?" He called one of the boys for a cup of tea.

I thanked him and said I needed a place to stay for a few days. I wasn't looking forward to being surrounded by backpackers, but it seemed like a better option than going to another ashram, which I knew would only confuse allegiances. And Hari set me up with a single room at a rate that didn't make me feel completely friendless.

I was doing eye rotations on the prickly lawn outside when I got swarmed by biting ants, and I jumped up swearing and making enough noise that soon hippie kids (or wannabe hippie kids) opened their windows to check out the commotion. I writhed my way down the road out of sight, and past the huge arch painted with gaudy flowers and hands pressed together and the words: Welcome to the Home of Eternal Bliss! My ex-ashram.

Covered in mini welts and mashed ant carcasses, I ordered breakfast at a modest, open-air restaurant—a soft-boiled egg, toast, and tea. "Comfort food," Karen would have called it. Whatever. I wondered if she and Benny had kids, if they'd bought a place in the suburbs to be bored happily ever after.

Washing up at a water barrel after I ate, I glanced in a shard of mirror propped on the shelf. Today I looked like an old thirty-three, sun-lined and hard-featured. "Never to be younger than Jesus again," a British girl joked on my last birthday. What was that supposed to mean? That's when I saw the kid Siddhartha on the rocks by the river. A lean, brown boy, maybe twelve, with white-blond dreadlocks, he leapt from rock to rock in only a white loincloth leading a troupe of other Indian boys. The product of an astrologically calculated union of a Norwegian woman and a big deal swami on the other side of the river, he was born with spiritual attributes that I'd be lucky to get a few lifetimes from now.

Siddhartha, huh. Maybe I should change my name to Shiva, the destroyer. The dahl-bucket destroyer.

I watched him run and play for a while before I headed up to darshan. Jana waved from the office. Apparently, not everyone knew yet. They would. I sat on the wall outside the meeting room and turned the beads on my mala with a low chant. The sun was rising fast, and I moved in closer to hug the shade of the building. Rachel sashayed up the path in a fresh sari, and seeing me, she fixed her eyes on the ground in front of her. Her hair pulled back, she had a book tucked under her arm, and she glanced at me as she sat down.

"Hello," she said and opened her book—it looked like religious philosophy.

"Rachel?"

"Actually, it's Durga now," she said, pressing her finger to the page, not looking up.

"Nice choice."

"It's Swamiji's," she said still pretending to read.

"I'm sorry about your dad's hand. I didn't mean to hurt him."

Her brow twitched as if she were unsure if she would respond. A squirrel scuttled across the roof and leapt into a nearby tree. Rachel dog-eared the page and closed the book. Her eyes were watery and her mouth a bitter line.

"Melvin, he's so miserable here, don't you get it? He never wanted to come here; he's not like you. The only reason he came was because he was told to. All he wants to do is go back to Pasadena, but he won't till Swamiji says he can. And you provoke him. Can't you leave him alone?"

"Rachel, Durga. Your father is perfectly capable of achieving crankiness without my help."

"You needle him. It's as if you want to prove he's not above your pettiness so that he can't go home. Why do you think I was sent here? I'm interested, or I wouldn't have come. But still, as I left, my mother said: 'Try to help your father along, so he can come home.' Do you have any idea how lonely she is? What our lives have been like?"

I took a deep breath and said, "Richard got here seven years before me. Don't you think that if he were so close to soul satisfaction, I wouldn't be a deterrent?" And, I felt like saying, Don't you think if you weren't here, *I* would be making a lot more spiritual progress? Even as she practically spit at me, I thought how pretty she was. Anger had raised the color in her cheeks and made her eyes flash greener. She rubbed a tear away roughly and sniffled.

"Hey. It's okay." I reached out to touch her bare, freckled arm, and she flinched.

"Don't touch me," she said.

"Okay. It'll be all right." I was trying to stay calm. People were coming, and I didn't want to get into more trouble. But Durga squatted down, away from me, dabbing at her eyes with the corner of her sari.

As people gathered around, the philistines passing through yacked loudest: "Where're you going next? . . . The best bhang lassis in Agra, they'll blow your mind . . . The Dalai Lama has a better vibe, but I'm interested in this stuff." Finally Surinder unlocked the door from inside. I was the first one in and sat three-quarters of the way back. Rachel, I mean Durga, sat up at the foot of Swamiji's empty chair, her back squarely toward me, and took a tape recorder out of her bag.

I would have felt sorry for her if she didn't believe that I was the cause of her family's suffering. Would I ever be allowed back in the ashram with her and her father around? Christ.

Swamiji came in, and while we prostrated, I peeked to get a reading on him: He seemed mildly bored as usual, as if thinking, Go ahead throw yourselves down if you need to.

As I arranged myself into full lotus—my knee felt better today— he asked, "Melvin, what are you doing here?"

"You said I could come to darshan."

"Have you found a place to stay?" There were throat clearings and coughs from around the room.

"Yes, at the Tourist Bungalow." More snickers from the holier-than-thou crowd.

"That's fine," Swamiji said in such a way that shut everyone up, thankfully. Rachel, now composed, gazed back at me with tender pity. I wanted both to cry and to smack her. Swamiji had turned to interview some new arrivals, and I was counting breaths to keep my cool, when the door creaked open and we all turned. A middle-aged Indian couple shuffled into the room, he with black-framed glasses and a worried face, and she with her eyes cast down, her tidy gray hair in a bun, both dressed all in white.

"What's wrong?" Swamiji asked.

"We have come from Calcutta to see you," the man said. "My wife is anguished because our grown son has been diagnosed schizophrenic." The woman stared mutely out at Swamiji.

"You have traveled a long way to get here. First you must rest. We will talk later. After you rest, recite these prayers." He pulled some pieces of paper out from under his robe, and the man came up to get them. Swamiji put his hand on the man's head, gave some instructions to Surinder, and the couple was ushered out, their sadness sloshing through the room behind them.

I felt as though I'd been kicked in the chest, hard. Seeing Swamiji care for these people, acting to alleviate their pain, made me see that I had been stupid with the bucket the way I'd been stupid with the letter a few years ago; both were gutless, penny-ante offenses with the worst possible repercussions. If only I could "do good, be good" (or, for that matter, "do bad, be bad" and get out of here altogether), but I couldn't. There was nothing for me outside. I decided I had to meet with Swamiji, with my renewed faith and new understanding, and convince him of my worthiness to return.

Sensing Richard behind me, I twisted around and smiled at him, but he looked stonily ahead, and I faced forward again. Swamiji was talking about "concentrating on the formless . . . Each bangle is made of gold, they are separate forms, but they are all made of the same material—"

"Please repeat what you said, Swamiji?" Durga asked punching tape-recorder buttons and holding a bean-sized mike in front of his face.

"Put that thing away!" he snapped.

I smirked. I didn't mean to. It's just such a rare moment that he comes down on Rachel or Richard. Then I felt the blaze of his eyes.

"Melvin, leave," he said.

"Wha—" escaped from my mouth before I resigned myself. Shaking out my leg crawling with pins and needles, worse than the ants, I staggered to the door and prostrated clumsily there.

Once outside the compound, a tingling took over my body, an old familiar feeling—not awareness—rage. I had put my life in his hands because he said I should in order to stop the bad karma accruing, to make a break from the lies and the vanity and the materialism, to be happier. And that made sense to me. After all, I hadn't been doing such a bang-up job of it myself. But it was hard work following someone else's plan for you. And after three years of giving it everything I had, he chooses Richard, that good-for-nothing wimp, and his smug daughter, over me.

On the bridge, I stopped and bought a bag of pellets to fling at the big, ugly fish below, and then I took off down the path on the opposite shore, past the garden of plaster statues of Hindu deities (think Technicolor lawn ornaments waving arms and baring midriffs), past all the ashrams, up the dirt path toward the hills. This was where people wanting real seclusion came to live, and I could see how that worked, without the distraction of others' sticky egos. Me, I need to be around people, to know I'm not the only one struggling, but right then I craved a fat break from it all.

Sweating felt good as I tramped uphill, following the steep path a long way before I reached a pine-needle-covered flat with a stone Shiva shrine. I sat down in the dappled shade looking over the river and hills, listening to the thudding of my heart. I lay back and gazed at the blue sky through the dark boughs twisting like a spiral staircase up the trunk. Birds twittered, and the wind in the trees sounded like sand being poured. But the sound of twigs cracking underfoot popped me up onto my haunches. I scoped the rutted downhill to gauge how fast I could take it when an old woman came out of the trees. Caucasian, wrinkled, tan. Standing up, I saw she wasn't more than fifty or so, her gray hair cropped in raggedy tufts, her eyes sharp blue.

She raised her eyebrows. "You look upset." Her voice creaked as if she hadn't used it in a while. She wore a man's tattered kurta pyjamas, and her bare feet were thick with callouses and dirt.

"I didn't know what the noise was."

"And so you became so much afraid that you were ready to flee or gouge my eyes out?"

"No. Yes. I thought I was in danger."

She kneeled before Shiva as if she hadn't heard me, smeared him with gold paste from a copper bowl, and placed some red flowers beside him, chanting. I picked up my bag to leave.

"It's no wonder you've been kicked out of your ashram, with all that fear and suspicion."

"Huh?" I crossed my arms.

"I can see it in your face. You're not at ease here, and you're not anxious to go back down. By the looks of your clothes, you're not a tourist or a sadhu. Which ashram?"

At least she couldn't read that from my face. "Eternal Bliss."

"Ah, Swami Vidvanananda." Swamiji! "How is that old rascal? I used to live there until about four years ago."

"He's fine, he's good. What happened?" I sat down beside her. Was this why I had gotten kicked out of darshan, so I could meet her? Swamiji works in amazing ways.

"Oh, I liked Vidvan all right. I liked him a lot in fact, but I needed solitude finally."

"Has it worked?" No one called him that, not even behind his back. I decided I had to be careful. I liked her, but I wasn't sure she was all there. I had seen it before among Indians and Westerners alike: how an all-out search for god could shred their faculties like toilet paper.

"Worked? Yes, I suppose it has." She looked far off across the water and hills. "I feel better than I did. I felt really terrible when I left. Vidvan accused me of running away. But I said he was equally guilty of penning me in. Why have you been asked to leave?"

I picked at a rock in the dirt. I wasn't sure I wanted to get into it with her. "Conflict with another resident."

"Not that old coot Richard?"

"You know him?" Uncanny.

"Sure, he's a big baby that one. Wanted Swamiji to give him his bottle four times a day when I knew him. What's he up to now?"

"The same, the same—" I clapped, relieved.

"But?"

"His daughter Rachel has come to stay and help him and—"

"You're attracted to her?"

I looked away.

"Does she sit at his feet?"

I nodded. I was starting to get creeped out by how much she knew.

"Let her go. You can't compete. And then try to accept this: You are weaker than all the weakness combined that you have met in your life, and when you give in to that, it will save you. Goodbye." She turned to go into the forest.

"Wait!" I called. She looked over her shoulder. "Do you need anything before you go?" I reached into my sack and held out money.

She scowled as if to say, "Didn't you hear a thing I said?" and I felt as if she had given me a shove downhill—I just dropped the money and ran.

I could hear the clicks of the padlock while Jana opened the safe in the back room of the Eternal Bliss office to hand over some of my savings. Meeting that old kook had reminded me I wasn't going in for the alms thing yet.

I went upstairs to find Surinder to ask him when he thought the best time to ask for a meeting was, but Swamiji answered my knock.

"Come in," he said, and I opened the door. I began to prostrate.

"Stop," he said. "And speak plainly."

"I want another chance. Please let me stay here."

"What's wrong with the Tourist Bungalow?"

"I'm not among my own there: sex, money, drugs."

"You know the tenets, resist them."

"It's not just resisting. How can I go forward in my spiritual practice? What's the point of even being here?" I had never been so frank, or so desperate, with him.

"Melvin, don't you see, the point is not the point. Forward, backward. There are no such things. All mental constructs. Yourself is not *your* self. When you begin to dissolve that self—especially these ideas of how you need my support and approval, and how you deserve them more than Richard or Durga—the pain you find yourself experiencing will begin to dissipate."

Easier said than done, I thought.

"As for the temptations," Swamiji continued. "They are real, and you must find ways to defeat them."

"Swamiji, please don't turn me away. I'll be good. I'll work hard. I'll make amends."

"Maybe later." He straightened his papers.

I stood up. "Can I meditate and chant here?"

"Satsanga only, no more darshan, and do not talk to the residents."

"Can I meet with you?"

"The first of every month."

"Indian calendar?"

"Yes, now get out please!"

I jogged down the path till I hit the corny arch and rested behind it, my eyes stinging. Fuck the motherfucker. Fuck him. *Fuck* him.

Bob Marley, pot, raucous laughter. What did I expect? I closed the curtain but left the window open. I would try to sleep. Maybe a nap would clear my head.

Couldn't Rachel love a guy like me? Or at least like me?

"No," said a distinctly inflected voice. Was it him? "Melvin, don't you see that your expulsion is all what you make it? Of course it's me."

"I thought it was suspension."

"Exactly, it's what you make it."

"So, what do I need to go back?"

"Patience and faith. Yours is a long, hard road. Everything cannot come at once."

I fell into a thick sleep then and woke up in the long shadows of the room to a pure voice singing, "Went to a party down a red dirt road, there were lots of pretty people there, readin' *Rollin' Stone*, readin' *Vo-ogue*."

I pushed the curtain aside to see kids playing cards and drinking tea and beer on the lawn, a girl braiding another's hair, lounging with their sunburned faces and rumpled clothes decorated with mirrors and embroidery. I needed to make peace with Richard, Rachel, and Swamiji. I knew I could do it. I decided I would start with Durga. Goddess that she was, that look of pity in her eyes must count for something.

Three boys tossed stones at a circle in the dirt at the ashram gates, and I asked one to deliver a note.

"Dear Durga, Would you like to have dinner?" I wrote and signed my name, like a date in the eighth grade, but all I wanted was a truce, and she was my way in, I was sure.

I pointed at the apartment sticking out on the hillside and told the boy to ask for Durga, to give the note to her alone, no one else.

I sat out of sight of anyone who might be looking down from the ashram, and watched a sooty white cow meander up the road, all sagging back and ribs. The boy returned quickly and handed me my note. "Not at home," he said. I gave him five rupees, wondering if it was true.

Outside a restaurant that does brisk business across the river, I heard a high, merry laugh, and I knew it was Durga before I walked in and saw her red curls bouncing around her face. She looked giddy and free, and then I realized her father was across from her, his shoulders shaking with laughter too. And suddenly I got a sick feeling that I knew exactly what they were laughing about. I wanted to escape, but she saw me.

"Hi Melvin," she said, opening her mouth wide and closing it, as if trying to stifle the hilarity rising inside. Richard turned around and nodded. I excused myself and sat down on the other side of the room, my back to them, and waited patiently for them to leave.

As I walked back just after dusk, satsanga prayers droned out of all the ashrams, and when I hit Eternal Bliss, I just kept going. At the Tourist Bungalow, I lay face down on the bed and clutched a pillow over my head as if I could smother the furious thoughts coming out of it.

I woke up with a start and everything was dark and quiet, except for the buzzing call of a bird somewhere. I put on my good sneakers—no leather in them. Ganga Ma would tell me what to do, and I left the hotel compound under the cover of the bird's steady noise. On the empty road, alongside the river, I listened to the water lap and burble in a way that I never could during the day. And then, ahead of me, was the ashram's garage, a smeary yellow cube under the orange streetlights. I still had the key to it on my chain, and I rolled up one of the metal doors. The 220SE faced me in the moonlight: sky blue and dusty with her familiar rounded curves. I opened the driver's door, light on its hinges. It was an old feeling, this, like coming home as I slid inside breathing in the warm, salty smell of the vinyl. The worn-down ivory steering wheel with its smooth grooves for gripping, the rounded roomy space of the interior, and the cool knob of the gearshift. I rolled down the window and breathed in the fresh night air and the concrete smell of the garage.

If the car hadn't been famous throughout the villages of Uttar Pradesh for belonging to a holy man—and she was—I would have just gotten in and gone, taking me back to car trips with Karen, not so long ago really, where we headed out into the wide open space of Iowa, her eating a green apple beside me, the map spread over her knees, sun shining off the bits of blonde in her hair. We'd go due west until the sun went down so that both of us were blinded by the last gold streams of light, unafraid of the world and each other for as long as the drive lasted. That too, I understood now, was something like bliss, but I didn't know that then.

I popped the hood and got out to study the engine. I found the distributor, and plucked it out, a chunky, greasy spider with its eight rubber arms. When they checked the car for Swamiji's trip to Delhi next week, and the engine didn't turn over, they would have to call me. They didn't know jack about this car. I would work day and night to fix it, and when no one was looking, I would pop the distributor back in, and then be duly thanked, maybe even allowed to move back in to Eternal Bliss.

I felt twitchy with the plan as I closed the garage door, and something like invincible as I skirted the sleeping beggars and ducked through a hole in the fence to the ashram. I thought if I could just catch a glimpse of Rachel, that furrowed brow, all would be right in the world. She didn't like me yet, but I was hopeful—the way she lit up when she laughed, even if it was about me. But when I got to their apartment, the place was dark, and the spell was broken. Suddenly, I was irritated for every reason at once, especially because I was trespassing where two days before I had every right to be. Those jerks, I thought. It was their fault and that's what they were and I threw the distributor at the window.

And if I could have hurled myself forward and caught it like a cartoon character I would have. But I couldn't, and the glass shattered like a dream; the lights snapped on and there was Richard rushing in, easing Rachel to her feet. There was blood on her forehead trickling down one side of her face, and she wore a strange and knowing smile that made me want to step forward.

But then Richard yelled out the window, the opposite direction of where I was standing. "I see you out there! You bastard!" He didn't see a thing.

"Shh, Daddy, please don't get upset," she said leaning against him and faltering so that he scooped her up like a baby.

"Help! Someone help!" he called, and lights flicked on around the compound. I bolted uphill toward a gap in the fence, leaping billy-goat style up the firewood trails till I was high above the ashram and the town below. There I perched on a flat boulder, waiting for hours, my ass getting cold, but no one came after me. Finally, in the silvery-gray light before dawn I began to make my way down toward the Tourist Bungalow, hoping I could get to bed before daylight.

His hand shook slightly as he banged the little plastic stirrer around. Bloody Mary. Bloody bloody. At the end of the birth class, they watched videos of births. Ted would close his eyes. Instructor Jane, and sometimes some of the other women, cried and exclaimed, "Isn't it beautiful?" Ted ran off to the bathroom, thinking he might throw up.

(Bomer, page 27)

Y2K, or How I Learned to Stop Worrying and Love the CD-ROM

Matthew Samton

Y_____ walked out of his house
On one of those crisp early spring weekend mornings
A clean sweater on his back
A smile on his face
And his left shoe untied
Before his sole hit the pavement a half dozen times
The world had ended.

X_____ raised the shade on the window of the red-eye from Los Angeles
A few minutes after raising her eyelids from her nap
The dawn greeted her over the Midwest
In front of her
The flight attendant set down a Bloody Mary
And pointed across the aisle
At the man's enthusiastic wave
X_____ sighed
Then turned back to the window to watch
The world come to an end.

W_____ was what her closest friends called her
But she let him call her that after just one evening
At the drive-in
Her hair was beginning to respond to the blow-dryer
When her little brother's desperate voice squeezed
Through the bathroom door

OPEN CITY

Before the pee made it all the way down his leg
To the thick shag carpet below
The world had ended.

Dr. Von UTS sat in his laboratory
His radio tuned to the choir
Half a world away
By the shores of the Great Salt Lake
The melodic voices were enough of a distraction
To keep him from his tea
For which the water was
Presently boiling over
Onto the hot plate
In the next room
If the Mormons were prophetic
They might have alerted their listeners to the impending doom
As it was
Von UTS was caught with his hair standing on end
In delight
When
The world ended.

"I can't stand it anymore!"
Were the distant words
Heard by the neighbors of the large tower
Up on the hill
The sun had not shone in the valley
For as long as most of them could remember
Again and again
The high-pitched protests from the tower
Cut the fog that separated it from the gray cottages
Below
Young R.
Born with a club foot
Let his cane drop
And pointed a finger at the light that seemed
As if on divine cue
To pierce the overcast sky

Suffusing the faces of the townspeople
With an ethereal glow
As
The world ended.

Q____P let the thoughts of suicide subside for the moment
As he thought about his mother
She would not approve of the sweater he had been wearing
Uninterrupted for the past five days
Inundated with cigarette ash and smoke
But "Fuck her!" he thought and the name she gave him
Which
In one final fell swoop
Would disappear
Along with all the other fuckin' humiliating baggage
He had acquired in this world
A long pause
When Q____P called his brother to say "goodbye"
He got the machine
Then remembered
His brother was out of town
Death might have to wait a day
He thought
This realization cheered him up a bit
And
As he lit what was to have been his final cigarette
The world ended.

O. (Opposable) "Thumbs" began to tap his namesakes
Against the steering wheel
As a familiar tune sang out of the car radio
In the passenger seat
N. (Nicky) "Knuckles" had his mind on more pertinent matters
Their trunk was still full of its cargo
"Knuckles" abruptly shut off the music
So he could think
"Thumbs" stopped the car short
There was a tense silence

OPEN CITY

In the car
Before
A faint tapping brought their attention back
To the trunk and its contents
However
Their "cargo" hadn't regained consciousness for long
Before
The world ended.

It was MLK's birthday
And all he could find on the television were reruns
It's The Man again
He thought
The wife enjoyed them
So he didn't make a scene of it
But
All that canned laughter was bringing a frown to his face
How many more years before they learn?
The boy was crying
In the other room
The dog was chewing
The nose of the boy's toy rocket ship
Never to fly again
But
By the time any acknowledgement was made of the fact
The world had ended.

A morning rain woke up the windshield wipers of all the cars
Passing J_____'s stop
With no bus in sight
Her yellow slicker covering her body
And The Book Review
Above her head
A protective halo
Allowing her mind to stray
To the previous night
Again waiting
For the telephone call

That never came
And still she waited
But the bus didn't come
No news is good news
She joked to herself
So
The longer she waited
The happier she became
Reveling in the reflection
Forming at her feet
And
Still she waited
In the living room mirror
A young woman
And a good book
Alone
In the middle of just another Saturday night
She waited some more
In no hurry to go to sleep
Tick tock tick tock tick tock
Went the windshield wipers
With a broadening smile on her face
She kept waiting
And still the bus didn't come
It was Sunday though
And she didn't have to get anywhere fast
And the world went on
At half speed
The Sunday drivers
Honking their horns
And shining their lights
For the pouring rain.

Later when I was alone in my bed
I thought one thing: What if it was true,
that in the end he was irrelevant?
(Bialosky, page 37)

Drawings

Ann Faison

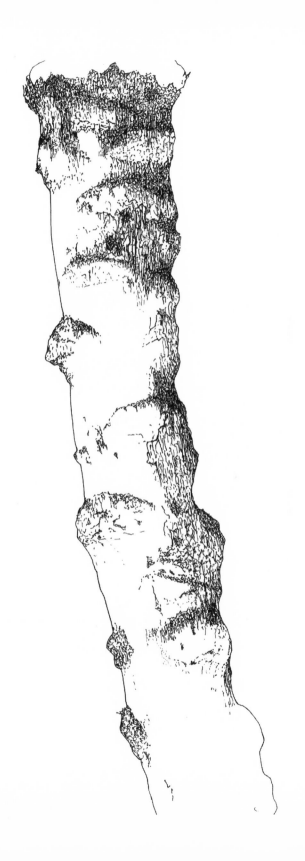

And On the First Day

Ben Doyle

the telephone cord snapped
from overuse. It was everywhere.
The refrigerator stopped its petulant
knocking; in the abandoned mailbag
I found the following letter:

chickenscratch in chickenscratch
in chickenscratch.

And on the second day,

all dogs I had considered adopting
        at the pound had been
"put to sleep,"
A drift of white fur was still
        in the corner of a cage;
I hid it in my mouth.

And on the third day,

we mated furiously on a cardboard mat
while the calico goldfish Marco looked on
levitating in his jumbo bell jar.
I knew soon we would say the awful thing
that would tether us like horses to saloons,
        so I went inside & bought a bottle of sour mash.
Later:
        I stepped through the rip in your screen door

& snuck Marco under your pillow as you slept
the huge sleep of someone
who had made a decision to, in the morning,
decide.

And on the fourth day,

it was overcast &
I awoke only in time for about an hour of that.
My clock-radio had become deprogrammed in an electrical storm.
I wasn't sure if noon was A.M. or P.M., & then those data
seemed very important.
Open to suggestions, I wandered to town
with a virgin credit card
singing "alleluia, alleluia" in my breast pocket.

p.s.: The sun was behind the green tarp.

And on the fifth day,

I mowed the lawn with a hangover.
I poisoned a three-point line
with used motor oil into the shorn grass
surrounding the concrete square
& worked on my jumper until the clouds drew whistles.

And on the sixth day,

a vault arched through the sky
& created a sunset somewhere new.
I scurried under the coffee table
like a crab who has seen the future

and on the seventh day,

it is the seventh day.

Push It Out

Lewis Cole

THIS WAS MY VERSION OF THE STORY:

Twenty-three, married to a Dominican furniture maker who wove rush chairs in a Dyckman Street garage, Delores took her two kids to a Lords mobile clinic for lead paint poison testing (this was 1969, two years before; "Serving the People" was the motto of the day): sample jars, instruction sheets, hypodermics, rubber tubing, anxious mothers, harried nurses, crying, bored, rambunctious kids, and funny, serious Ramón.

She likes the way Ramón acts—he pats her son's hair—and looks: pouty lips, troubled, passionate eyes, a regal nose.

Everything's a mess, a wonderful mess: short-staffed, the Lords need someone to hold a baby, answer the telephone, explain the procedure in Spanish to wary, intrigued grandmothers. Delores helps out. Nice to work with the quick, self-assured nurses, speak to the women who, like herself, worry for their children—she understands their problems, says comforting things. Yes, the Lords don't know what they're doing. Kids themselves, all the party members jabber too much, take much too much for granted. But she has to give them credit because they've organized this marvelous thing and without them, the van, doctor, nurses, desks, files, and the fact that kids who might be in danger will actually be treated would never happen. And, besides, there's Ramón . . .

"You'll be here next week?" she hears herself ask Ramón when she can no longer delay bringing the kids home for their nap. *Qué dices?*

she thinks. Just like that? You ask him just like that? You're thoughtless, *sin vergüenza*, like Aunt Dahlia used to say, shameless: You'll be here next week?

And, as soon as he answers, she promises: "I'll help you, I'll be here at ten."

Her life has changed—she's come to America; found out she's pregnant, fallen in love; she's no longer herself, Delores, housewife and mother, but restless, confused, a woman with a silent, accompanying presence in her life: her promise to work at the tests in five, four, three—the next day.

She arrives early, helps them set up. So much to be done. She corrects everything the Lords do. They're children, full of instinct, enthusiasm, and energy, but they know nothing about people or practical craft. They listen to her. They need her. She feels fulfilled, the kind of flesh warm, flesh-swelling fuck that has made her want to pull and push her husband down and around inside her, except now there's no cock around which she wraps herself, but a blossoming inner satisfaction: they need her.

"We're meeting to discuss some things. Can you stay? We can really use your help." Ramón, innocent at the end of the exhausting day, not that much taller than she is, the slightest hint of a risky smile at the edge of his kissable lips.

She thinks: the kids. No, they're taken care of, parked with her mother-in-law. Ramón jokes with her. Between them a small flirtation—she corrects his Spanish, he buys her a *café con leche*, nothing duplicitous, certainly not on his part, he's in awe of Delores—she's a prize for the Party, a working mother whose membership would be more living proof that the Party really makes sense and can triumph.

The long speeches frustrate her; the smoky air in the room chokes her; the general talk of contradictions, revolutionary nationalism, mother country, peasantry, and bodega-owning "comprador bourgeoisie" (her uncle? he owned a store) confuse her. She feels insecure and stupid. But the spirit in the room thrills her. There's nothing small or defeated about these people; they glow with purpose; they inhabit the world.

Then the meeting is over. What to do? She stands around. No place to go but home. Steps outside into chilling air, harsh wind, pulls up the hood of her green-wool loden coat and lingers a moment to light a cigarette. She sees herself walk past the gilt-framed family photos and bookcase topped with votive candles and pictures of Santa Barbara that line the long entrance hallway of her mother-in-law's Audubon Avenue, Washington Heights apartment. Smells of fish, beans and coffee. A doll and ball scattered in the impeccably clean, plastic-covered living room. The sound of her children. Home. A happy death. What is she thinking?

"We're going to a party. You want to come?" Ramón again.

I had heard the story a couple of times when Ramón and Delores stayed the night with Karen and me getting high and talking late. For some reason I always imagined this moment vividly, Delores on the top step of the mobile lead-testing van, Ramón underneath her, looking up, both their faces raw and red in the winter wind so that his question extends outside itself and really asks her: Don't you want to be inside, warm, with me—come, come!

It's her wish come true, something that doesn't happen often. It's also a big choice because she should go home, see her babies, kiss her husband, relieve her mother-in-law. But she wants and needs to stay here, needs to stay here, it's been a long time since she's been without babies, husband, and family. And besides there's a new element now. Ramón who charms her—magic words, soft laugh, glittering eyes. She can tell he wants her; he can't take his eyes off her; it's been another long time since a man had needed her like this.

They walk to the party, talking, all the time, talking—she's never heard anyone with so many words, never been asked so many questions. It's strange for her to pass the stoops, street signs, and stores of her youth with a man other than her husband. She remembers old boyfriends, kissing in hallways. Ramón pushes the familiar black-painted, iron-grill door that opens into a vestibule decorated with a No Loitering sign, mangled mailboxes, and a framed tenant Directory listing many apartments and only two names. From above Santana sings: *Oye, como vá?* The grating buzz frees the lock on the inner lobby door and they meet familiar smells and the hiss of steam heat. Up the stairs, Delores first. She turns to hear something Ramón says and the magic moment of desire passes between them. Sudden silence. Ramón looks quizzically at her, moves to try a kiss. She surprises him, opens her full lips. Ramón stops: he has no experience with other men's wives. And she's also a mother. He pulls back, asking, Are you sure you know what you're doing?

"Check out yourself," she tells him. They kiss—high-school kids making out, the staircase landing as their bower. In the stale, cold air, his hand clutching leaflets presses through the wool of her shapeless loden coat to the small of her strong back; her palm feels for his stiffening cock against the soft denim of his dungarees; the only skin that touches between them is their chins. Still, they can't stop.

He tells her to wait, bounds up the stairs.

Alone in the stairwell, she stares at the worn, chipped, marble steps of the rising flight of stairs, and considers the possibilities: leave, never see him again, let her life return to its standard pattern, no danger, no risk.

But she doesn't want to go.

Stay.

Her thinking stalls. What does she want?

The heat radiates off her body, baking her. She tries to make sense of the purpose, confusion, and desire that charges her up and leaves her waiting there, stock still, and this is what she decides: The words she's heard all day—self-determination, collective action, oppression—define her life. And this man, man-boy, cares for her, wants to help her. So sleeping with him wouldn't be wrong. Not sleeping with him would be wrong. *Not* sleeping with him would be continuing her unhappiness, her oppression.

Meanwhile Ramón—already in love. As he takes the stairs two at a time, he imagines the brown, full breasts he has felt under the wool, sees her intelligent, passionate face, a real woman, not a college girl: he will save her, he thinks, transform her life.

A friend at the Party lends him his apartment in the same building.

A moment's foolish, strained delay at the door with the key and they're inside and naked. He starts to make love like other men, arousing and controlling her. No, she doesn't want this, not with him; she wants him inside her, losing himself. She holds his ass, squeezing him against her, squeals and laughs with pleasure, moans with love, gets him harder, whispers he feels good, grinds against him, stares the whole time into his face, not releasing him until he closes his eyes, stalled above her for a moment, and explodes.

Women Lords believe its their revolutionary to bring Delores into the Party.

She joins.

She has something new in her life, a child and a love, something she can feed and fuck; she bursts with new womanhood. She plans her days around meetings, Party work; she spends her nights with Ramón at a Party member's apartment, making love, talking until early morning. She wants to escape the drab dead end of her married life. He's fascinated by her hardheadedness and passion, her "working-class qualities," as he says. She listens to him riff about the Vietnamese Communist Party leader, Le Duan. He asks her about growing up in the Ponce slums. Did her cousin really try to sleep with her? When did she have her first razor fight? She's completely different from the girls he's known in college, quick-tempered and loyal, passionate and practical. Ramón loves the working class, loves the very idea of working class.

"What are you doing?" her husband demands.

She tells him he understands nothing. Of course she's not fucking another guy. What kind of stupidity is that? He doesn't understand politics: The only explanation he can find for her behavior is that she's off with another man.

She isn't lying; she believes this: What matters isn't Ramón, but Ramón's world, the magical place she enters when she's with him, the realm of the Party in which she's powerful, special, and listened to, the universe where she's free from the one-bedroom cave where she's ignored and used, exhausted and unhappy.

"You're a whore," her husband yells one day and slams her against the door.

She meets Ramón later that night. The choice is clear—stay with her husband and children or leave home. There's no hesitation. To go back is to shut the door on everything she had promised herself in the last months. She must leave; to stay because of the kids is false consciousness. Her husband hunts her down, shouts and slaps; Lords intervene, threaten him: "Don't make us do you some hurt."

She breaks with family and friends. Each day brings new loss. But to her the losses are choices, the sorrows self-assertions, the loneliness her right to determine her life. In her mind, she's not drifting further from shore, but swimming closer to the other side.

I know what you're thinking: These people were losers, the politics were boring, the cause hopeless, the leaders inept, the decisions disastrous.

Okay, okay—I don't want to sentimentalize us. I hate the sentimentality of the Left—the fake expressions of comradeship, the self-satisfied righteousness of "I fought the good fight,"the cloying, self-congratulatory idealization of our parents practiced now by currency traders, school board directors, and art gallery owners who as children watched I Love Lucy, Gunsmoke, *and* You Are There *in living rooms decorated with Gwathmey prints and Ben Shahn woodcuts and sat around the red and white-checked, oilcloth-lined kitchen tables listening to desperate discussions of the Khruschev revelations.*

(Remember when they weren't to be heard, our parents, the generation of the nineteen-thirties that we now love to honor? Remember when for us they betrayed the promise of revolution, sold out to Roosevelt, the CIO, the Democratic Party, and Israel? No charming kitschy figures memorialized by Anne Bancroft in Sidney Lumet films or heartwarming New Yorker *stories then. They were economistic (Lenin) Mister Joneses (Dylan) who didn't understand Blacks, Vietnamese, rock music, Che Guevara, Régis Debray, acid, the Jefferson Airplane, or the primacy of Third World struggles and watched television and paid mortgages.)*

Worse than the bullshit of the Right—because at least we should know better. Okay—we had our illusions.

But what about yours?

Around 110th Street, police barricades blocked the avenues. We left everyday time and entered the world of action, the land of sit-ins, marches, teach-ins, speak-outs, conventions (in Lansing, Austin, Cornell, wonderful provincial state capitals of education), demonstrations, and strikes, a place of cluttered side streets, mounted cops, carnival smells of horse shit, barbecue, rubbish fires, and pizza, rushing crowds, and the pulse and noise of music, chants, and shouts. I felt the familiar rush of excitement, anticipation, and fear: Slogans, meet, march, speech, march, speech, slogans, meet, every gathering, march, picket line, seizure, and strike turning around the question, What will you do? But with a character of their own that evolved as the action proceeded, so that I always felt I was experiencing something I knew very well for the first time. I must have planned and participated in a hundred actions and they had become a routine part of my life, but their drama still caught and held me. *Opening act exposition*—discuss (purpose of action; long argument: Do we really want to present the petition, see John Mitchell, take over the ROTC building, and use it as a freedom school for the neighborhood, or do we simply want to trash things?), dress (boots and jeans, jacket, wet handkerchief for gas, optional helmet, no earrings or jewelry if you were a woman), and gather (organize your affinity group, split up into twosomes, decide when and where you'll meet again). *Second act complication*—arrive, sense and try to master the situation. What sort of crowd? Huge and chaotic? Throngs of people, disorganized and angry, wanting a fight? Huge and happy? Chanting, dancing hordes jamming the streets, waiting to flood the main avenue, exuberantly believing it impossible for anyone to disagree with them on this brilliant, sunlit day? Small and sober, clear and determined in its purpose? Or small and ugly, only ourselves, everyone decked out in combat gear, helmets and boots, forcing ourselves to do damage, but actually scared and hoping the cops would go away? *Third act resolution*: a burst of action, cops charge us or we scream and run into them, or desultory failure from a lack of focus or energy, a general drifting away, you want to get something to eat? Hippies and peace activists splashing and cavorting in the fountain at the Mall or Central Park trying to cool themselves, a ragtag meeting in a local activist's living room to discuss what should happen next, or some private gut-check when an affinity group member dared me to toss a brick at a cop or through a plate-glass bank window. Actions were a landscape for me, a setting of edgy, suspicious cops, overweight, longhaired, bearded onlookers and stragglers, intent leafleteers wanting to confront and convince you about the pivotal importance of Raya Dunyavaskaya's vision of democratic revolutionary socialism, G.I. organizing, political prisoner defense work, the vanguard status of the Chinese Cultural Revolution (PLP, the Progressive Labor Party), Trotsky's theory of world revolution (YSA, the Young Socialists Alliance), combatting white skin privilege (SDS, Students for a Democratic Society), or working for Gene McCarthy, and the middle-aged and my-aged tense and bored crowd of whom none were sure what they were doing and all were certain they could be nowhere else. I went to actions by the season, month, and week and they were as varied and surprising as any repeated part of human experience, except that for me whether they were peaceful, violent, or sexy, or whether they bored, stultified, inspired, frustrated, instructed, or exhausted me, they all ultimately moved like a nightmare landscape back toward one vanishing point, the always-anticipated moment of confrontation, and the question that circled, swirled, and spiraled around it: *What would I do?* They scared, thrilled, tested, and bested me, and I loved them.

Let's make a deal.
I'll trade you—my vision for yours:
From the absurd mix of triumphalism and sophistry of the last twenty years, what sentimental dreams do you surrender?
One bannered polka-dotted antiwar demonstration declaring: WAR IS NOT GOOD FOR CHILDREN AND OTHER LIVING THINGS; STOP THE WAR!; FREE ALL POLITICAL PRISONERS; POWER TO THE PEOPLE; HO, HO, HO CHI MINH—*the energy of people warming them in the subfreezing weather, all glorious fellow-feeling and hope, the moment we surge into the streets, the reverberating echo of* Out to the street!/Onto the jail!/The people's power/Is the Panther's bail! *filling the downtown avenues, black-and-white photos of kids spilling out of school in Montgomery, yelling at soldiers in Saigon, dashing into the streets at Prague to set Molotov cocktails under the treads of the approaching tanks*—The Pig is the Same All Over the World . . .
For:
An evening's sanctimonious chatter on Charlie Rose *or* Nightline, *Charlie or Ted sober to the point of pontifical, all the usual suspects arraigned for commentary, grave and arch, experts and insiders, George Will, erudite and effete, Peggy Noonan, blowzy and ironical, the conservative as mensch, un-self-consciously fixing her bra strap while dismissing two hundred years of worldwide struggle and thought as juvenile indulgence compared to the penetrating adult vision of Ronald Reagan . . .*

We decided Paul and Karen should drive around while I contacted Ramón and arranged to deliver the sandbags; we had brought them for the Lords, jammed in the back of the car, at their request as defense against a police attack on the seized settlement house. We piled out, Cassie, Marcy, and Laura going ahead. I walked behind them with Daniel and told him Karen was now definitely coming to Atlanta.

"What are you going to do?" he asked, his eyes not on me, but the street ahead where the women approached the police checkpoint.

"I want to be alone in Atlanta with Cassie," I said.

"Then you've got to tell Karen about Cassie," he said.

"I can't," I answered.

"Then you'd better make sure there's no space in the car for Karen."

"Watch out for stray bullets," a young cop flirted, as they sidled past the saw-horses.

"Jerkoff," Marcy shouted back, "watch out for stray bricks." She draped her arms around Cassie's and Laura's shoulders, an ugly duckling in the middle, and the three flounced off.

"You know what amazes me?" said Daniel.

"No." No need to ask; I knew he'd supply me with the truth.

We entered the edge of the crowd. Stray leafleteers passed out throwaways announcing a rock concert, a people's tribunal to judge Abbie Hoffman, a lecture by Lyndon LaRouche on the General Strike, another on *First or Third World Revolution: White Skin Privilege and Trotsky's Theory of Combined and Uneven Development*, and rallies to free all political prisoners, demand an end to torture in Iran, protest sexist hiring practices at CBS, the racist firing of a Harlem principle, and the trial of three ex-Panthers charged with holding up a gas station. The smudged, banner-headlined front pages of *Worker's World*, *P'alante*, and *The Militant* carpeted the street. Fires burned in open-wire garbage baskets and food vendors hawked *helados* and hot dogs. A crowd of kids rushed by, heads bobbing, as though they had just been released from school, heads bobbing like buoys, running to the television news announcer; behind him the spotlights converted the narrow, littered street into a dramatic black-and-white canyon.

My chest tightened. The Tingler: My private campy joke name for the demon of fear that came alive inside me at every action, adopted from a silly black-and-white low-budget Vincent Price thriller Karen and I had seen on late-night television in which a lobster-looking beast implanted itself in victims and squeezed out their life. Some joke. The fact was the Tingler stirred in me at every action. He gripped and choked me, growing stronger and larger as we neared a confrontation, a physical presence of my fear, swelling inside me, scaring me into wrong, stupid, shameful choices, until everything exploded, and I was in the sea, panicked with nothing to do except kick out and swim for land or drown.

A crazy came up, a short man with wild, gray-white hair, a shirt that covered him like a housecoat and sandals that flopped like dead fish as he walked, the straps broken around his heel, and toes. He held two disintegrating shopping bags heavy with books and newspapers. "I'm in pain from Novocain. Everyone thinks he has a plan. But Rockefeller's not smart enough to rule the world."

"I know," said Daniel, and stepped around him into the action of the street. He searched for the women, momentarily out of sight. "They're beautiful," he said, answering his own question. "You won't find a lot of groups with such gorgeous women."

"Marcy's ugly," I said.

He pushed deeper into the crowd. The groups of people thickened. A band of students stood in the middle of the block, chanting, *El pueblo, Unido, Jamás será vencido!* A scraggly, thin-armed kid with matted corkscrew hair and thick glasses laughed, shrill, on edge; his girlfriend told him to get his shit together. Camped on a tenement stoop a group from the Lower East Side droned Buddhist "Om's" to a beat of tambourines and one steel drum while their leader in black granny sunglasses shouted about John Lennon and Abbie Hoffman conspiring against real anarchists. Next to them men in white skivvy shirts and Bermuda shorts played dominos, slapping the tiles down on a folding bridge table. Hurrying around us, a mother in a house dress and high-heeled shoes hustled a kid into their building. I tried to look over the crowd and locate the settlement house and Ramón.

"Aren't I right?" Daniel insisted.

We shouldered our way past members of Newsreel, the revolutionary film collective. In the group, a tall, bald-headed guy with wire-rimmed sunglasses smiled at a furious Asian woman who cursed him:

"Don't smile at me, motherfucker, because you are not smiling inside."

"I'm trying to work with you."

"You need to check out your attitudes, asshole."

Through the crowd I glimpsed a two-story-tall Caribbean Indian torching a *finca* with an orange blaze—the Lords had filled the brick wall of the deserted lot opposite the settlement house with a spray-painted revolutionary mural a few months ago.

"You mean Laura," I said.

"She's the most beautiful woman I've ever met. Where does she come from?"

Now the others, leftovers and fucked-overs: Print Collective, Klonskyites, and Avakianists, the last members of Up Against the Wall, Motherfuckers! Defense committees demanding support for Martin Sostre, Ahmed Evan, Lee Otis Johnson, the Fort Dix Three, the Puerto Rican Nationalists, John Sinclair, radical journalists from the Liberation News Service, a contingent of blacks wearing dashikis, some action groups from now-defunct SDS chapters and newly formed all-women's collectives, members of the Living Theater and the break-off Joe Chaikin group (and the women's group that had broken off from him), and groups from Weathermen collectives who instead of being asked to go underground had been requested to form New Morning collectives and lived together in Brooklyn and Vermont, supporting themselves by dealing dope while waiting for clandestine calls from their old leaders to help them hide for a month, secure an ID, lend them three hundred dollars. One woman looked lost, alone; earrings: She was new. Other than her, no one else, only hardcore, no one from the larger antiwar organizations, no professionals or church people.

I was pissed he thought Laura prettier than Cassie. "A peace movement fund-raiser," I told him.

"What else?" Daniel demanded. "Don't hold back."

"She went after stars," I told him. The errant, lost-looking crowd frightened me; I thought I had to talk to Ramón, tell him he needed to organize things better.

Daniel wanted more: "And? And?"

"She fucked Robbie Gold."

"Robbie Gold."

"Only once," I said, remorseful already for my indiscretion. "And she hated it. I'm sorry. I shouldn't have said anything."

He answered immediately. "I don't care who she slept with. She matters to me. Robbie Gold won't get in my way." He bit his moustache, hands on his hips, and marched off, angry and determined, ready to do damage.

Or :

Ho Chi Minh, Lumumba, or Fidel—nothings after all, school teachers, students, minor government bureaucrats dogged by exile and prison, penniless, armed with false passports and confused ideologies, leaders without parties, individuals who came from nowhere, no pedigree or preparation, geniuses of history who imposed themselves on our memories and conscience. (Remember Lumumba's carved ebony face? ? Framed by Trotsky glasses, his piercing eyes stare from the back of the jeep where he sits handcuffed and helpless, furious at his fate.)

For:

Rupert Murdoch? Michael Eisner? Barry Diller?

We pushed through the final clot of people. Hard television lights glared at the brick-bound, poster-colored, larger-than-life revolutionary stares of Che, Fidel, Lolita LeBrun, José Marti; weird wavy shadows from the garbage-can fires spread and shut over Zapata leading the Indians. Gangs of kids snaked and bolted through the crowd planning mischief in rapid-fire Spanish; I caught individual words—*el techo, basura, pendejo malecón*. Police formed a barrier between the crowd and the settlement house; behind them someone had pushed a few wrecked cars into the street, a people's barricade of rust and naked wheels. The kids played chicken with the cops, walking straight toward them, then dashing away, disappearing behind corners and cars. Another twist of the Tingler, harder this time.

The police barricade stopped us. Across the street, behind the junked cars, Delores commanded the settlement house's top step, tight-lipped and stormy-eyed, her Afro bursting from under her Party beret. Behind her a line of Lords guarded the sanctuary, arms crossed over their chests, faces set as humorless masks. From the platform of a flimsy folding chair, a Party member harangued the crowd. Lawyers, cops, and reporters filled the street. I shouted and waved to Delores. Kifner, the *Times* reporter, approached, a veteran from another side; his uniform: tie and blazer as always, moccasins without socks, photo ID dangling idly around his neck, notebook in hand.

"What do you think?" I asked, my fear wanting him to offer me the reassurance that some sort of sanity would prevail; we had been together through three years of these.

No luck. "City won't budge; they're not leaving; we're in a box." He grimaced, not liking the flat, professional judgment he offered. "You wished you didn't know what was coming," he said.

"You don't know what will happen," I answered.

"They don't know what they're doing. It's no good. I'm going to see what the captain says."

I turned to Daniel, but he was already gone, ducking under the barricade, headed toward the women who chanted and clapped across the street. I yelled and he answered he was right there if I needed him, pestered by my demand.

Delores pointed, summoning me. Cops and Lords security at the barricades negotiated my passage: Where's his ID? We need his ID, Balaguer intervened, minister of something, older, always diplomatic; I liked him. Handclasps and hugs. Good to see you, brother, he said. We sidestepped past the wooden horse and entered the moat of action, the sealed-off street before the settlement house, anxious reporters immediately wondering who I was, lawyers nodding hello, raised clenched fists and revolutionary salutations from others. On the steps, a Lords security and a burly television camera crewman gut-checked each other—Nobody keeps me from doing my job. This is off-limits. You can't stay here. You do your job, I'll do mine. Stay out of my way, pig. Shoves; the Lord flashed a karate kick. The burly guy—Woodstock T-shirt; lots of them were cops—lunged. A rush of people converged on the spot like a diagram of healthy cells surrounding an infection; shouts and argument; everything settled as quickly as it broke out.

Delores listened to me explain that the sandbags were still in the car while staring upward, concentrating on a roof, a warlord already, preparing for battle. Inside the settlement house, Ramón marched toward us through the confusion, thin-faced, haggard, arguing with someone in Spanish. Delores turned: "This is really something, isn't it?"

Before I could answer, a distraction; angry whispers to the Party member who had been arguing with Ramón. "You stay here," and I was alone, commanding the steps. I looked on the open street; chants echoed off the building walls; fires and lights baked the breathless air.

At the center of any action things tumbled and careened; I could never measure their flow, chart the progress that led from an over-filled classroom meeting to a desperate run from the cops. Even what was happening in the movement seemed a jumbled flow without any easily pinpointed start or finish; sometimes I tried to imagine how things had changed, the whole unfolding of our transition from triumph to this now sad state in which everything seemed a presentiment of defeat, thinking that if we could stop for a second and survey the scene we would see things out of the rush, capture some perspective, and begin to put things in their proper place. But it was as hopeless as stopping a riot. Instead the only thing that came to mind were pieces, snapshots, not movies—the moment of the meeting, the dash toward the cops, the telephone call at midnight or early morning that thrust me into a new world where Fred Hampton was dead or Cambodia bombed. *What are you going to do?* And now the snapshots started to appear. Cops left their posts, walking away, letting people fill the street. There was a blur of concentrated energy—a kid racing up a fire escape, toward the roof, taking the iron steps two at a time. In the front of the crowd a group sang the Panther anthem, *Power to the People!* Outside the energy swirled and spiraled. Inside the Tingler contracted and squeezed. *What are you going to do?*

"Why did you tell Daniel I slept with Robbie Gold?" Laura was at my side, her arm wrapped around my waist.

"He asked me." From inside, Ramón spotted me, waved; he'd be outside soon, we'd talk.

"Don't make trouble, Mark. I like Daniel. I really do. There could be something special between us. Don't hold that stuff against me. It's not fair."

Now Cassie came up, eager for news, cheeks flushed a freckled strawberry red and her hair loose and thickly curled in the damp heat: "What stuff?"

"Before I left. I slept with Robbie Gold a year ago and Mark thinks I should have slept with him." She turned to me: "You were with someone else. I would never do that."

"That's not the reason," I said, refusing to let her gut-check me. "I didn't worship you enough."

"What's wrong with that?" asked Cassie. "Every woman wants to be worshipped."

"Tell that to Robbie," Laura said. "Talk about depressing sex. I'm thinking, This guy isn't interested in me, he's interested in *acting* like he's interested in me. But I'm going along with it. What is that? What allows me to do that to myself? This is not a man I'm attracted to. He's not handsome. He has no soul. He talks too much and thinks he's much too irresistible. So why am I going off with him? I'm lying in bed and thinking, You don't love this penis, you don't like this penis, you don't want this penis in you and you don't like what it's attached to. It's not even like I can tell myself I'm having fun. I just want to go to sleep."

"And you did," I said, pissed at her attack on me.

"He told you that?"

Cassie was laughing. "He must have hated that. I was always afraid to."

"You slept with him?" Laura was delighted by the news.

"When I joined Weather. I thought he was vulnerable. Or maybe I was star-fucking." She looked at me. "Sex is crazy. Sometimes I think we should just put everyone into a room and let them fuck each other and get it out of their systems. Is something going to happen here?"

I welcomed the change in subject. "I don't think they know what they're doing."

She wagged a mock reproving finger. "You've got to have faith in the people. The kids in the street are stockpiling bricks."

Laura surveyed the street, looking for Daniel I guessed. "Can I say something? I've never understood the idea of a shoot-out. Is the idea actually to shoot police? Because then why don't you ambush them?"

"I was in a shoot-out once," said Cassie. "An almost shoot-out. We were visiting the offices of the Chicago Panthers and the cops surrounded the building. Everything was organized; everyone had a task. I was supposed to distribute handkerchiefs soaked in water if they tear-gassed. I was scared, but in a weird, calm sort of way. I told myself if I just kept thinking about what I was supposed to do I would be all right. They finally worked out a deal with the police without any shooting, but I almost felt disappointed because I wanted to be part of our group and show them we weren't afraid."

"You're amazing," said Laura. She hugged her; they had been roommates for a short while before Laura left for Kubrick and Cassie flirted with Weatherman.

I saw Daniel approaching from the street. "He said you have beautiful breasts," I announced, jealous of their mutual-admiration society.

"He did?" Laura was surprised and pleased. She pressed her palm against her chest, squeezing her breasts, as though checking to see if he were right and protecting herself at the same time. "He said that?"

"He's right," said Cassie. "I love your breasts."

Another hug. "I love this woman." She held Cassie's face between her palms and kissed her on the lips. "Isn't she the best," she demanded.

"She's the best," I agreed, Laura's implacable shamelessness always making an idiot of me.

"Can I say something?" said Laura. "When are the two of you coming out of the closet? Everybody knows you're lovers. When is that going to happen?"

"I'm getting some bricks," said Cassie, freeing herself from Laura's embrace.

"I don't understand why you should sneak around," said Laura.

"Who's sneaking around," asked Marcy. She stepped up from the street into the glare of a television light and looked sallow and greedy in the artificial whiteness.

"Nobody," said Laura. "I have a big mouth."

"What's going on?" asked Marcy, looking at me and Cassie and smelling trouble. But Daniel interrupted the moment, a bearded, exuberant doughboy offering us a bag of *cuchifritos* and asking when the riot was starting.

"Get serious," said Marcy, still watching me with a slight smile, indicating she knew my secret.

"Why should I get serious?" he said. My mind of course was on Ramón, the sand, and Marcy's nosiness, but I realized something I had never understood about women and men: Laura liked Daniel for the reasons I did. "You people always want serious. Revolution is fun. You're taking your life into your own hands. Serious is for Norman Podhoretz."

"Norman who?" Marcy asked, as though once again he was talking about a friend or SDS organizer she was excluded from knowing because of male chauvinism.

Or:

One feel-good patriotic celebration (the U.S.A.-All-The-Way! hockey team, lionized teenagers, none good enough to make the pros, say, or the Broadway parade after the Gulf War, the literate warriors, Colin Powell and Schwartzkopf in the lead, or the vets, that staged homage of carnage, the past as unrecognizably shredded as the confetti papering Wall Street, an impossible to disentangle mess of sorrow, resentment, courage, hate, pride, and manipulation)—
For:
One stupid, stoned discussion with my old friends.
Enough. Back to bed. Know when to shut up.

A cheer rose as Ramón mounted the rickety speaker's chair. He started his speech. He wasn't a great speaker and didn't particularly inspire a crowd. He lacked Mario Savio's originality and poetry and Fred Hampton's murder-mouthing defiance. But he had another quality which possessed its own power. He liked to talk, to work out his ideas; he got an almost adolescent satisfaction from arguing his point of view in front of an audience. He exercised an enjoyment so obvious that his pleasure became contagious, his energy and passion overwhelming any illogic or dogmatism and drawing you to him— whether before a mass audience or me, in my kitchen, at two in the morning.

Same now. His speech was almost a private dialogue, an attempt to convince himself that the action could succeed and made sense. *Thesis:* an inventory of all the internal, strategical, tactical, and external reasons, and all the among the people, between the people and the pigs, primary and secondary contradictions that would stop the action from accomplishing its goals. *Antithesis:* the fact that there was a force more powerful than any of those reasons, the presence of the people in history. *Synthesis . . .*

Cassie appeared. Standing beside me, she plunked her arm across my shoulder and rested her head on her arm, an intimate, comradely gesture that stilled and gratified me, accepting me and making me part of her. I looked around as Ramón exhorted us, What do we have in common? he was asking. What brings us all here? His obsession alone: None of the domino players planted by the entrance to the bodega in their Bermudas and woven shoes, crucifixes and Saint James medals swinging across their naked barrel chests, taxi-cab drivers, butchers, Department of Parks and Sanitation employees, numbers runners, gas-station and car-washing attendants, carpenters, and guys who simply were the other man in the truck, the one not driving whom you passed in the street as he unloaded and tossed onto the conveyor belt the cartons of milk and soda, cereal and paper towels that would fill the shelves of your neighborhood store, the mothers and grandmothers in their housecoats, skin-hugging dungarees, tank tops and black sacks of mourning, storekeepers, teachers, the unhelpful girls behind the counters at the Bueno Bargain discount shops that lined Broadway and the hippie, flirtatious ones who served you *café con leche* at the Cuban-Chinese restaurants, bank clerks with long nails and silent, ghost-like *abuelas* who made a little extra money for the family sweeping the dingy halls of public schools, the kids now wearing bandannas looking furtively through the crowd for their buddies who would enlist in the Army, start a band, learn electronic engineering or become dealers, and even all of us, Marxists, anarchists, believers in the vanguard party or adherents of the theory of the General Strike, Third-World tailists or mass-movement inclusionists, gay liberationists, feminists, and simple I-like-a-riot street people from the Lower East Side cared about Ramón's tortured Maoism. But his talking held us. His desire and conviction silenced us and concentrated our energy. The music and gossip vanished. The street vendors stopped fussing with their carts. The only thing you heard besides Ramón's hoarse, tired, boyish voice was the faint static of police radios and the whinny of horses. The silence, in turn, charged Ramón, steeled his voice, strengthened his stance, giving him a power to transfigure us, if only for a moment, a magic that froze and freed us and transformed the squalid street into high, heroic ground and our ordinary selves into champions of an immemorial struggle.

"Warriors!" he shouted, the words going beyond their immediate meaning into a realm where feeling made sense. "Not brothers! Not sisters! But all the same—warriors in the struggle!"

The television lights outlined his raised fist, the sign we wanted, the signal for which we had been waiting. We burst out, *El pueblo, Unido, Jamás será vencido!* The people! United! Will Never Be Defeated! Our unison rose. I looked around. Goodwill brightened and burnished our faces. We weren't that many, or powerful; the crowd thinned by the middle of the street, and I wished the group were different, moved to come by new conviction, rather than the sense of obligation (daunted or determined, hopeful or harried) that now haunted every movement function. Still, Daniel bumped hips with Laura, turning the revolutionary rhyme into a silly seductive dance, and Marcy worked the crowd, pacing in front, revving their cadence with her fist pummeling the air, her anger for once directed out toward the world rather than at us or herself. We experienced a moment of joy, carried by a wave that lifted us up and beyond ourselves and offered us a new view of the world, below and spread out beneath us, ours to conquer, a world without end.

Then a silence. Inexplicable. The stillness I had felt with Cassie a moment ago vanished; the Tingler returned, squeezing; a delirious thrill held me as I waited for the next moment. No Lords around except for the security; I don't think they had realized the drama had come to its climax.

But Ramón knew. He lowered his hand; paused; and as we watched—everyone in the silence, one breath, one focus—his arm unfolded upward again.

He was holding a gun.

Or did the shadow of his clenched fist against the backdrop of the settlement house's concrete wall look like a gun?

Ramón, I thought, leading us into battle? *When had he become a general?*

"I don't like this," Laura said, and tucked her arm under Daniel's, "what do you want to do?"

"Come on," Cassie whispered. "This is a trap."

The Tingler tightened; I breathed, not wanting to panic; I would be all right as long as I stayed in control.

"Take it easy," I said. "Let's go to the settlement house."

People moved around us, a jostling, purposeless eddy pulled by some unseen, but present and building force behind it. I knew there were only seconds before the tension broke and felt torn, wanting to stay on the street to see and take part in the action, and knowing we should protect ourselves.

"Keep moving," said Daniel.

The presence grew, a presaging swirl of whinnies, shouts, and curses. The crash of smashing glass, a siren. In the crowd, kids jumped up and down to see what was happening. The Lords security tensed; monitors cautioned people not to panic while a police bullhorn instructed everyone to leave the street or we would be breaking the law. On the chair, Ramón started chanting.

"What's going on?" Laura asked.

Above the crowd, I glimpsed whirling red lights, the back and forth between people and police at the far end of the street. I heard more noise, then another shattering smash. Flames splashed across the street from a thrown garbage can. The police charged and everyone ran, our beautiful, single, massed energy split and shattered into a delirium of scattering, screaming, laughing, shouting people.

"Don't run!" I yelled, "don't run!" The pressure continued to build inside me to do just the opposite. Cassie gripped my hand, snatching looks behind her.

Someone yelled that the door to the settlement house was closed; Lords security guards motioned people to the rear entrance down the block. On the steps Delores shouted at Ramón; behind them a hotdog vendor pushed his cart against the wall of the empty lot, looking for a hideaway; a red light flashed; Laura looked to me: *Mark, what are we going to do?* I kept repeating my order not to run while groups rushed by, going toward the police; yelling in Spanish, kids hopped like jumping jacks to see the action. From the roofs fell chalk-filled socks, firecrackers, bricks, bottles, plants, telephone books, their pages opening like wings, some tear-gas bombs; firecracker smoke soured and thickened the air; fires burst out of trash cans, orange flames blossomed in white gas.

We turned a corner into a momentary calm; Cassie grabbed my forearm and asked if I was all right. "You're brave, Mark," she told me. "You're brave."

A crowd raced up the block toward us, police following them. Daniel grabbed his face, screaming and stomping. Laura held him upright. He cursed he wasn't shot; he couldn't see, he was blind. Kids dashed into vestibules, cops chasing them. From the middle of the block, Lords yelled for people to come inside, they had to close the doors, Get in! Get in! A horse reared as a tear-gas bomb twirled on the street, spewing fumes.

The hard black of a nightstick landed on my shoulder.

"He's blind, you asshole!" I shouted at some cop—my usual plea for a special case. "He's blind! He's blind!"

I wrapped my arm around Daniel and Cassie pulled me; we gained a step on the cops, nearing the settlement house. Laura clung to Daniel, pushing his face into her shoulder, flailing at any cop who came near with her free, nail-lacquered hand, shouting at them to stay away in an imperious, desperate voice, a mother protecting her child.

We reached the door with hundreds of others. No one could get in. People shoved and pushed, others saying to cool it, *tranquilo puta malecón*. Daniel writhed, cursing and stumbling, as we burrowed into the crowd. A line of stunned-looking new Lords, none of whom seemed to be over fifteen or had any idea what to do, guarded the entrance. I need water, Daniel kept saying, just get me water. I started to explain the situation to the Lords, but they were lost without orders. Cassie led us toward the other end of the street, but a line of police approached. The people at the door chanted louder, the call to let them in somehow becoming directed against the police who now stood in a straight line behind a captain announcing through a bullhorn that we had to disperse.

"We're not going anywhere," Marcy cried, revving the crowd, a scrawny fury in her T-shirt, fist pummeling the air. The cops listened, edgy, sneaking looks behind their backs. One young cop pointed a finger at her, staking his claim; Marcy yelled back; war games in the television lights.

I let go of Daniel's hand for a moment to try explaining the situation one more time to the Lords guarding the doors. Delores appeared, ignored me, and shouted orders toward the roof where some kids were pushing a refrigerator over the parapet: I hadn't realized the fallout of junk was the Lords' organized artillery. I shouted to her about the doors and was pushed by a wall of people, first toward the cops, then back. Cassie grabbed me as I thought, *Lead them! Charge the cops!* and the glut of people at the entrance melted, flooding the entrance to the settlement house.

I stood in the doorway—neutral ground, I guess—and saw Daniel dance in the street, a cop locked on his neck, dragging him away.

What are you going to do?

I froze. I wanted to go to Daniel's aid, but my mind was already creating a story: *Daniel was in the police wagon, a cop hit me, I couldn't get there in time.*

Laura yanked me into the street. I don't think she realized I wasn't moving, simply that I hadn't yet started to move. Ramón shouted some slogan and a crush of people pushed me from behind so that I fell upon Daniel who was twisting and turning, furious and ridiculous with his belly exposed and his eyes streaming tears, trying to break free from the cop.

"Let him go!" Laura yelled.

She and Cassie threw themselves on the policeman, Cassie grabbing the arm about to strike with the nightstick while Laura pulled at Daniel. I stood behind, still paralyzed by the Tingler, without any plan, shamed by fear, my failure, and my extreme awareness of my failure: I lacked some basic instinct to help. Even Laura, petted and self-petted with her nail polish and fancy underwear, jumped into the fight; springing to help him was something before thought or feeling, a simple gesture of her soul: I'll help you. And I, unlike her, had all the reasons to move, ward off his attackers and lend him a hand, books and arguments, heritage, and a completely self-imposed personal morality, stood there, possessed by fear and an instinct of self-preservation that took precedence over everything else, an ugliness of spirit, small and clenched, despicable. You have to do something.

I stuck out my hand—a gesture toward holding the cop. Two other officers hurried up, nightsticks raised, trying to pull away Cassie and Laura, but Jeff and some others ran at them, one kid seizing the cop from behind.

"Leave him alone!" I yelled. "He wasn't doing anything!" (Reminding myself: He hadn't, we hadn't.)

Cassie shouted for me to get the cop and I listened, putting both hands on the cop's arm. I smelled sweat and starch, the greasy, sweet odor of hair tonic, noticed some dandruff on the cop's collar. We swirled and danced. Blue arms and hard hands, shouts, the cracked concrete rising. I wanted to let go of the cop and thought of my excuse: *I couldn't get nearer, Laura was between the cop and me, I tried, but couldn't hold on to him.*

The cop tossed Cassie to the street and Daniel spun around and twisted free.

The gun fell from the holster and smacked the pavement.

Terrified, certain the cops would think we wanted to shoot him and try to kill us, I reached for the thirty-eight, intending to pick up the gun and give it to the cop politely: Here, Officer, here's your gun, it fell out of your holster.

"Don't touch it!" the cops yelled.

The three of them froze, one holding his revolver, the other two crouched toward the gun. I didn't move, leaving my hand outstretched, hoping they'd see I was harmless. Daniel and Laura had disappeared; Cassie was gone.

One of the cops started forward and someone shouted. Instinctively we all looked up. On the roof, the refrigerator seesawed on the edge, over the street. Some kids gave a final push and the door opened like the wings of a great bird. For a moment the weight hovered in the air, suspended, floating next to the building, as light as a feather. Then it plunged as the kids cheered and we all dashed to safety, clearing the area as shelves, plastic casing, wires, and glass shattered and smashed on the street.

With a yell, some Lords ran forward and Cassie yanked me. My legs wheeled backward. I stumbled and fell, trying to regain my balance. In front of me, the Lords scattered and the cops filled the street. My hands flailed at my sides, trying to touch the pavement and halt my backwards reel, but I couldn't pause long enough to right myself, and I staggered, legs, feet, arms tripping over themselves, like some out-of-control marionette, into the settlement house.

"Are you all right?" Cassie asked.

Everything around us was movement and noise, swirls and rushes, a bursting bubble of joy and fear, desire and exhilaration. People yelled and shouted; packs of Lords and kids cut through the crowd; announcements bounced off the walls. Cassie laughed, her ocean eyes vibrant with energy. Our words rolled over each other: You took his gun. I thought we were going to be killed. I was trying to give it back to him. You're crazy. In the rollicking turmoil of the breaking wave we held and hugged each other. My hand felt the folded, muscled curves of her back, she rubbed my arms, and a foam of dust exploded at our touch, dried, gray tear gas billowing out over our clothes. More laughter, helpless in tears as we tossed and shook her hair, fluffing thick red curls with our hands: I can't stop. Let me get it off you! She hadn't understood what I had told her: You wanted to give it back to him! she kept saying, You're so crazy! *I love you!* Love; she meant all kinds: *I love you*—the flip, casual love we said to each other high off action; *I love you*—deeper, the meaning you reserved for someone special, said with a conviction that always sounded to me as bordering on sorrow; *I love you*—the final, a desire that grew from or led to the other, to hold and inhabit you, press soul to flesh. I love you, I answered, and we kissed, her tongue like the inside of a fruit, cool somehow, fresh and soft against mine. Around us, the room whirled, flashed and ebbed. I found myself thrown and tumbled, as though the risk I was taking were a surf sucking me down and around, and I floundered to get air by trying to come up with the arguments I'd use with Karen if she confronted me, thinking, *The kiss meant nothing,* (breathe), *we were excited,* (breathe), *it doesn't matter, I'll never do it again,* and my head was again above water, sustained by an argument that ashamed me even as Cassie and I renewed the kiss.

"Wow," Cassie said, "you have a problem."

"What's that?"

"I love the way you taste."

We were back in the real world.

Laura yelled to us from the rear. I saw her standing over Daniel who sat on a bench, stripped to the waist: a walrus hunched over his beefy flesh. Where were the others? Cassie took my hand—a harmless gesture I assured myself, already trying out the explanations I would offer Karen: *We were together,* I'd explain later, *just after the riot, it didn't mean anything.* We wound our way through the crowd. Kids distributed pails of water and wet rags to tamp down the gas. People cried. Cadres debated what to do next, Avakianists v. Klonskyites: Take an exemplary action or build a base and struggle sharply? At the door, the Lords had erected a makeshift barricade of upended rusty lockers, chairs, and boxy wooden desks. On top of the heap, stringy haired junkies and kids with feathery mustaches perched as lookouts and yelled moment-by-moment reports on the activity outside, each contradictory message—the cops were ready to charge, the Mayor was sending a representative—a bomb that set off shock waves of worry, jubilation, or anger through the room. I noticed the new girl carefully untangle her sweater from her hoop earring. A hand-printed sign on the wall already announced unisex bathrooms and broken toilets. Other phalanxes of Lords cut through the crowd, repeating a mantra: Get your people together! We've got to get together, people! Some older Lords marched down a staircase marked by a dim red EXIT light covered with a protective metal mesh shield. The place with its tarred floor and white-tiled walls smelled of stale sweat, urine, and steam heat mixed now with the sweeter aromas of marijuana and tear gas.

Cassie detached herself to greet some friends from a women's collective. I stood alone and the feeling of being inside a building came back to me, a mix of triumph, community, and also anxiety— because the weird part of seizing buildings was you became the aggressor by being besieged: As soon as you got into a building all you did was talk about how you would get out.

And how were we going to get out? Did the Lords really want a shoot-out? I looked around me. There were no obvious candidates in the scattered frantic energy of the cavernous place for beating a police attack. The Lords appeared and vanished, talking to themselves, or, even worse, stood around, a young cadre, silent and suspicious-looking because they didn't know what to do without orders. No binding force drew us together, created a sense of our being part of something larger than ourselves. I felt a tightening twinge of panic, the Tingler again, come back to life. I wanted to keep busy, make plans, find a way out of here.

Or was I wrong? Maybe this was exactly the way shoot-outs began, not with the perfect combination of people and circumstances, but thrill-seeking kids, professional troublemakers, desperate leadership. That was the point: You didn't and couldn't know how things would work out. There were no rules; people who tried to impose them ended up without triumphs. I had to go along. But where and who was going to lead us? Ramón? Delores? The cops and motley collection of Movement people, community activists, and street kids inside the settlement house might imagine Ramón and Delores as warriors—Ramón and Delores might even believe themselves capable of leading people into battle, but I didn't. I pictured Ramón slapping a clip into one of the wooden-stocked M-1s that *The Anarchist's Cookbook* and half a dozen more rudimentary, hand-stapled, crudely drawn pamphlets instructed you in converting to an automatic rapid-fire M-16, and the panic inside me grew. *Nothing to fighting*, I told myself, remembering Omar's advice, *You just shut your eyes and let the black take over.* One night in Harlem at the Panther Party head-quarters a year ago; we were on an all-night security patrol to make sure the cops didn't trash the place. I hadn't understood. The black? I asked. Omar was silent, not looking away, avoiding something, but going inside himself; sometimes his quiet was so deep I thought he was lost in himself and would never come back. The black, he answered. You know. The shit inside you. You just let the black take over. Doesn't matter what you weigh or what you know—very few people are going to take you down. I was scared then but calm because I trusted Omar and his decisions—the police really killed Party members and he knew guns and death from the streets and Vietnam. Not Ramón, I thought. The Lords weren't ready for that sort of battle. I reminded myself of the rule for these events: The more militant the occupation sounded, the more peaceful the evacuation. I told myself that by any realistic assessment, we were in for a night of threats and counter-threats, the community going up versus the law coming down, and felt betrayed by my own logic; I was a leader, but was thinking of why we should leave instead of stay, negotiate instead of fight, cool things down instead of heat them up.

I spotted Balaguer and Ramón in a corner. They spoke with their heads bent down, their hands making short, rapid gestures, their focused intensity separating them like a force field from the pandemonium of the room. Ramón yelled at me to get my people together, and pointed to the red EXIT light, meaning he would meet me there in a moment. His notice boosted my flagging sense of purpose and self-importance and I moved through the crowd, gauging the mood: Up Against the Wall Motherfuckers took impassive long drags on unfiltered Camels and waited for something to happen, a *Worker's World* cadre told me it was important we stay, the anxious blond-haired Weatherman sympathizer appeared, forehead dabbed with pink, white T-shirt stained with blood, appeared out of nowhere, a stuttering prophet announcing the people were ready, the youth were in front, we were making the people's army! I ducked him and passed the college kid with corkscrew hair arguing with his group: Sometimes you've got to stand up. This is the moment. You have to draw the line. A girl answered him: It's not an individual decision. It's my life. You are such an elitist!

Laura tended Daniel, daubing his hair with a damp cloth to smother the gas. Puffy black bags sagged under his bloodshot eyes. I wanted to be alone with him, confide and confess. No chance for that; even if I asked Laura to go away his head would stay with her.

"This isn't good," he said to me as I approached, and erupted with a violent sneeze. He stuck his head in a pail beside him and emerged like a bearded moose, water streaming off his hair.

"Close your eyes," said Laura, and knelt, steadying herself with one hand on his chest, her carmine nails pushing into his blubbery-white skin. He sat obediently, stiff with anticipation, an overgrown child waiting to be asked the next question in the spelling bee. Laura wiped soot from one eyelid, and stood back, checking him.

"What?" he asked her and waited for her to say something, enchanted and mystified by her steady quiet. "What?" more insistent and frustrated this time, the question opening onto a world of new meanings: What happens next? What do you feel? What do you want me to do? What should I do? The questions for his lifetime.

"I like this face," she decided, and pressed her lips against his mouth, hard, as though wanting to imprint herself on him. He gulped, unprepared for her assault, then opened, receiving her, and just as quickly backed away, hand to his nose, and sneezed.

"I'm sorry," he apologized, looking upward at her in adoration.

Laura grabbed his bearded cheeks in both hands. "This face!" she exclaimed, and looked at me, forcing me to be part of their communion, a witness and approver of their mutual declaration: "I love this face! How can you not love this face!"

In her grip Daniel squirmed and looked at me, pleading, helpless and delighted, as though saying, *Don't blame me. It's not my fault. What can I do? She's in love with me.*

"You're right," I agreed, despising her manipulation and powerless to resist it, enmeshed in the complicated weave of her desires.

She put her free arm over my shoulder. "I love being here. This is so special. We have to go to Atlanta. It's crazy to let the Movement be destroyed. We can't let that happen, can we, Mark?"

Yes, I wanted to say, *actually we can*. In fact, this time it would be a lot better to let things go, give up the fight, forget our political, social, and drive straight over the Brooklyn Bridge to the Belt Parkway and pig out on hot dogs at Nathan's. There's nothing here besides desire—the Lords for a successful action, mine for a movement, Daniel for you. This isn't what I want; this is desperate, lost, a waste of everything we should want to preserve and you're part of it.

"No," I answered, silenced by my lack of heart. "Of course not, we won't let that happen."

The three of us embraced and I wanted to cry. Laura asked if I was okay, but I couldn't answer because comradeship or love wasn't moving me, but a sense of irremediable loss, a soft sinking of hope inside me, its place taken by a stupid and necessary determination that I told myself would carry me through to the end.

"What is this? A scene from *Battlecry*?" Marcy came up, Jeff and Cassie behind her. "We're all supposed to fuck before we go off to war?"

"What's the plan?" said Daniel, and put on his shirt.

I looked over to Ramón, still engaged with Balaguer in a private dialogue of nods and gestures, and a flood of action began, things turning and jumbled, a sudden wash that picked me up and carried me along, leaving only snapshots of frozen moments:

Paul and Karen marched through the door, a smirk of satisfaction on Paul's long, thin face: "Contradictions of capitalism. The police let us through. They even helped us unload the sandbags."

Karen, elated, giddy, and flushed while Marcy told her about the fight: "You guys!" she said. Her maddening nod met me as I told her my worries: "You've got to give it a chance. You don't know what they are really going to do."

Everyone's arms around each other: Cassie's slipped around my waist, Karen's slung over Cassie's shoulder. One big family.

I looked to Ramón; gestures, nods; he saw me, raised a hand: one minute more.

"Less revolutionary smooching and more revolutionary doing," said Marcy. She was revved, a wired engine of enthusiasm, cigarette smoke pouring from her mouth. "We need to raise the level of energy."

"We're revolutionaries, not nutritionists," Jeff answered, skeptical and distant, vaguely dusting off his sun-yellow ponytail. "We raise the level of struggle, not energy."

"Definitely," Marcy agreed, too happy and eager to let anyone get in her way. "*El pueblo unido*" bounced off the walls, shouted by a group on the other side of the room. She jumped on a bench and joined in, communicating with the chanters, sending their words back to them, cheerleading the rest of us. "I'm ready," she told me. One big family.

Ramón signaled me over. Hug: How are things going? Good, good, good. He spoke from another world, distant, seeing something completely different from what he was talking about, mouthing his answers automatically: good, good, good. Words from a Creeley poem came to my mind: The darkness surrounds us/And what should we do But . . . I had heard them recently in *Drive, He Said* one of the new bad movies trying to capture the Sixties: *Drive, he said/And for God's sake,/Look out where you're going.* Ramón did, immediately attending to business, official policy focusing him like a lens snapping a scene into crisp resolution. He gave me the Party line, none of the points making any real sense. *The occupation*: a success, mobilizing a new sector of the community. *Next stage of the struggle*: a deal with the city—the Lords could remove their guns secretly if they surrendered peacefully. *Problems and contradictions*: Where to store the guns? Not in the community; the police would bust any of their established safe houses immediately. They needed a transfer point. What to do with Ramón? The C.C. (Central Committee) had decided he couldn't be arrested because the city would press gun charges against him and his trial would become the focus of organizing, not the community demands. They wanted to smuggle him out with the guns and hide him. *Solution*: me. Could we take care of the guns and would I drive him to the hideout? He was going to the Crosscups.' Did I know him? Jules Crosscup, a Communist Party historian—

Of course I knew him. His big, thick, dully colored multivolume sets documenting the slave revolts, labor struggles, socialist communities, and tradition of radical thought that made up the left-wing version of American history, had filled my parents' library when I was a kid, part of the cabala of left-wing intellectual culture, though now of course the sets were required reading in college courses and you came across their newly printed paperback editions in dorm rooms and student lounges.

I nodded my head, mirroring his seriousness and hiding my relief: Ramón's problem was my solution—Paul's collective agrees to hide the guns, I miss the bust and Ramón usurps Karen's place in the car to Atlanta. I caught Karen's eye and motioned to meet with them.

Ramón was going on, telling me about Crosscup. "We always argue," Ramón said. "He thinks we're left-wing adventurists and don't understand about parties. But you learn from him because he's a walking encyclopedia of American history. Did you know a socialist was mayor of Bridgeport in . . ."

More nods and Delores came up, pulling her brown hair tight behind her in a ponytail, wanting to know what was happening.

"See," said Ramón after we told her the plan, "I told you everything would be cool. Don't worry." He hooked his arm around her waist and tugged at her. An old rock and roll song came into my mind: *Come closer, darling, hear what I say*—seductive and slinky words—*you're mine forever, forever and a day* . . .

She snapped the rubber band around her hair and removed his arm. "You do this shit and then you tell me not to worry. You got a real problem."

A duel—he claimed possession, his hand on her neck: "What's your problem. This is what we want."

She twisted free. "Not me. Not us. You like this playacting. That's what got us into trouble before." Then, to me, ignoring him: "When are you ready to go? We got to get out of here soon."

I went over to Paul and Karen, explaining the plan. Everyone joined us in a general discussion. Grave nods and serious-sounding questions from Karen: When? How many? When? Where? What about the security? Daniel argued, This is a heavy thing they're asking us. The rest chimed in their opinions, a big family, arms draped over each other's shoulders, Paul in the center, enjoying the attention, his face taut with worry and fear.

"Tell them to come," Paul finally said, and our attention was distracted by Ramón and Delores still at it:

"No *mámi*, last time was commandist, but now the Party acted in accordance with the masses."

"Get your hands off me, motherfucker. You'll hang out in Pennsylvania and I'll go to jail. We had this whole action planned perfectly. You messed things up."

A bodyguard shifted his stance; a tall Up Against the Wall Motherfucker, construction boots, Fu Manchu beard, and steel-rimmed glasses, a dog-eared paperback copy of *Saint Genet* sticking out of his back pocket, intervened, saying, Chill, we've got to deal with the cops. Delores ignored him, one hand telling him, Get the fuck out of here, her stare never leaving Ramón, harsh, accusing: "This was perfect and your macho messed it up."

"That's mechanistic thinking," Ramón said.

She slapped him—a quick, light reflex, reproving and warning, the way her grandmother and mother must have disciplined her. Immediately she put her hand on his cheek, the soothing touch, the one to take away the hurt.

Now Ramón was unforgiving: "You're undisciplined. We're going to deal with this in the Central Committee."

"You don't say what the C.C. is going to do. You're not on the C.C."

"Mark," Laura whispered, arm tucked into mine, insistent: "This is bad, do something."

What? *What are you going to do?*

I called Ramón; he ignored me, the two of them going off into Spanish, trading accusations. "What are they saying?" Marcy asked, insistent, fascinated. Next to her, Jeff watched, a cool observer, smoking; his tongue flicked out, lizard-like, and wet his lips. From outside came bullhorn announcements; floodlights swept past the windows. Perched on the piled-up lockers, the scraggly lookouts called out warnings: Something was happening in the street.

Balaguer now stepped between them and told them to back off. No good. It was a school-yard duel, neither of them speaking to the other, both addressing Balaguer:

Delores: "I'm sick of his elitist shit. He thinks he can do what he wants because he fucked me . . ."

Ramón: "She's sick."

"Big-time lover. You think no one knows you have a dick? Everyone knows you can't deal with a woman unless you fucked her. You're still scared *mámi* might find out you fuck. I'll smack you again. This time I'll hurt you hard, motherfucker."

She was right. Ramón was no match for her. She was in the street, hard and sullen as concrete, drawing all the attention of the scared, thrilled kids looking on; Ramón only answered her, jammed by her attack, not able to fight or walk away, a kid with pens in the breast pocket of the starched white shirt his mother had ironed for him. I remembered Omar: *You just let the black go.* She pushed past Balaguer, a straight-edge razor blade revealed between her thumb and forefinger. Instant turmoil, everyone galvanized, interceding, trying to stop the melee; arms and hands flailed and restrained, separating them; threats and curses from Ramón and Delores; Balaguer pushed and yelled at them, directing Lords to hold them in different corners, saying, What is the matter with you? You let the pig get to you? What is the matter with you?

Lords told everyone to get back, we needed security, the pigs could be coming, we had to stay tight. More bullhorns boomed from outside; lights flared through the iron-grated windows; lookouts announced cops, cars, and mounted police massed on the street. I stood, hating the instant opinions about the fight I was hearing: It's not a bad thing, it's a good thing, you got to take the struggle to a higher level. Karen looked undone, eyes alarmed and body stiff with fear, cigarette perched anxiously at the far edge of her mouth, listening to some internal monologue she would never share with any of us, Daniel stood at my side, as abashed and eager to talk as a child who has just witnessed his parents fight.

"I'm not talking about it," I said.

"Absolutely," he answered. "Can I say one thing?"

Balaguer knifed through the crowd, getting my attention, calling me to follow him. All I wanted was to get out. I gathered the rest and tracked Balaguer to a staircase landing. He sat huddled low on the steps by the wall, cornered in darkness. Whispering, he told us the plan. The cars were parked outside. We carry out three bags, all supposedly filled with guns, but one holding Ramón. At the safe house, Paul's, we split everything up.

Marcy listened hard, a sudden revolutionary tactician, her sharp face swaddled in smoke: "What happens if they follow us?"

"That won't happen."

She shrugged, unhappy with the answer but afraid to keep insisting. Paul next: "I need to know when you'll retrieve them."

"Immediately. We'll take care of our pieces." He looked around. "This everybody? Let's go."

We split up, Paul and Karen going to check on the cars. "You'll be all right?" I asked her and got a scowl and dismissive wave of the hand as an answer: embarrassed at my attention or simply angry at me? They went out and the rest of us followed Balaguer down the smelly staircase. The chants, bullhorn announcements, and general alarm from upstairs faded. The space shrunk around us. The staircase had been designed for kids, with low ceiling, steps, and railing, and I felt small and trapped between the cantilevered roof formed by the projecting underside of the steps above and the metal mesh wall dividing the flights.

Balaguer entered a brick-red painted door labeled BOILER ROOM, leaving us waiting.

"You don't think we should trust them?" Marcy came into someone else's whispered conversation.

I heard more muffled noises from upstairs, excited chants, and things being dragged; the vague commotion scared me and I told the others if they didn't want to help with Ramón and the guns they should leave now.

Cassie reproached me, her soft, firm hand touching my back discretely in the dim light: "No one's saying that."

"What are you saying?"

Jeff tossed his hair back, shaking his head in disapproval: "Can we play the mind games later, please."

Daniel giggled and apologized: "This is so heavy. I'm sorry. It's so heavy."

A Lord opened the door and we entered. The boiler-bomb room. I had lived with the idea of bombs for so long I had forgotten that I had never actually encountered them. Talk about them—yes, they were part of our lives, like weather, Molotov cocktails, homemade antipersonnels of nails and staples like the ones that killed the Weathermen on West Eleventh Street, dynamite packages stolen from highway construction sites and detonated by the simplest fuse of a folded paper match tucked outside the rest of the book, and more complicated, timed devices deposited in banks, police stations, libraries, and government buildings, set by friends who turned out to be strangers, and strangers I knew as well as friends—a guy I first met as a migrant-worker organizer for Friends of SNCC in New Jersey, the woman I flirted with at a meeting about the bombing of Haiphong who said we should ally ourselves with consumer and transit user groups, a kid from Seattle who crashed one night with me and Karen before wandering north to Fort Kent, Maine, where he was arrested for blowing up a Dow research lab in Corning, New York— their explosions linking us with striking coal miners in the 1880s,

Wobblies, Spanish anarchists, resistance fighters for the last hundred years including the students in Prague (*The Pig Is the Same All Over the World!*), and provoking theoretical debates about the efficacy, efficiency, and ethics of possibly blasting holes in people's heads and hearts: harmful or helpful? Organizing or alienating? Bombs scared people. You needed to give people an alternative. Not the point, not the point at all. Of course you needed to educate and mobilize, but sometimes righteous rage forced you to act: It was humanly, unacceptably disgusting to allow Kissinger and Nixon to carpet-bomb North Vietnam, or Mayor Daley to assassinate Fred Hampton—you had to show people you could resist, present them with a simple. clear refusal that said all pig lies and explanations were useless, the killers were accountable, we were a witness to the truth, like the old Civil Rights song claimed, *All their lies will be forgotten/Carry it on/Carry it on.*

The truth. All the talk had yet to prepare me for the presence of the actual thing. Not major bombs, either—no sticks of dynamite or any exotic explosive material. The Lords were simply destroying stocks of Molotov cocktails, gasoline- and detergent-filled bottles capped with Tampax whose limp strings dangled over the sides and served as fuses. Piece work: toss the Tampax into a plastic garbage bag, pour the gas and detergent mix into the large, enameled janitor's basin, deposit the bottle into the waiting cardboard carton with the immediately identifiable logos of Hellmann's Mayonnaise, Bumblebee Tuna, Goya Rice, or Scott's Toilet Tissue stamped on the side. They performed the task with a steady, conscientious quality that reminded me of school children doing an assignment, even stopping to arrange the empties as they added to them. The thing that impressed and scared me was the sheer number of devices; hundreds of glass-walled Cokes, Pepsis, Seven-Ups, Rheingolds, Millers, and Buds, light and regular, thin-necked and wide-mouthed (several Tampaxes filling the gaping maw), gulping family-sized magnums and one thirst-quenching-swallow baby-bottles, an arsenal the Lords must have manufactured from the empties stacked in the alleys behind every neighborhood bodega, artillery they had intended I guessed as the opening round in their standoff with the police, a glass-sharded wall of fire they would shoot through with the impressive amount of weapons they had stockpiled.

Daniel breathed heavily, a dramatic gasp for our benefit, indicating his thought: This is heavy. He looked at me, eyes eager and scared: *What are you going to do?* I had no idea. I looked behind us as the Lord who let us in—chubby; soiled T-shirt bursting out where his stomach couldn't be contained by his worn, tight jeans, sparse wiry-haired sideburns covering his still-baby-fat-filled, jovial, plump acne-scarred cheeks—turned a dead-bolt lock that barred the exit door. My hand was pinched: Cassie, standing behind me, her fingers holding mine for a second. Marcy stomped out her cigarette, some embers falling through the grated-metal landing on which we stood into the weave of white-painted pipes that covered the floor below. I couldn't breathe: fetid air stinky with gasoline, sweat, fuel oil. Quiet: a buzz from a dull, blinking, naked, florescent suspended from the high ceiling, the splash of running water in the industrial sink, and Delores telling the bomb-makers and gun-packers to hurry up, come on, we only had three minutes. A spectrally thin guy who wore a sleeveless flak jacket decorated with an embroidered map of Vietnam on the back looked up at her from his work dismantling some rifle, an expression of mild disbelief on his face. Next to him several other Lords worked on the last piece of the image: a bed of stocks, muzzles, clips, pistols, shotguns, cartridges, and boxes splayed out over a large Winnie-the-Pooh sheet.

I turned and a flash of light bounced off a bank of blank-eyed, narrow, rectangular windows that stared out into the street. "You have five minutes to vacate the premises"—the official, stern warning announced by the police through the bullhorn. The outside noise and movement were impalpable and real, a wave passing under the ship when you're inside a windowless cabin. Marcy coughed and Cassie lifted her hair up from her shoulders, the gesture asking what I thought about the whole situation. I stepped onto the first open, iron-grated stair leading down, and the floor wavered. The flak-jacket guy was dismantling a gun: break down the carbine, swaddle the muzzle in a towel—there was a stack several feet high; where had they gotten so many towels ?—and load the baby into one of several large hard, plastic, sheet bags spread out on the floor. I noticed other ordnance now too, piles of chains, iron rods, sacks a Lord filled with nails and rocks. *Get the guns,* I told myself, *get the guns, Ramón, get out of here, time to go.*

I gathered myself: down the rest of the stairs, metal vibrating underfoot. Behind me Cassie touched my hand, but I didn't respond.

I felt outside myself, as I had in jail, keeping myself together. Ducked under a pipe at the last step, resting my hand for balance against moist, flaking paint slimy to the touch. For a moment I was lost. The pipes seemed everywhere. They covered the puddled floor and extruded from the lumpy, white-washed walls, bristling with valves and knobs, stretched and angled in a sort of industrial cross-word puzzle. A hand-painted sign showed an arrow pointing to FURNACE, and I maneuvered around, through the maze, guided by the sound of Delores's repeated injunctions to hurry up, we had to get out of there, the cops were coming. Near the unused iron box of the furnace, I squeezed past a thicket, the skin of the pipes pasty with condensation and slick with mold, and came to the clear section I had seen from the landing.

"Where is he?" Delores shouted past me.

I looked up. Balaguer now stood on the grated landing I had just left and answered Ramón was coming. Over the machinery of the room, he and Delores exchanged smiles, a stolen moment between them that I happened to see: *Thesis* (hers): exasperation and indulgent annoyance; *Antithesis* (his): pleasure at her impatience; *Synthesis* (theirs): the enjoyment of the other only possible because they were in love. They're screwing each other, I thought, and with a cascading clatter of steps, shouts, and crashes down the staircase, Ramón appeared, tense and focused, asking where the gun bags were, the cops were getting ready, they had to go.

Lords zipped up the two large plastic bags. The wave of noise outside gathered, a sustained, building, threatening arch of sound ready to break into action. The skirt of windows at street level, portholes to the passing world, went dark, the television lights changing their orientation from the settlement house to the crowd. We waited. Behind my back, Cassie's fingers stroked the palm of my hand, an absent-minded, feathery touch; I turned and she smiled at me. Jeff wandered over to the sink where the chubby Lord emptied the final bottles: "Detergent," he explained to Marcy, offhand, unconcerned, "good idea. They ignite faster that way. Really explode." Daniel whispered secrets to Laura. They had just met a few hours ago. How did he manage to have so much to say to her?

"Come on," said Delores, as soon as Ramón appeared. "Let's get him out of here."

"This is a body bag," Ramón said, meaning the carryall prepared for him.

"Army surplus," the flak jacket explained.

"Two minutes to vacate," the loudspeaker announced. The cops must have been lining up; I heard crowd shouts, sounds of pushing, cries of protest. Delores insisted: "Let's go, motherfucker, I've got to get upstairs!" The cadre lifted the two packed bags by straps at the front, back, and side; between them the sack swayed like a hammock.

"I've got to pee," Ramón said.

I wanted to leave and Delores started to argue, but Balaguer interrupted: "Man has to pee, *mámi*. Chill."

Down with the sacks, Delores and Balaguer arguing in Spanish as Ramón disappeared behind a thick, white-painted wooden door decorated with a girlie calendar, two circles drawn around the tits and the scrawl: THIS IS WHAT I WANT. Another clatter of steps and a Lord on the landing shouted Spanish, Delores answering. Daniel looked up to the windows, fur-lined lips pursed in fear. Words from songs kept coming to my mind: *Something's happening, and you don't know what it is, do you, Mister Jones?* Full of mischief, the chubby Lord opened another door. Warm air and the scent of barbecue and tear gas drifted by as the sounds outside suddenly amplified: the door we would take to the street. Balaguer yelled to shut it. At that moment the fluorescent died; there were cries and shouts from upstairs and outside; Marcy squealed like something had bitten her; my stomach flopped as the Tingler clenched, a jolt of panic as though the plane had suddenly dropped, my arms and legs steeled against danger. Balaguer instantly reassured us it was nothing, the cops had told them it was going to happen, and banged on the door: Ramón, man, hurry up! We stood in blue and gray shadows cast by street lamps and television spots. The street crowd howled a protest. Spooky, Marcy said, and Cassie took my hand. *The darkness surrounds us.* I needed to pee too and looked toward the bathroom.

"One more minute," said Balaguer to me. Then added, almost as an apology: "We'll miss him. The Lords owe the man a debt that can't be paid." A short exchange between us, a weird suspended pause when we spoke our dense private language, understanding each other perfectly, comrades, in a minute assessing the movement and agreeing everybody needed something: whites, more discipline; the Third World, leadership; gays and women, political education. Balaguer praised the new recruits, but said the Party couldn't do without its old members. "We have to consolidate ideological preparedness with instinctive class consciousness," he said. "Otherwise we risk political deformation."

"What is he doing in there?" Delores asked. "We got to move."

Ramón came out, shaking water off his hands. "My stomach," he apologized. Balaguer motioned, no problem. "That was really good," he said to me, and opened the bag for Ramón to climb into. "Let's get together when all this is done."

"You have one minute to vacate the premises," the bullhorn announced. From outside, a huge, answering, defiant cheer, whistles now, screechy and shrill, ululations, high, bird-like eeks repeated faster and faster, the sounds of horses clopping, shouted commands, the crash of shattered glass, a swirling clamor circling around itself, drawing new noise into the vortex.

"We've got to go," Laura suddenly put her foot down, the responsible one, the adult: Fear makes people act in funny ways.

"We'll call you in Pennsylvania," Balaguer said to Ramón. "All power to the people!" An embrace; Ramón crawled into the bag. "Don't drop me." He scrunched on his side, burrowed into a corner, a man becoming a baby; Balaguer drew the zipper closed. Ramón curled and crunched in the space, eyes shut, "my body bag."

We organized ourselves and formed the line to go outside; they hoisted the bags again, Balaguer, flak jacket, and chubby one, an idiotic smile still pasted on his face, taking charge of one each. Outside more sound, danger approaching. *Hope you have got yourself together/Hope you are quite prepared to die/Looks like we're in for stormy weather/There's a bad moon on the rise*—a year ago they had used it on a pamphlet: *Bring the War Home Now!* I grabbed Cassie's hand behind me and Marcy laughed because I held her small, smoke-drenched fingers instead: "You've got the wrong girl." There was a screech as a Lord opened an iron door and the bottom scraped against the concrete floor. Hot, breathless air and the scent of tear gas and fires rushed in. Delores took the lead—Chicks up front! We coupled off, Marcy next to Jeff, Daniel asking Laura whether she was okay in his troubled, anxious whisper. I ignored Cassie's fingers try-ing to take my hand from behind; I was scared her touch would dis-tract or soften me in the next minutes and brought my hands in front of me, cutting off any contact; then she pressed her palm against the small of my back, propping me up.

The outside stairs to the street level were steep, narrow, white-washed; tiny specks of mica sparkled in the scratchy, dark, sharp, rock walls. At the top the noise of the crowd rolled like a surf, one chant replacing another: *The People! United! Will Never Be Defeated! Po-wer! To the People! Off the pig!*

The slogans tumbled into one another, creating an eddying wash of sound. We surfaced into a rush of noise, light, movement, atten-tion. The crowd had grown since we entered the settlement house. Sisters in struggle: A wealthy Westchester middle-aged anti-war activist who flew regularly to Hanoi stood next to a woman in a tank top and bolero pants who was beating out the rhythm of the chants with a fork on a metal pot while performing a salsa on her spiked heels. I didn't like the antiwar organizer; she was a sickness of "selves"—satisfied, interested, and approving. But she had come; she was present when so many others were not; I turned her—and my—very deficiency into a reason for pride, as though we were to be laud-ed precisely because of our frailties, as though our conviction was all the more unusual because it arose from such starved and meager roots. My pride stiffened and swelled inside me, honored by the din: we were heroes, leaving the battle, full of loyalty, purpose, fear and pride.

In the tumult, a cop captain appeared, harried, suspicious, anx-ious, the hard edge of his voice a warning that he wouldn't be fooled with: "This the package? Let's get it out of here."

We entered the street. Cops lined the wooden street-barricades. Behind them the crowd thronged. People shouted instructions and questions, waited by the cars. I dared a surveying glance around me—a real dare: I was so concentrated on getting down the street that I was scared any shift in my stance would stop my forward progress.

"The drivers?" the captain asked Balaguer. Paul and me. Down the block I saw the flurry of horses readying, snorting, anxious muzzles tossed in the air. The cop demanded our licenses. We froze, uncertain what to do, afraid to identify ourselves. He noticed this and looked at the bags to inform us he knew the identity of our packages. "You got a problem? Licenses, licenses."

"What do you want them for?" Daniel appeared at my side, a blustery dragon; his belly popped out of his shirt, smoke foamed from his mouth.

The captain ignored him and addressed us: "I need to see your licenses."

Daniel interposed himself again, now putting his bulk between us and the cop. "What's your badge number?"

I intervened, opened my wallet, telling him to stop, thinking, *Don't let him turn this into a scene*, and met his furious face and whisper: "That's wrong. They'll know who you are. They'll know where everything's going."

"They can follow us anyway," I said.

"Don't do their work for them."

Louder shouts from the crowd now; they knew something was happening. The Lords carting the bags looked exhausted, school children made to wait on line. A young movement lawyer with a lisp like Daffy Duck and blond ringlets like Shirley Temple joined the argument; he fulminated and gesticulated, squawked and stalked before the crowd telling the cops their business, saying the delay was outrageous while Paul and I stalled, instinct more than reason insisting we disobey them. New voices entered the argument:

Laura: "What's the problem, officer?" Laura: good touch—officer.

Delores: "Why do you need to see their licenses? No one ever said anything about licenses."

Balaguer: not speaking to the cops, only to Delores, trying to pry her away from the confrontation, "Let the lawyers handle it, *mámi*; come on, come on."

Then Kunstler took charge, his straw-dry, long hair pulled back in a ponytail, his voice a pleasant rasp, superbly self-assured in his sober self-effacement: "Officer, my name is William Kunstler. I'm a lawyer and an officer of the court. These men are my clients and I represent them in all dealings with the law. What is the issue?" Meanwhile Daffy exhorted the crowds to maintain control, warning them not to bust through the barricades; he knew what was going on: If they busted through, we would get caught in the melee, Ramón in the bag.

The captain and Kunstler sparred: They're not leaving without licenses. I understand; will you trust me to ascertain their validity? The captain surrendered. Eyes peering above his wire-rimmed glasses, Kunstler made an elaborate show of painstakingly examining the documents. Are you the person identified on this license and no other person? Yes sir. Who resides at the address printed on this license? Yes sir. Then an equally detailed report to the captain. As an officer of the court I proffer for your approval the certain identities of the men on these licenses. The captain listened in seeming exasperated amusement and finally walked away waving his hand, the signal to open the barricades and let us through.

The Lords placed the bags in the two trunks while Daniel whispered why he had challenged the police: You see? That was what I was afraid of. It was practical. I didn't want them to identify us. He couldn't stop, even in the car, hunkered in the back with Laura and Marcy, repeating the same point: You see? That was what I was afraid of. I nodded, and agreed, Cassie next to me, as I turned on the ignition. From the other car, Paul waved, hand back and forth in the open window like a pendulum, long face goofy with a frozen half-moon smile. Behind him, Jeff chanted, grinning as he surveyed the crowd, as though contemplating a pleasing possibility. Next to him, Karen bit her lip and opened her eyes wide to show worry and hope, You really think they'll let us out? But I thought something else, Cassie beside me: *If Karen wanted me to love her why did she always let me stray?*

"Keep your hands on the wheel," Marcy said, interrupting herself from shouting cheers to the crowd out the window when she noticed my palm touching Cassie's thigh.

The police escort took off, some cops walking in front of Paul's car. We followed, a two-car cortege crawling at a coronation's pace, five or six miles an hour. As we passed the crowd, the tumult of noise spiked, everyone applauding as though we had run a race; some firecrackers were tossed toward the cops, the explosives popping in the air. Marcy thrust herself out the window, revving the chanters with her fists, and I joined her and stuck my arm out the window to pummel the air.

"Hit the horn!" shouted Daniel, and Cassie leaned over, her breasts pushed wonderfully against my hands, and pounded the rubber center of the steering wheel to throw a silly beeping sound into the din.

We stopped to let the cops open the wooden horses that blocked off the street. The noise boomed and careened. In the glare of the television spots, tossed before me as she beeped the horn, Cassie's hair glowed an impossibly passionate, thick-bunched and free-falling amber red. The car bounced in time to Daniel's and Marcy's chants. Behind the barricades, a little boy, his father keeping one watchful hand on the kid's tiny shoulder, flung himself from side to side, delirious with excitement at the adults going crazy around him. I caught his huge brown eyes and chanted in his direction, as though speaking to him, shaking my fist in unison with the words: *The people! United! Will never be defeated!* He answered with nonsense words while his little arms boxed back at me, his small face set seriously as though he were in a karate match. Holding his attention, I mouthed the words I was saying, instructing him, and he answered with a roar, opening his mouth wide and showing his teeth, pretending to be a lion. His father—plain, round face, skeptical eyes, stiletto moustache; I imagined he had spent more time playing baseball than attending political rallies—joined the instruction and lifted his son, holding the boy's arm and leading him in the chant. The boy started to get it right, the little voice wedding the crowd's; then the wonder and power of what he was doing overwhelmed him and, safely enclosed in his father's arm, he leaned his body out over the railing and shouted: "Goodbye Mister Silly People! Goodbye Mister Silly People!"

"Let's go!" said the cop, waving us on.

I followed Paul around the corner into the emptiness of a deserted, dark street. There was a pop and flash behind us, the receding wave of some crashes and noise, the frenzied sound of police sirens. Paul accelerated and I checked if we were being followed—nothing except a volley of light. A police car and its siren raced past. We turned onto Fifth Avenue. We were free.

"Check Ramón," I said.

Daniel leaned over the back, calling his name. No answer; Marcy yelled to pull over while police cars and wagons went by, ignoring us. No one would know us now; we were part of the traffic, one of many cars. Daniel tugged at the zipper while Laura told him to take it easy.

His voice fogged and confused, Ramón roused himself out of the opened bag. "Where are we? I fell asleep."

We took my favorite route, the East River Drive to the Brooklyn Bridge, cruising past the filigree of city lights that hemmed the wave-charged river. Cassie fiddled with the radio, skipping around the half-minute headline updates. We caught the broadcasters over gusts of hot wind and traffic noise that blasted through the open windows; there were references to arrests, a riot, Delores saying something about cops, but nothing elaborate, the static-ridden reports obviously intended to play down the incident, and soon everyone fell silent. I watched the blinking red eye of the Wonder Bread factory smoke-stack on the opposite shore and felt myself separate from the rest of the group, float away from them into a vague, exhausted reverie in which I imagined driving to Atlanta, speaking to Karen, rescuing Ramón. Cassie must have felt my distance because she put her hand on my knee, a lifeline of feeling pulling me back toward shore; but when I looked at her, she also seemed distracted, smoking, staring out the window, her hair arrayed behind her on the headrest.

"I see that, you guys," said Marcy, meaning Cassie's hand on my knee. "You guys are really hot for each other and don't think I haven't noticed it."

"It's none of your business," Cassie answered her.

"I thought we were a family," said Marcy.

"We can still respect each other's privacy. Mark and I are friends. It doesn't mean what you think. I wouldn't treat Karen that way."

"It looks pretty hot to me."

"When and if that's what's happening, I'll let you know," she said and clamped her hand harder over my kneecap.

Her behavior relieved and confused me. Marcy wouldn't dare challenge Cassie. But were we lovers or not? I had imagined she accepted my living with Karen. Did she want me to leave her? Did she want Karen to know about us? For the last several hours I had lived in a world separate from my usual one, acting like our special cir-cumstances excused my touching her. Soon we would be out of the world of the car and back in Brooklyn. I would have to say something to Cassie or Karen. What would I say?

We curved and climbed onto the bridge and shimmied over the metal-grated roadway toward the tenements and warehouses that filled the protruding belly of the Brooklyn shore; shimmering red taillights of cars disappeared into the broad lap formed by the dark, brooding warehouses. A different view behind me: the austerely elegant, yellow, white, gray, and black sparkle of the Wall Street towers waiting for dawn. Be a hero, they said. In the back, Daniel whispered to Laura; yet another secret. How come they had so much to say to one another?

I remembered a winter's drive with Daniel: We crawled at five or ten miles an hour swaddled in a white wind, the headlights carving out horizontal columns of furious snow ahead of us. Daniel insisted we drive through it: You can always drive out of the weather, he said. The road disappeared. We joined a line of other cars that tagged behind a snowplow, a caravan of strangers, and passed abandoned trucks and colored lights whirling in the dark whiteness. The car became a smoky cocoon. We talked about the heroes of white kids. We were coming from a depressing visit with Sam Melville, the bank bomber, in Attica, an hour in a locked visiting closet hemmed in by humorless guards and clanging gates. Melville gave long, pausing, one word answers to our questions. His huge eyes swam behind his reading glasses as he stared at the yard outside enclosed by walls constructed of medieval-looking rock. Was he a hero? A father of two small kids, he had formed his own affinity group and planted bombs at night, propaganda of the deed that protested and commemorated Fred Hampton's assassination, the bombing of Cambodia, the murders at Kent State. I remembered him from that time, a vivid picture because I didn't know of course that he was meeting at night with his group of five to plan the dynamite purchases and disguises. Instead he seemed dreamy and distant to me, still longhaired, though balding, a vaguely romantic, artistic type who strummed a guitar through a meeting and seemed incongruous hanging out with ex-college radicals fifteen years younger than himself. How can he be their hero? asked Daniel. Working class kids don't even know who he is. Okay. But who *were* their heroes? There were Americans who had sacrificed— John Brown, Big Bill Haywood, Mother Jones, the members of the Lincoln Brigade. Daniel was incredulous. That's who they *should* be, he said. Their real heroes are Elvis, John Havlicek, Roger Maris, James Dean—and you know what? It's not so bad that they're their heroes.

"Remember?" I asked Daniel, telling everyone about the exchange. "Elvis?" said Laura.

"Why not?" said Daniel. "You don't have to know Mao on contradiction to be a hero. Elvis takes risks. He isn't afraid to stand up for himself. That's what a hero does."

"He has no ideology."

"He's a working-class kid with a lot of guts. I respect that."

He debated Laura and Marcy, holding them at bay while we exited the bridge. We entered Brooklyn driving toward a single lit sign announcing MOBIL at the end of a wide, dark avenue. Inside, I continued to drift toward worry and anger, a sea of feelings I didn't want to be in—the power of Karen's coming presence: bad moon on the rise.

"I wanted to stay that way forever," I finished telling Cassie, speaking about my feeling in the snowbound car. "But by the time we got to Albany the snow had turned to rain. We went to some diner—"

"The Big Chief," interrupted Daniel. "Off the Taconic. Near Lake Taghanik. It's a terrific diner."

"—and had cherry pie."

"*Great* cherry pie," Daniel corrected.

We turned onto Paul's corner; the other car had already arrived and the house was lit up with a bright and busy, festive look. People wandered in and out of the open door and I heard music and Marcy's voice through the open windows: *Are you ready for a brand-new beat? Summer's here and the time is right for dancing in the streets.* Karen drew the curtain over the living-room bay window, a precaution against surveillance. I parked and Ramón woke up, drowsily asking questions about what would happen next. Everyone got out, except Cassie, who waited with me for a moment.

I turned to the house watching shadows pass behind the shades. This was home, where I knew everything that was going on. The idea of joining everyone left me feeling heavy and hopeless. "I don't want to go in there," I said.

"You have to," she said. "You'll help Ramón and we'll go to Atlanta."

I turned to kiss her. A measured gamble: We had a moment's grace, I figured, before having to meet the others, and, if she did realize we were absent, Karen wouldn't go out of her way to risk the public humiliation of finding us. I shifted in the seat, poised between the gearshift and steering wheel; she waited for me, curious and silent with an observant, pleased, tolerant smile: *What are you going to do now?*

A red curl, touching her cheek, distracted me. I tucked it back, freeing her face. She smiled, accepting me. Something soft stirred inside me, a muted hint of caring I had not known before. I didn't speak, but stared and cupped her waiting face. She shined and receded from me. I pushed one amber strand back, then another, as though I were keeping a tide at bay, and her face emerged in the streetlight. I felt as though I had never seen it before: high forehead and determined cheeks; soft, prescient mouth; daring, scared eyes. She held the tumult of hair back and I touched her face, feeling the high, pleasing firmness of her forehead and sweet cushion of her mouth. I wanted to embrace and absorb her, touch and honor her magic core of heat and light. I felt lifted up and held, high and outside my life. The feeling reminded me of moments during demonstrations when the sense of everyone's separateness joining in a great single mass moved inside me like a wave, carrying me toward a sea of such wild fullness that its inspiration scared me. I was also afraid now, wanting to say something, and scared that my words would waste the moment.

Behind us the house waited. The silence that swelled and stretched around us threatened to break. We couldn't stay here, suspended in this sea of quiet forever. I moved to kiss her and she ducked, eluding me sweetly, her palm covering my mouth.

"Say something"—me, desperate.

"I don't know what to say." She put down my hands and we embraced, clumsy, awkward, smelling of the night's tear gas, fire, and smoke. I imagined terrible things as I held her, visions of the two of us dead in the car, crashing, and also some dread sense of Karen admonishing and yelling at me: *What would we say to everyone?*

"I'll see you in Atlanta," she said, and left the car.

I floated, alone. I was aware of the house, but saw something else instead, a sense or wash of change, like a color or the motion of wind or current, a terrifying movement of dread and isolation. The sense was inside me, living in my imagination and emotions, but I couldn't control it. It swam before me, vast and unthinkable, as though a delirium of fear inside my head was taken out and made real. Whether my eyes were open or closed, it filled the space around me—losing

Cassie, staying with Karen, an image of all of us continuing in the same way for years. I hung in its hold, weightless and trapped, afraid any movement might change its balance or presence, while, at the same time, thinking that my fear wasn't real, something this irrevocable and hard didn't happen, death was outside, not in me, and if I got up and walked out of the car, up the stairs, into the noise and light of the house and the troubles, angers, and worries of Ramón, Karen, and Daniel, I would leave this fearful bottomless power and be on land, whole and real, myself once again.

I left the car and started up the stairs. *Thesis:* save myself. *Antithesis:* as soon as I felt myself within the pull of the busyness of the house, I missed the fear I had felt in the car—a moment, wanting its reality. *Synthesis:* I forced myself up, thinking, *It will be all right. Later. Do and decide everything later, after tonight, Ramón, the fall strategy conference in Atlanta. You're safe. Cassie won't say anything. Later. That's your plan. Later.*

Inside the house Karen told me the news, no coolness or resentment on her part, even taking my hand. A mini riot had broken out in East Harlem, fires and injuries; looters and cops had skirmished at the Ninety-Sixth Street boundary between the ghetto poor and doorman rich; the leadership had let themselves be arrested peacefully, but the police were still looking for Ramón. "Total breakdown in security," she whispered, and pointed to two Lords sitting at the dining room picnic table talking in Spanish who presumably were picking up the guns. "They could have been cops. Total breakdown."

The phone kept ringing. Laura had taken charge of communications, receiving calls and arranging interviews. Daniel assisted her; furious and delighted, he yelled at a reporter over the phone. More people wanted to go to Atlanta now; Marcy organized rides. People lined up for the bathroom and shared towels as they showered off gas and smoke. In a corner Ramón talked to some lawyers. There was a flurry of private conversations—Lords, Ramón, lawyers, Paul, Daniel, everyone—and we organized moving the guns: Paul, Daniel, and Laura acted as decoys and drove away the two cars in which we had arrived while the Lords and I loaded up another car that came around from the back. After the car left, I waited a moment on the street, exhausted, and thought: *You have nowhere to go and no one to go with you.*

The long night unraveled. Inside the house, I wandered around searching for something to do. Paul returned from the decoy run, but not Daniel and Laura. In the kitchen Jeff scoured the cupboards for food, Cassie at his side. People kept calling him or Ramón to the phone; the two of them were leaders, in demand. The people who lived in the house met in a bedroom upstairs. I went outside and Cassie followed. She tossed herself into my arms, took my hands and placed them on her ass so I could press her closer to me. In my ear, she whispered that she loved me, then left with Jeff for an all-night diner. When I went back inside, I felt like a stranger at a party and Marcy complained about male chauvinist elitism and demanded we hold a self-criticism meeting.

Ramón asked me to come with him.

"You see what I mean," Marcy said.

I ignored her and followed him to a corner, his importance creating a shield around us.

"They're charging me with incitement and attempted manslaughter," said Ramón. "But the thing is that the Party has to get itself together."

I said something about the fight with Delores, fishing for information.

"She's all right," he said. "She gets a little out of control now and then."

He changed the subject to Ho Chi Minh and the Trotskyites. People traipsed downstairs from the house meeting, stoned and happy, offering everyone joints. Ramón and one of Paul's housemates discussed the demerits of western medicine. Ramón dragged deeply on a joint, agreeing that European medical practice was a rip-off. "The body is like a political movement," he said. "You have to work within its negative and positive capabilities."

Paul came over, his eyes pinched together and shining, his silly half-moon smile lighting his face. He hugged me, saying struggle was a wonderful thing. Cassie returned with Jeff.

I went to shower. Karen joined me, wanting to know what was happening with Ramón. We spoke while I bathed. I wondered whether she didn't care about me and Cassie or maybe really didn't know. I asked as casually as possible if she still planned to go to Atlanta. Now she was excited about the trip. The plan was to take two cars, one for women, and the other for the guys and Ramón. We would reconnoiter every two hundred miles or so and stop halfway at Hampton's Farm, a collective near Roanoke, Virginia. I listened, drying myself, self-conscious before her gaze.

"You look good," she said.

We kissed. I expected her usual lovemaking, lips pressed tight against her teeth; she often closed her eyes as I entered her, not daring or wanting to look, sometimes shielding her face with a bent arm, as though guarding even her closed eyelids against my sight. I suppose we both thought sex would get better between us, a category of behavior like loyalty or class consciousness, capable of constant improvement. Instead our passion remained true to itself, middling and cool.

Tonight she wanted to fuck. She positioned herself against the porcelain sink and we groped each other for a while, getting ourselves hot. I thought about Cassie for a moment, but lost her in Karen's tight press of a kiss. We tiptoed downstairs. The living and dining rooms were a jumble of bodies sleeping on beds improvised from chairs and cushions. We laid some sleeping bags next to each other and she burrowed below and stripped off my pants. I never expected her to take me in her mouth; when we first became lovers she had sometimes kissed me, but never sucked to make me come. Now she licked and nibbled, scratched my thighs, bit my stomach. I wanted to enter her and pulled her toward me, doing our special position, my thigh pressed against her cunt; a lesbian testimonial had promised this helped orgasm. She smiled with appreciation, then put my hand between her legs. Her lips were wet, heavy, and open. She closed her eyes, with pleasure, not caution, rolling on top. I entered her silently. In the street-lamp-lit darkness, barely moving, watching me, she squeezed and released, then reached down and held me; I started to come and she pressed against me hard, bringing herself to climax.

"Is that you?" I asked, my hand closing over her quivering cunt.

"That's you. You do that to me," she said.

Then, later, a kiss before I drifted off to sleep: "My guy."

When we woke everyone was already up. I dressed inside the sleeping bag and found Daniel in the kitchen surrounded by a happy mess of empty egg and milk cartons. He was sharing a joint with Jeff and Cassie. She welcomed me with a smile, but I worried about Karen and complained that the pot broke security.

"Lighten up," said Daniel, offering me the joint. "Ramón was smoking all night."

"I've got to get myself together," said Cassie, and she and Jeff disappeared.

"What are you mad at?" Daniel asked. "I'm smoking dope with him, not marrying him." He dreamed over the eggs for a moment while I wondered if I should go after Cassie. I felt as though something had broken between us.

A new burst of energy, Daniel giving a final stir to the pan. "Laura and I talked all night. We're going to Hollywood. We're going to produce movies."

He was crazy. He knew as much about movies as I did about selling cars. "You think you can make movies?"

"I love movies." He spooned out the breakfast on paper plates.

"Did you sleep with her?"

"I'll tell you later." He looked around the empty kitchen and shouted into the living room that the eggs were ready.

I went to wash and met Karen and Marcy. Marcy looked miserable; her sallow face was swollen with lack of sleep.

"Marcy heard us last night," Karen said. "Having sex. She told me she's never been so humiliated in her entire life."

"It was as though I wasn't there," Marcy said. "You don't understand anything. I call you "brother." But you don't understand me at all. You don't want to."

I waited for Karen to defend us and tell Marcy to mind her own business. Instead she apologized for our behavior. "He does," she said, taking Marcy's hand. "I think he does."

"You're so blind," Marcy said. "Don't you know he's fucking Cassie."

I started to interrupt, but Karen shut me off, telling Marcy this was not her business.

"I'm insulted as your friend. It's an insult to me that he treats you like that. I'm not going to be quiet like our parents. You've got to deal with this; I'll make you deal with it. What are you going to do?"

Karen took off her glasses and stared at Marcy. "I'm not contributing to my own humiliation."

She walked away. "This is your fault," Marcy said. "You've come between us."

I went after Karen. She was staring in the mirror, thinking, lips pressed together. She held out her hand, warding me off, but placing its warmth on my chest, covering my heart. I wanted to hold her and ask forgiveness, and also be away from here. *You're an idiot,* I thought: *I can't make her feel better about what I've done.* But I wanted to, and my incapacity to make things right—to do what I wanted and have her understand and approve—paralyzed me. I tried to embrace her again, and she twisted away.

"Go," she said, her face small and pinched, trapped, angry, and scared. "I know what you're thinking. I'll be all right. Ramón needs you. Go. Go."

Push it out.

(We used to say this in meetings all the time: "Push it out." Sometimes I think our equivalent of teenage knife fights was debates over the Black Nation.)

Push it out—carry the NLF flag into an army base during a demonstration, disband the organization, declare all monogamous relationships inherently oppressive to women, reveal the contradictions (latent, real, primary, and secondary) that make up everything in the world.

Why don't you acknowledge the contradictions? Good question. There are three possibilities.

1) You don't see them—they're too small, undeveloped, insignificant. Fair enough, Sir, I'll buy that.

2) You see them, but you're afraid to recognize them. Example: Cruising in Mercedes air-conditioned comfort on a hot, summer Monday morning down from Santa Barbara with a trust-fund millionaire friend with all the right opinions—collects Lucian Freuds, supports the Palestinian demand for a separate state, sends his daughter to a single-sex school—we pass a beer-gutted, sweat-stained highway construction crew taking a cigarette break. "Look at them," friend says, about to earn more for the hour he'll spend today behind his Milan-made desk than the louts will receive for a month breaking and pouring concrete in the noise and dirt of the freeway, "they never work."

What do you do? You say nothing. Fair enough, Sir, I'll buy that.

3) Or you're so afraid of recognizing them that you pretend they don't exist—"false consciousness," like unions, the Democratic Party, our parents' entire generation, making their pathetic deals with the ameliorations of capitalism.

Plus there's another element in Push It Out, the:

American impulse, wild and free, going to the Alaskan extreme, the tallest building, the biggest screen, the crowd urging the cowboy to ride the bull for the extra second, the Apollo audience applauding the sopra-no who holds the high note.

Push It Out:

Joe Hill faces the firing squad, a dough-faced man with sky-blue eyes alone against a wooden post in the courtyard of a granite-walled Utah prison: "Don't mourn for me: Organize."

Push It Out:

The horizontal scroll of words wrapped on the white marble walls of the Jefferson memorial: "I have upon the alter of god [small g] sworn eternal hostility against every form of tyranny over the mind of man."

Push It Out:

Huey Newton and Roger Williams, Coltrane and Emerson, Malcolm X and Abraham Lincoln: "Fondly do we hope—fervently do we pray—that this mighty scourge of war may speedily pass away. Yet if God wills that it continue, until all the wealth piled by the bondman's two hun-dred and fifty years of unrequited toil shall be sunk, and until every drop of blood drawn with the lash shall be paid by another drawn with the sword, as was said three thousand years ago, still it must be said, 'the judgments of the Lord are true and righteous altogether.'"

So—PUSH IT OUT:

We were all there?

No.

I don't think so.

If we were all there then how come Cambodia was bombed? Fred Hampton murdered? Allende overthrown?

These things happened.

So:

If we were all there, then why are we here now?

(More later. I'm hungry. Time for a break. How about some mid-night risotto?)

Hobo Deluxe, A Cinema of Poetry

Text and Concept by Max Henry

Photographs by Sam Samore

The Grapple

Twelve Noon: He awoke to the acute burning of a toothache, achingly rehashing the details of their well-documented drunken debauchery that had lasted till dawn. That morning they had fought over stupid things; unfolded linen or an unwashed dish. They had argued; *he* only to accommodate *her* desire to do so, a melodrama filled with invectives and small insults aimed at maiming him emotionally. It crippled him for an instant; it was enough to make him bolt her comfortable bourgeois apartment building with concierge and laundry room.

He walked into the bracing cold; the dirty, decaying cobblestones felt as hard as they were old and the morning gently gave rise to a superb azure noon sky. Maybe this would be the last time he would see her—he thought about her silken blouse the night before—perhaps he would see her again after all. He walked on, past the hobos warming themselves by the trash-can fire. He imagined how the hardness of the wooden bench slats felt against their necks and shoulder blades. He remembered robbing a bodega, some underage chick had left her money on the counter after a purchase, she was in a hurry, the store clerk with his back turned. As he pulled out a cheap cigar, he heard the chick say the money's on the counter, the clerk was on a rickety stepladder, the amount for a six-pack and a pack of cigarettes. The clerk was so slow; he grabbed the eight bucks and bolted. Hey, the clerk shouted, but he was gone. He jumped the turnstile at the Bowery and caught the J train.

Later that day *she* called, leaving him messages, imploring him to come back, to her. He ignored her apologies, besides the other Jane had finally called back. He wasn't about to miss an opportunity for a new affair, these things were hot and cold, he was on a hot streak. He knew it like he did when he played the horses, all he had to do was show, if she was mellow, they would hit it off they would beguile each other for days drink cocoa and cognac listen to music and the muses laugh naked and shower together order takeout delivery and do it over again and again and again. They would mesmerize each other; her slender waist tattooed along its side winding toward her derriere a tantric symbol of female virility, at least that's what she claimed. Still he could not help but think of *her*, his orgasms had been intense and deeply fulfilling. This, he

valued much from a woman. The adoration, their beauty, their longing for a man, the perfume they wore, the charming clothes which costumed them, the slit in the skirt, the sinuous limbs.

She had a sixth sense that he'd been seeing another woman, so the first thing she did when he ran into her at the café was smile at him. He smiled back and walked toward her. When he was within range she slapped him—all wrist no elbow still it stung and it bruised his ego. A small thick welt formed on his cheek. His face contorted for an instant as they stood there awkwardly while the patrons murmured to them-selves and the waitress giggled. A slight smile rippled across her face, she had the advantage, he couldn't do a thing. As he stammered an apology she slowly turned and exited, he couldn't help but notice her legs and remember the smoothness of her thighs at the instant she departed.

At last I can move on from this man, get on with my life, she thought as she walked north along the commercial boulevard, still she felt afraid for a second, she had been in love or perhaps it was lust she debated what had turned her on to him remembering the crook of his elegant neck as she orgasmed one afternoon during a midday rendezvous, she had taken two hours away from the office, she'd been possessed. It was the height of their passion and now she was walking away from this man who had been her lover. She shivered as she stood at the traffic light a taxi swerved close to the curb honking and speeding off into the distance. She had corralled her girlfriend about him. She knew her friend had gone down on him once or twice. Dump him he's a hobo she exclaimed, he doesn't work only writes those stupid texts, he doesn't want to have a normal life like you. You're much too good for him. She remembered her girlfriend's drunken pronouncement: They should have a meaningful ménage à trois. She remembered kissing her passionately in front of him—go ahead, he said, make out with her, grinning widely, enjoying the game. The girlfriend had grabbed his crotch when she went to the bathroom, I'll get you later her girlfriend teased, combing her hair in the antique mirror as she returned to the room. They were smoking hash that evening excusing her girlfriend's behavior letting her off the hook secretly turned on by the idea of the three of them she remembered her girlfriend in a bodysuit at Yale but he had passed out on the vintage velvet sofa.

Weeks go by, I've been thinking of you . . .

He'd read past dawn but arose early only slightly bedraggled from the lack of sleep, still clearheaded enough to mull over the possibilities the potentialities the firmness of the burgeoning changes at hand. How long had he lived now? It seemed now all the pages that formed the basis for his life were a consecration of blankness, dissolution, removal, and ad hoc. The grapple was the wedge that kept nagging at his conscience, a topsy-turvy extant, inconspicuous but there. He was mentally fit despite the fact. There would be days when he would sleep past noon not from laziness as his mother had assumed but from a dreadful incapacitation, a deeply rooted nineteenth-century musical melancholia which only scads of sleep could even begin to nurse. His dreams led sometimes to a colorful prose. There he touched the garment of a nebulous presence; its pool of cool violets and warm pinks was frightening awesome and boundless. Without fleshly body to hinder it, it hovered and swirled slightly above and the text *draw nearer to nigh* formed but where from? And then a human-like voice said but without saying he had read it as if a TelePrompTer:

While all the world's asleep, I whirl I whirl ascension . . .

What kind of a being was it? And what could compare in a dense waking state? His faith was nil in pharmaceuticals; thus did he slumber and reel.

The rooming house was lived in and homey with the smells of Nigerians cooking down the hallway. Colorado lived at the end of the hall, a whoop-it-up drunk and a bad cook. Teddy the old-time southern black lived next door, he was half deaf, everything was a shout, in the spring-time he would wash cars for neighborhood residents. The ones with money on West End. His neighbor Ballentine used a rickety air condi-tioner in the middle of winter. This made the most annoying sound. Sometimes vociferous disagreements occurred in the stairwell. He didn't care. He could sleep through almost anything except for distinct noises at low decibels. It was good to observe silence in a metropolis filled, even at its most quiet, with an inconceivable array of sound human and/or machine. The inorganic hum was a natural to the pace. In the grapple roil, he determined to remain equine and serene. No one could

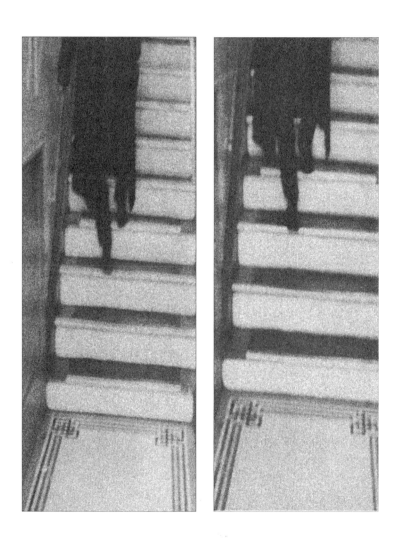

touch him, he'd had a vision and stuck to it over the years. Now he was building a fortress of strength. The rainbow was visible, he would make the grade and be vivid with an incomparable blankness, he was going to lead! The naysayers would crash and burn. The glossy Janes would undress for him. He would have them. He would have them all.

But somehow he knew he would pare down to a pallet and a Vedic book. After a taste, he would find a gateway past the grapple; beyond the grapple: The long lines/the long lives of verse would formulate a discourse on the refinement of the soul.

Her head rested on his clavicle as she slept breathing rhythmically. It was the breathing of a lady who felt satiated and content after sex. He lay there thinking blankly as always. The lo-fi hi-fi played at a low decibel, a crooner wistfully sang about love. He listened intently his physical thoughts merging with the song. Thoughts are physical he thought again. Her hand brushed against his thigh as she turned on her side. Aroused he decided against the violation of her sleep, the endless articulate montage played on. What is real time to real thought he thought musing about thinking in general. He gauged her in the dimness; her breasts exposed the dark outline in her compliant angles.

That morning he was grouchy having nodded off around dawn. The glossy Jane had departed he discovered turning over to kiss her. He regretted not having seen her off to work. What a good lay. He sat doe-eyed in bed. He longed at the pillow. Perhaps a few more minutes of sleep. It would be noontime when he awoke.

The calendar passed alternately speedy and slow; there was a conjunction of the moon or some other such planetary activity. A monsoon-like weather pattern emerged melting glaciers and snowcaps sudden hail falls repeated dry spells, torrential all. Despite this rubric the exoteric world manufactured a chimerical posture to be doled out and consumed by the electronic watchers. A suffusion of light and sound maintained by a secret vessel of indeterminate largeness.

She had shown weakness, this made her vulnerable and edgy. Why had she slipped so miserably at the snappish affair? It would have been fine if she sipped a ginger instead of that confection from a silver tumbler. They had seen her tanked they knew she was drunk—alone her social

graces caved in to slurring soliloquies about the meritocracy. Her old acquaintance had worn an ostentatious beaded dress, much too beady for the informal gathering at the Brilliant Lounge. Her once-friend even had the audacity to comb her bad haircut in the middle of the room, making calls from her handy. This idiot fostered hope of an allegiance in cultured conversation. Buzzified enough to lose *her* politeness she realized no one else wanted to talk with this dumb Jane, so, with a deft move to the bar she overcame the impending "so how have you been" line. Why are people so insipidly insensitive to each other she thought noticing the conversations in twos, threes, the sideward glances, the smiling faces making sport of the uncouth woman. All the pretty faces are here she thought to herself thinking about *him* at that instant.

He had no caress toward the follies of the world, he who had roused and roamed the slurry byways of September ravings, the indistinguishable apparitions, the callow and uncouth ambitious appointees, the blurry and contagious diseased, he had no caress:

No one surrenders their delusions on the keeper that the keeper will come to you as a founder of the compelling wordless reconstructions and relevant analogues unimaginable to the holy query the nectar pressed deep into the flesh the novel importance of ancient betrayals and of course the benevolence of the good gods; o hum something noctagonal and warm and let the afterglow of heaven's aroma form those words he didst not hear that he did hear those words did not hear the weeping icon the supper gourd the mirror in the sun your sun the mirror the maker your own mirror maker in the future framework wrested from the world in the future people are composed and pacified of intent. He would ask to meet the gods in good circumstances . . .

He walked buzzified by the soft drizzle, the light gray mist felt well about his face, he was humming a big band song; fingering magic in the breezy cool air. Lost in the hyperreality, he embraced the mind's exits and entrances with aplomb:

Take off your clothes he said to her, he pondered this thought for a while before casually asking her to remove her logo-less clothing. Obliging him, her garments scattered around the lacquered divider to the bedroom. A kindness packaged in her naked body, the offering made apparent and wanton, the luxurious wantonness unrestrained in the bedroom, the bedroom painter engorged for the coupling the laptop afterwards wedged at the leg in communion with the characteristic heroic transcriptions of their naked adjoining perfume, leisurely entertaining unencumbered thoughts on profuse launches at anything female that moved . . .

She thought something must be wrong with him. He sat up thinking blankly thinking she was asleep she thinking blankly herself thinking he thinks I'm asleep ha I'm not as he stared at the fourth wall; *this went on a few seconds*, there, he continued the blankness—a vial of immeasurable constitution and vigor, the largeness of minutiae. She touched his loins. Yes his starlights were abuzz, and the gaze plummeted to her derriere. And thus later, her letter all that time his companion; her spirit in longitude.

He wrestled with her infertility and spell-casts sometimes staring at the cleavage she indulged for his attenuate circumstances her pleadings and longings in the lair ignited by the budding tension and the mere appetites of desire, of depths profound and wondrous, those ignited by tension and depths irregular despairity. He wrestled this . . .

She called twice a week leaving long dialogues reprimanding him for not calling her often enough if at all, she sent postcards from Marseilles and Montmontre, the handwriting neatly compact, all efficiency. She hinted at a Parisian lover during the fashion shows. This had enraged him. He imagined flying off to that romantic city, making a dramatic entrance into her room at the Ritz, catching them in the midst of an afternoon delight. He imagined this as a cinema, with soft porn lighting and color. After a moment's pause, he was smiling, knowing a laissez-faire response was best, what could he do, he wasn't the jealous type was he? He didn't like games of love, too much effort, or nonchalance. He liked passion in his women, passion and demurity. Self-deprecation was cool, warmth welcome too. A quiet femme knockout. That would make a man notice. That would make him notice. But this is what drew *her* to *him*.

"Take me to the movies tonight," she asked.
"Talk into the mike, I can't hear you."
Audrey leaned closer and in a deeper voice demanded,
"Take me to see something Italian."

(Kennedy, page 137)

We Used to Breed Remarkable Percheron Twitch Horses

Creston Lea

I'LL CALL ANYBODY ANYTHING I WANT, BUT NEVERTHELESS I HAD a donkey because I thought they were kind of cute, and it got sick and I had to stand there and nurse it for a week, drain its catheter and give it cranberry juice from a baby bottle. Nipple-feed a donkey! It sounds like a Christian picture, but there was wet donkey shit and wood shavings all over my legs and my own back was hurting like a fork was in that spot above the hip. I had pain, too.

When are you supposed to allow that your own pain maybe dwarfs the pain of the suffering wretched? I didn't know, but I hung water with a half gallon of Ocean Spray in a new bucket from the hook in the stall and took my rest. The donkey died in the night and I cried like a pussy when they put it in the ground.

meantime I watched two
distant lights halfway up
the snow-covered moun-
tain, the sadness of solitude mixed with the sad-
ness of the snow-covered
mountain and those lights
halfway up and I asked
myself if I would ever
manage to sleep in that
lonely bed, at the top of
the tower, almost balanced
on those flights of stairs,
squeezed by the looming
mountain, with its ghostly
lights, but all these questions and reflections did
not warm me up

(Longo, page 153)

Against Witness

William Wenthe

One of us must have a gun,
I said.

Four cars stopped on a desert road,
it's only likely: statistics.

The horse that had been tossed
from the toppled trailer,
writhing, slammed his skull
teeth-first against tarmac.

It hurt so much
to watch: How can I presume
to write it down?

Two shots released him.
Blood. Urine. Shit.

A rope around the neck,
and four men trying to haul
1,100 pounds off the road.

It would not give.

My inner anvil's muffled in velvet
    (Starkey, page 73)

Stills from *The Naked City*

Miranda Lichtenstein

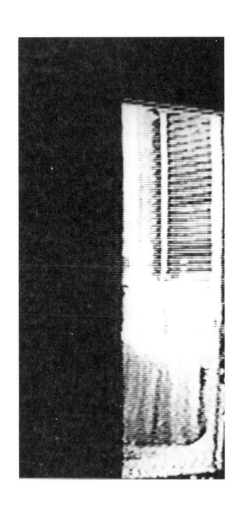

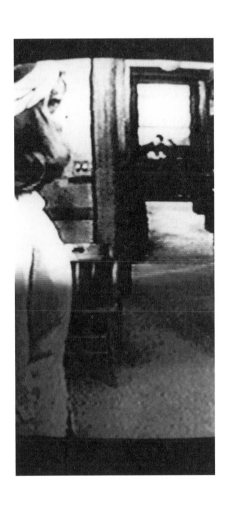

Largo

Rachel Wetzsteon

"Look for someone to make you slow."—Elias Canetti

They are ogling the stars in an outdoor garden,
and the night's infectious energy
makes them bold, makes him grab her hands and declare
A brilliant chapter begins tonight:
I have novels in me, whole realms of feeling
that your eyes prize open. To which she responds
I'm a changeling, darling, in your masterful hands;
this morning I was one of eight million stories
but now I'm wearing freshwater pearls
at the end of a pier, in the middle of summer—
race me there, and the waves will envy our speed.

A sudden hush descends over Café Largo
and a low voice whispers, Be all these things,
ring all these changes on each other
but slowly. The brain that races tonight
will end up a frowning skull in a viewless mansion;
you'll wake up in bare rooms, horrible jewels in your hands.
Walk, instead, past never-finished cathedrals;
light one cigarette from another;
find, if you know what's good for you, endless answers to whether
the table is really there when you close your eyes.

Gusts

Rachel Wetzsteon

An agitation shakes the trees:
this tumult always seemed to me
the oldest motion, the turbulence
all others copied. As blossoms drift
down through the moist air, so blessings come
to those who wait long enough; when
pollen falls, the flight recalls
a fragile friendship dying. I never thought
that when petals touch the ground
the plentitude might stop there, the fragrance
be neither portent nor memory, but only
sweet smells lasting as long as the walk home.
It is spring; flowers are flying everywhere.
And all night a low voice chides me
for never giving my all to the moment;
a question forms and grows urgent
and won't take no answer for an answer:
if I gave up stories, what would become
of the gust, and the scatter, and the stillness after?
Would the trees be robbed of what made them priceless
or let their riches loose as never before?

Inside the Tube

Meghan Daum

THEY GATHER IN SMALL, BLONDE CLUSTERS AT THE GATE, SIPPING coffee from the Terminal C Nathan's Famous, their clean hair swept carefully out of their clean faces. They cannot possibly be real, these uniformed creatures, these girls with matching luggage and matching shoes, these warm-blooded extensions of that hulking, spotless aircraft.

Neither passenger nor pilot, the flight attendant is the liaison between the customer and the machine. She is somehow blonde even when she's not blonde, a girl even when she's a guy. Part bimbo and part Red Cross, she is charged with the nearly impossible task of calming the passenger down while evoking enough titillation to suggest that there remains, even in the twenty-first century, something special about air travel.

Flight attendants are fetishized and mocked in equal measure. They are both fantasy and punch line, the players in hackneyed sex jokes and the guides through smoke and fire to the emergency exit. Since the beginning of commercial flying, back in the 1930s when flight attendants were required to be registered nurses, the profession has symbolized an unearthly female glamour. Until the 1960s, flight attendants were not allowed to be married. On many airlines they were required to have a college degree and speak a foreign language. Their skin was periodically checked for blemishes, their hair was not allowed to touch their collars and, if they were, say, 5'4", they could not weigh more than 115 pounds. Until the 1970s they were called "stewardesses," real girls who were treated like ladies.

There is no small amount of perverted nostalgia in all of this. When people today talk about what's happened to flying, about why any given transcontinental flight bears a heavy resemblance to a Greyhound bus ride from Memphis to Louisville, they often claim to be talking largely about the absence of ethereal waitresses serving seven-course meals in first class. No longer does the starchy hiss of the uniform sound a note of almost military kinkiness. Back in the old days, flight attendants were as sleek and identical as F-16s flying in formation. Back in the old days they may as well have all been twin sisters. There was a time when you could pinch their asses and they'd buy you a martini. These days they will stop serving you drinks when you've had enough. If you do anything that they feel interferes with their duties, you could be charged with a felony. There are handcuffs in the cockpit should such an occasion arise. These days you have your fat ones, your ugly ones, and worst of all, your old ones. It used to be they had to quit when they turned thirty. Today, with no retirement age, there are a few as old as seventy-seven.

But even now, perhaps even this morning when you boarded some generic flight to some generic airport, you looked at them in search of some whiff of the past—you looked for a cute one, someone who might like you more than the others, someone to whom you pretended you might give your phone number. You wanted to consider these possibilities but chances are those possibilities simply weren't there. She's not in your league. Her sole education requirement is a GED. She's some bizarre relic. And, like the fact that your flight was oversold and delayed and some used-car salesman in a Wal-Mart suit inexplicably ended up seated next to you in business class, you are more than a little heartbroken about the whole thing. This is because the sex appeal of the flight attendant, like the sex appeal of flying, is gone forever. As much as you act like you have it over her, you somehow still long for an earlier era, back when there was no question that she had it over you.

The sky is a strange place to be. Eustachian tubes are tested up here. The human lung is not designed for the air outside. The food is nuked, the forks are plastic, the dirty words have been edited out of the movie. There's a good chance that the flight attendants, who may be hamming it up during the oxygen mask announcement and giggling in the rear galley like sauced-up Tri Delts, have not met each other until they boarded the plane.

When I board an evening flight on US Airways from Philadelphia to San Francisco, accompanied by a flight attendant who agreed to participate in a magazine article, no one else on the crew has met me or had any warning that I'd be coming along. I tell them that I am writing a story about flight attendants for a glossy men's magazine (the story, in the end, was killed by the editor because it lacked the prurient details he'd hoped for). After a few requests that I change their names—"I want to be called Lola!"—we are getting along like old high school pals. They're connoisseurs of bonding, high skilled socializers. If a reporter showed up to my workplace and announced that she'd be there for the next thirty-six hours I'd duck out for coffee and never come back. But there's plenty of coffee here already. They can't leave and their ability to deal with this fact is pretty much Job One.

This is called a turnaround, a day-and-a-half stint during which this crew will fly from their base in Philadelphia to San Francisco and then to Charlotte before returning to Philadelphia. We are on a Boeing 757—a "seven-five," in airline speak. All of the flight attendants are in their thirties or forties, four are women, three of whom are married, and two are men. All have been flying for at least ten years.

To contemplate what it means to be a flight attendant for ten or more years is to consider, after getting past the initially ludicrous notion of serving drinks at 37,000 feet, the effects of the relatively recent, popular tendency to put flying in a category that also includes walking and driving. To say that flight has become pedestrian is something of a Yogi Berra-ism. But to say that air travel has infused itself into the human experience without leaving marks or building up potentially problematic immunities is to view technology in a Pollyanna-like manner that may have gone out of fashion when applied to phenomena like the Internet and surveillance cameras but continues to thrive in the realm of travel. When it comes to technology's hold on our quality of life, cyber porn may be insidious, but jetliners are by now almost quaint, older than Peter, Paul, and Mary, as common as the telephone.

This is true and not true, a dilemma that often emerges when, as is the case in air travel, the glorious evolves into the stultifying and we are forced to come up with ways to re-experience, if not the original novelty, some form of entertainment. This is where the flight attendant appears onstage. When flying began, she was part of the show, as slick as the aircraft itself. Even through the 1970s, passengers were moneyed and expensively outfitted; ladies wore gloves on DC-4s. To deplane using a movable staircase was, for a moment, to do as rock stars and presidents did, and respect was paid accordingly. The idea has always been that the persona of the flight attendants should reflect that of the flying public. In that respect, little has changed. The only difference is that today the flying classes seem a little more public than in the past. The flight attendant, too, is given to the bad manicures and bad perms of any girl next door. She's still part of the entertainment, it's just that this is a lower-budget production. This may gnaw at passengers, but those holding $99 tickets to Miami may do well to look at the larger picture. Perhaps the flight attendant wouldn't remind us so glumly of the girl next-door if so many of us didn't live close to the airport.

Still, passengers pay attention to flight attendants, not during the safety announcements, when they're supposed to, but later, while flight attendants are eating dinner or reading *Cosmo* or doing normal things that are somehow rendered out of sync because of the uniform. During our five hours and twenty-six minutes to San Francisco, we hit some "light chop" twice—airlines discourage pilots from using the word "turbulence," which frightens passengers—and the seat belt sign goes on. Passengers get up anyway. They visit the flight attendants in the galleys. They ask for playing cards and more drinks and hand over their garbage to be thrown out. Wayward business travelers amble around the first-class galley and take stabs at the same kinds of conversations they impose on people sitting next to them. "Where do you live? Do you like it there?" and then "Could you get me another drink?"

Even as he accepts an empty pretzel bag from an unshaven, Reebok-wearing passenger, Carl, who is working in the main cabin tonight, manages to put a spin on his role as service provider. "We're a few notches below celebrity status," he says. "The moment people see a crew member, their eyes are on you constantly. People will come into the galley and just stare while you eat dinner. You have to watch everything you do and say."

Carl is thirty-six and has been a flight attendant with US Airways for twelve years. I am asking him questions in the aft galley ("aft" is used to describe anything located behind the wings) where he and Jim, his friend and colleague, have fashioned a seat for me out of a stack of plastic crates because I'm not allowed to sit in the flight-attendant-reserved jump seat. They have poured salad dressing left over from first class into a plastic cup and are eating it off of their fingers. "We have a needy bunch tonight," Carl says. "But not as bad as if we were going to L.A. Certainly nothing like Florida."

A lot of call buttons have been ringing tonight. A lot of people cannot seem to figure out how to use their headsets to watch the in-flight screening of *Tomorrow Never Dies*. A fleshy, spacy eleven-year-old boy repeatedly visits the aft galley asking for more soda, more peanuts, some ice cream. "You're a pretty demanding kid," Carl says with just enough smirk so that I notice but the kid does not. Carl and Jim disagree as to whether the boy qualifies for the unofficial passenger shit list that is compiled on every flight.

"He's a pain in the ass," says Carl.

"No, he's obviously slow," says Jim. "I feel sorry for him."

Still, no one is punching anyone in the nose tonight. No one has threatened a flight attendant with bodily harm or become obstreperously drunk or engaged in the sort of activity that would merit a presentation of those handcuffs stored in the cockpit. The fact that these sorts of incidents are ascending at an alarmingly steep angle, mostly for those pesky reasons having to do with the invasion of a public mentality into what was once perceived as a private space, dominates much of what is written and discussed about flight attendants these days. It is part of the reason that I am here in the aft galley dipping my finger in salad dressing tonight, the other part having to do with discerning whether the deglamorization of the job is the cause or the symptom of all that aggression.

What is at first most noticeable about flight attendants is the chronic disorientation that follows them both on and off the job. With work space measured by aisle widths and hours either stolen or protracted by virtue of time changes and date lines, flight attendants occupy a personal space that must prove stronger than the artificial and ever-changing scope of "real" time and geography. Flight attendants are always tired and usually bored and, though they are required to

wear a working watch at all times, understand distinctly the difference between knowing what time it is and feeling what time it is. A
forty-five minute break on a transatlantic flight demands the ability
to fall asleep instantly on the jump seat. They must learn to literal-
ly sleep on cue.

But there is another layer in the psyche of flying that transcends
the burdensome working conditions of flight attendants. It's a set of
notions that has a lot to do with life on the ground and yet can best
be unpacked by examining the ebb and flow of life on an airplane.
Just as air pressure will make one martini in the air equal two on the
ground, the malaise of modern life extends its claws in cartoon-like
proportions on an airplane. It's a sickness aggravated by tiny bathrooms and recirculating air and laptop computers that allow no
excuse to take a break from work. "What I hate is when passengers
won't put the computer away when I try to bring them dinner,"
Theresa, a sinewy Mexican-American flight attendant for US
Airways, tells me. She is in the first-class galley eating chocolate syrup
out of a plastic cup. "They never look up, never take a break to enjoy
the flight. They never just look out the window and see how beautiful
it is."

This is a disease of plastic and its discontents. It is what happens
when sleep becomes a greater novelty than gravity defiance. It is what
happens when the concept of New York to London seems more like
changes in a movie set than a journey involving thousands of miles
of empty sky, five degrees of longitude, an ocean. It is what happens
when the miraculous becomes the mundane, when we are no longer
amazed by flying but bored by it at best and infuriated by it more
often than not. And it is this hybrid of nonchalance and aggression
that has largely come to define the modern air traveler. It's what causes passengers to punch, slap, spit, swear, make obscene gestures,
grope, and fling food at flight attendants and each other. It's what
makes people dismantle smoke detectors, throw tantrums when they
don't get a meal choice, and threaten to get a crew member fired over
such infractions as not having cranberry juice. That the flight attendant must act as an agent for the big, impenetrable aircraft as well as
for the small, vulnerable passenger is both a corporate conflict and a
metaphysical conundrum. As boring as the airplane may be at this
point, its technology remains distancing and unnerving, sometimes

even terrifying. And whether the flight attendant is aware of it or not, her duty is to bridge the gap between the artificiality of the cabin and the authentic human impulses that play themselves out in that cabin. She has to shake her ass yet still know how to open the exit door.

The more tangible reasons for her condition have to do with numbers. Every year more seats are squeezed on to planes, seat width has become narrower, flights are oversold, and cheap tickets attract passengers that would otherwise be taking the bus. Flight attendants blame the overcrowding on federal deregulation, which occurred in 1978, and essentially legislated that airlines were allowed to spend as little money as possible per flight as long as they did not violate federal safety standards. This introduced significantly lower ticket prices; it costs an average of twenty-four percent less to fly today than before deregulation.

Out of this was born the era of the $99 ticket. It also meant an abrupt end to luxury air travel; the pillbox hats were traded in for unwashed hair. "We're taught in training that people can't get on board if they have curlers in their hair or no shoes on," said Tracy, another US Airways flight attendant. "And if they have to publish that [in training manuals], that's frightening."

"They show up wearing jogging suits," Carl says. "And I doubt that they're wearing any underwear under those things."

"I hate it when people in the exit row put their feet up on the bulkhead," a Delta flight attendant told me a few weeks later. "If you were a guest in someone's house, would you put your feet on the wall?"

It seems like such a small complaint, but then again this is the sort of gesture that shapes the psyches of those who work in the air. This is *not* her house. And yet it is. This is not a house at all, and yet it's the place where a huge number of people spend a huge amount of time. As more and more Americans carry the detritus of earthbound life to this tube in the air, measures must be taken to make them feel at home without allowing the frontier to become lawless. "When the door closes, we must play every role," said Britt Marie Swartz, a Delta flight attendant who began her career at Pan Am in the late 1970s and actually cooked eggs to order in 747 galleys. "We're doctors, lawyers, travel agents, therapists, waitresses, and cops. No one would demand all of that from a normal person."

The first thing aspiring flight attendants learn when they attend a recruitment meeting at the American Airlines training school near the Dallas/Fort Worth airport is that, if hired, they will make a base starting salary of around $14,000 a year. The second thing they must do is fill out a lengthy questionnaire designed to give recruiters an idea of their basic character makeup. When I visit the training facility, I am not allowed to see this questionnaire, although I am told that the nature of their answers will lead to what interviewers call "probing points," wherein candidates are asked to talk about themselves in ways that may or may not indicate personality traits incompatible with airplane social dynamics. "There was one grammar outburst," a recruiter says as he emerges from an interview. "I think I detected a double negative." Although I must sign a release saying that I will not print or repeat any of the questions asked of candidates, I am allowed to print the answers they give. And as I spend an hour watching a sweet and painfully sincere twenty-four-year-old from Arkansas hang herself on the basis of about two answers, I am amazed at what an art the recruiters (all of whom are former or working flight attendants) have made out of selecting their co-workers. The candidate, carefully outfitted in an Arkansas version of a power suit, complete with Fayva-type pumps and a neckerchief, seals her fate based on the following responses:

"I would say 'I don't find that type of humor funny' and walk out of the galley," and, "If nothing else worked, I wouldn't lie. I guess I would say, 'Your feet seem to be causing an odor. Can you please put your shoes back on?'"

The woman is sent back to Arkansas with the promise that she will be notified by letter within six weeks, which means that she most certainly will never be hired. Though the recruiter, who looks and speaks almost exactly like the weatherman on my local ABC television affiliate, cannot put his finger directly on what turned him off to her, he tells me it has something to do with apparent inflexibility.

During the week that I observe training, I spend most of my time with a class of sixty students. They have been selected from an original pool of 112,000 applicants, all but 4,000 of whom were eliminated via an automated telephone screening system. American has one of the most rigorous training programs in the industry—flight attendants from other carriers frequently refer to them as the "Sky Nazis"—but it is also among the most sought-after employers, both for its reputation and its pay scale, which is high by industry standards.

The training facility is an awe-inspiring complex. Occupying a large building next door to the flight academy, it contains a hotel, conference center, and salon, as well as a multitude of offices, lecture halls, and several life-size cabin simulators. The simulators, which fill up large rooms, look like movie sets of airplanes. They hold real seats, real galleys, and real doors. The windows are filled in with painted renderings of fluffy white clouds. The flight attendants practice serving real food to their classmates and are observed closely by their instructors. Part of their training involves getting accustomed to erratic hours and last-minute schedule changes; their day can begin as early as 3 A.M., and individual students often receive telephone calls in the classroom from a mock crew scheduling unit, which informs them that drills or simulated flight times have been reassigned. Business attire must be worn at all times. This means jackets and ties for the men and no skirts above the knee for the women. Flight attendants both in and outside of American have referred to this training program as Barbie Boot Camp. New hires consult at least once with the American Airlines salon manager, who suggests suitable hairstyles—the French twist is especially popular—and teaches the women how to apply makeup, which is to be worn at all times during training. Several of the students privately refer to the image consultant as Sergeant Lipstick, who is known to keep tabs on the freshness of application.

Throughout the week I am escorted at all times by a representative from the corporate communications office, an impeccably groomed and perfectly nice woman who leads me through an itinerary that has been set up specifically for me. Almost all of the classes I observe have to do with aircraft evacuation. One class involves food service, another is centered almost entirely around a device called the Automated External Defibrillator, which American recently acquired for most of their overseas jets and which, I am told several times, many other airlines do not have. To my disappointment, I have apparently missed the phase of training that involves personal appearance standards. When I ask twice if I can relocate to the hotel at the training center in order to interview the experienced flight attendants who are housed here for their annual recurrent training, I am subtly put off both times; like a demanding passenger, I am denied my request without ever hearing the word "no."

It seems to me that flight attendant training has relatively little to do with the actual job of flight attendant. Although the trainees have ostensibly been hired based on a vibrancy of personality and the good sense not to say "I don't find that type of humor funny," there is something so sterile about the vibe of this education that it's hard to imagine how their lessons will ever mesh with the reality of dealing with actual people in the actual sky. In an entire week of observing classes, I never once hear the word "crash." Instead, a strange semantic code seems to be in place. Several times I hear the phrase "crispy critter," which, apparently, is what the flight attendants will be if they can't maneuver a clear path through fire. "If you do not go through the protected area and there's a fire," chirps an instructor at seven-fifteen one morning, "who's the crispy critter? You!"

Though American may have earned its "Sky Nazi" wings by maintaining a somewhat overzealous tone when it comes to corporate culture, their personnel bear little resemblance to the "coffee, tea, or me" drones of the past. Recruiters say that they work hard to hire crews that will reflect the demographic makeup of the passengers and from the looks of things, they're succeeding. The class I observed had several men and women over forty and a number of people of color, including a thirty-six-year-old former North Carolina highway patrolman with two children who said he just always wanted to fly. "The times that I've felt down about being here, I just go to the airport and watch the planes take off and land," he says in a group interview that's been set up for me by company supervisors.

That's a poetic sentiment, and American Airlines doesn't mind that kind of sound bite. But the theme music they really want played is all about "customer service," a term that the company repeats like a mantra, much like "Be Prepared" is to the Boy Scouts. Things get tricky, however, when it becomes clear just how difficult it is to uphold Ritz-Carlton-like service philosophies in an arena that is accessible to almost all walks of life. Customer service may be the gospel here, but it isn't necessarily the law. "Our company no longer holds fast to the policy that the customer is always right," says Sara

Ponte, a flight attendant recruiting supervisor. "If a passenger consistently causes a disturbance, then that's not a passenger we want on our airline." Although no one at American will confirm or deny any rumors, company myths have it that a few celebrities, including Kim Basinger and Charlie Sheen, have been banned from the airline because of in-flight misconduct. Basinger's tantrum was allegedly sparked after she was refused ice cubes made from Evian water.

Herein lies the central conflict of flight attendant training, and it is the conflict that factors most heavily into the larger identity crisis of airborne life. Cabin crews are supposed to maintain an aura of exclusivity by making passengers feel special. But how can this be done when the very customers they're trying to please are anything but exclusive? By definition, the public is not private, nor are flight attendants high-priced personal assistants who consider the maintenance of freshly starched shirts a higher priority than feeding 173 people in under one hour or, for that matter, being able to evacuate 173 people in less than ninety seconds. That airlines continue to advertise themselves as luxury watering holes that, it so happens, will get you across the country in five hours is both a disservice to the flight attendant and one more way that the passenger is distanced from the actual concept of flying. Singapore Airlines, which is considered to have the highest level of customer service of any carrier in the world, has long touted their flight attendants as their major selling point. In the 1980s, the airline's slogan was "Singapore Girl, You're A Great Way to Fly." While it's doubtful than any United States carrier could get away with this kind of ad copy, all flight attendants carry the burden of this kind of public image. They are expected to represent the sex in their airline while remaining utterly nonthreatening. They are symbols of technology and symbols of flesh, and this is where their religion and their rules begin to come unglued.

When new hires are asked to leave American Airline's training program, they always disappear instantly. Students can be eating lunch together only to find a classmate gone permanently an hour later. In this class of sixty, seven left early, some for reasons no one quite understands. When I try to talk to the students, they happily accommodate my questions until they realize that everything they say will be within earshot of my escort from corporate communications. A woman waiting to practice a drill tells me that she was forced by the company salon to cut her hair and now feels bad about it. Back in the classroom, half an hour later, she clams up on me. When I press her, she finally slips me a note that reads "I can't really talk now."

Though I cannot be sure, I have inklings that my escort from corporate communications is keeping an eye on me when I visit the ladies' room. We eat lunch together every day. We walk down every corridor together. As I throw questions at anyone I can find she lingers next to me, reducing every flight attendant to the bland politeness of the first-class cabin. Though my escort has offered to pick me up at my hotel and drive me to the training center every morning, I have a rental car and assure her that I can find my way on my own. One afternoon, after parting ways in the parking lot, we get separated by a few cars as we pull onto the road that leads to the freeway. As I drive along I notice that she's pulled over to the shoulder so I can catch up. "How nice," I think to myself. "She's making sure I don't get lost." Hours later it occurs to me that she might have been making sure I didn't sneak back to the training center to interview people without her. I had indeed considered staying behind by myself, only to discard the idea for fear I'd be sent home.

Back on our US Airways flight to San Francisco, I learn that Carl and Jim have a penchant, during mid-flight seat belt checks, for taking note of male passengers who have fallen asleep and developed erections. They then go into the galley and whisper something in the neighborhood of "Check out 26C" and send other flight attendants, one by one, to do the old corner-of-the-eye glance while moseying on by. This is considered a necessary distraction and an entirely acceptable way to wile away the hours. They also play a game called "Thirty-Second Review," wherein they have thirty seconds to walk through the cabin and make a note of the seat number of the passenger they would most like to have sex with.

As I research this story, I am told about flight attendants who work as prostitutes on the side, flight attendants who give mid-flight blow jobs to pilots, flight attendants who are transsexuals, and flight attendants who carry separate business cards for their drag queen personae. A friend of mine can tell a story about a flight attendant who gave him a hand job in the business-class section of a 747 during her half-hour break on a flight from New York to São Paulo. A cab driver who took me home from the airport a few months ago described meeting a flight attendant on the way to Orlando and shacking up with her for a week at a hotel near Disney World. "Of course, I had to pay for everything," he said to me as we careened over the Triborough Bridge. "She had it all figured out."

None of these actions or examples, weighed on their own, register enough scandal to send the airlines into collapse. As sensational as some of them are, these are the exceptions that prove the rule that most flight attendants are regular people with regular aspirations, many of which do not require business cards at all. But the fact that such tales are recounted so readily, both by people outside of the job and by flight attendants themselves, reveals a trait that is shared by just about everyone who works in the air. As the remoteness of the sky threatens to render them something less than human, they have no choice but to make themselves almost exaggeratedly human, hyperreal characters who rely on wild behavior and raunchy mythologies in order to outsmart the numbing effects of the airplane.

These stories, apocryphal or not, serve to sustain humanity inside the artificiality of the tube. A particularly dark plotline involves the widely held belief that the so-called Patient Zero, to whom over forty of the first AIDS cases were traced back, was an Air Canada flight attendant named Gaeten Dugas. More common are ambitious passengers seeking membership into the Mile High Club. Carl recalls a couple from Dayton who sheepishly offered him $20 to allow them to enter the lavatory together (he waived the fee). An American Airlines flight attendant recounts what he swears is a "true rumor" about identical twins who worked as flight attendants for Eastern Airlines in the 1980s. The sisters worked together on wide-body aircrafts like the DC-10 and L10-11 that had lower level galleys accessible from small elevators, which could, in effect, be locked by keeping the door open downstairs. Together they would solicit a male passenger and take him down into the galley for clandestine three-way sex. Afterwards, they would serve him champagne.

Such rituals have been in place since the inception of commercial air travel. Pan Am stewardesses regularly taped centerfolds to the backs of safety cards when flying United States troops on military-contracted flights to Vietnam. Even into the late 1970s, flight attendants on Pacific South Airlines wore uniforms that featured miniskirts and go-go boots. The difference today is that these rituals are played out on the sly. As airlines fight harassment and discrimination lawsuits, keeping strict watch over potentially solicitous pilots or questionable behavior on layovers, these antics are mind games more than parlor games. There is considerably more talk than action going on. The influence of gay male culture cannot be ignored either. It is perhaps no accident that stereotypically gay male styles of social behavior seem custom-made for the flight attendant lifestyle. "For a lot of the gay guys it's been a wonderful ride," says Carl, who came out the same year he began flying. "The airlines have been a friendly atmosphere for being ourselves. But it's more social than sexual."

Jim, who is also gay, is quick to jokingly add that there is no better job for him *because* he is gay. This is a valid point, but not in the way that probably first comes to mind. While there are plenty of male flight attendants who are not gay, the cabin is dominated by an unquestionably campy sensibility; the boys help the girls with new hair styles, the girls loudly evaluate the boys' asses. It's a vibe that points toward the tolerance on which flight attendants pride themselves. But it also scratches the itch of their central contradiction. They are at once erotic figures and cartoon characters, raunchy talkers who wouldn't be out of place in the cast of Up With People. Their penis jokes have the ring of a junior high school cafeteria; words like "meat" or "fruit" cannot be spoken without some degree of sophomoric innuendo. Flight attendants live in a state of permanent chaos, and thrive in it. Unlike their passengers, whose systems are still adjusting to the transient new world, the flight attendant has successfully adapted to surroundings that are neither here nor there. For better or worse, she represents the nervous system of the future.

Kew Gardens, Queens, near JFK and LaGuardia airports in New York City, is the sometime-home to approximately two thousand flight attendants and pilots. I visit an apartment complex that houses two hundred of them in dorm-like apartments that are cleanly furnished with drab sofas, Formica dinette sets, and the perfunctory $24 halogen torch lamp. The building's landlord actively seeks out airline personnel, who each pay a monthly rent of $150 for their maximum stays of seven days. Each unit has two or three bedrooms that hold two sets of bunk beds with the exception of the errant, single-occupancy pilot's room, one of which is elaborately outfitted with stereo equipment, a computer, and a wall-mounted, large-screen television affixed with a Post-it that reads "Seinfeld 11:00." A lot of pilots, however, drift in and out of a nearby place nicknamed Animal House, which is considered a prime spot for crew parties and fraternity-style debauchery.

But things are pretty calm tonight in unit C-2, where several flight attendants, many of whom have just returned from places where today is still yesterday, are gathered in the common room watching The Weather Channel. Janet is thirty-eight, divorced, and worked on the ground for Delta until she got a company transfer and began flying in 1993. She commutes to this crash pad from her home in Atlanta, and, like many of her colleagues, admits that her transient lifestyle can get in the way of her personal life. A typically prepubescent maxim in aviation goes like this: "What does AIDS stand for? Airline Induced Divorce Syndrome." For every crew member who relishes the personal space inherent in her job, there is another who feels her relationships have been sabotaged by it.

"A lot of the girls from my class are divorced now," she says, finding herself unable to keep from getting up to refill my drink before I even finish it. "Guys you meet think it's kind of fascinating, the whole mystique of being a flight attendant. I dated a guy who I swear wanted me to wear my uniform when we went out. But they don't really want to have a relationship with someone who is gone so much. They'll come home at five o'clock and you're not there."

Later we go across the street to Airline Night at the local dive bar. There are hundreds of flight attendants and a few scattered pilots ordering two-for-one drinks and rubbing each others' shoulders. Even out of uniform, there is something about the crowd that is unmistakably airliney. With their clean fingernails and neat hair, they seem like they come from nowhere, as if they're extras in a made-for-TV movie. Like people in an airport, they are a smorgasbord of regional accents and styles. Though most will fly together only rarely, they tend to touch each other a lot, giving bear hugs and wet kisses and pulling familiar figures aside saying, "I remember you from the seven-two, a couple years ago."

Not unlike the main cabin of an airplane, this bar is jammed with representatives from every town in every state. Hired to assist and identify with the country's disenfranchised, disoriented air travelers, the primary job requirement seems less about handling an emergency than diffusing the side effects of hours spent in the hothouse that is the plane. Very few say they fear an accident, and most maintain a Zen-like philosophy about the possibility of crashing. "I figure when it's my time to go, it's my time to go," a thirty-two-year-old flight attendant named Len says. Of all the flight attendants I spoke with, about half had experienced incidents like engine explosions or faulty indicator lights that required returning to the airport. Within that group, only a tiny fraction had ever evacuated their plane. Britt Marie Swartz says that early in her Pan Am career she was scheduled for a trip that she had to cancel at the last minute. "The plane crashed. After that I was never afraid. I figure my time will come when it comes."

No one is allowed to die on an airplane. The worst thing you can do to a flight attendant is try to die on her. It won't work. She'll have to give you CPR no matter how evident your passing may be. Upon making an emergency landing, after they cart you away, the plane will be impounded. There will be the inevitable lawsuits.

"We are told unofficially that no one is allowed to die on the airplane," a Delta flight attendant in Kew Gardens told me. "Maybe they died on the jetway, but not on the airplane." Flight attendants are not allowed to declare death, and doctors, if there are any on board, are often reluctant to speak up when called for because of liability issues. In 1997, Lufthansa lost a one-million-dollar lawsuit against the family of a man who had died of a heart attack on the plane.

There is an unparalleled creepiness about airplane deaths, perhaps because we most often associate them with the gothic horror of news footage when there is a crash. But while air crashes occupy a far larger place in the popular imagination than they do in realistic odds, medical emergencies are relatively common. Every flight attendant in this story described situations which were sometimes harrowing enough to rival an episode of *ER*—strokes, seizures, childbirth, psychotic reactions to drugs, broken bones, a catheter that needed to be changed in heavy turbulence.

In the sky, denial is not just human instinct, it's a job requirement. A flight attendant for Canadian Airlines remembers an elderly man who, unbeknownst to his wife, died in his sleep. "I put a blanket on him," she says. "His wife was right beside him and I let her believe he was asleep until we landed. It was the best thing to do given the situation."

"A colleague of mine said that last week a woman traveling with her husband knew he had died twenty minutes into the flight," says Shannon Veedock, a Chicago-based American Airlines flight attendant. "They had made a stop in Dallas, stayed on the plane, and continued on to New York. She kept telling the crew he was asleep. She'd even called her son from the plane and told him what was going on. She was determined to get him home."

Here again, lies the contradiction of flying, smatterings of the grotesque on a sublime canvas, heroism one minute and *Beavis and Butthead* behavior the next. A flight attendant with a major airline explains to me how she and her co-workers spent two hours and forty-five minutes giving CPR to a passenger who was vomiting on them and saved his life. Five minutes later in our conversation she recalls a particularly nasty passenger who demanded an extra lime for her gin and tonic. "She'd been snapping her fingers at other crew members, snapping her fingers at me, and so I took her glass into the galley, got two pieces of lime and shoved them up my nostrils and wiggled them around. Then I plopped them back in the glass and cheerfully brought it back to her."

The night I am flying home from my turnaround with the US Airways crew, I find myself overtaken with an uncontrollable urge to become a flight attendant, to join the living up here among the sleeping, to wear the uniform. It's the uniform that gets me where I live, that hideous, dazzling, itchy ensemble of unnatural fibers, that homage to country and corporation. It embodies all the contradictions of airplane life, contradictions which, in the end, make more evident the crisis of national identity: the need to be free versus the need to be sewn inside an organized structure. With their insignia and their rebellion, I can't help but think that flight attendants are, in a sense, quintessential Americans. They are at once rootless souls and permanent fixtures, vagabonds who can't stay anywhere too long and plain folks trying to restore equilibrium to a crowded, light-headed world.

This 757 is a tube of intersecting lives, a pressurized cross section of the entire population, a flying nation. In a few hours we will land at an airport that looks like a shopping mall. We will stay in a hotel that gives no clues as to what city we're in. In a world whose pace and legroom is controlled by the speed of technology, a glance down this length of darkened cabin gives a pretty fair indication of the shape we're in. One hundred ninety-four passengers are curled up asleep in what little space they have, their coats tucked under their heads, their knees tucked under their chins. Laptop computer screens are glowing. The air smells of coffee and peanuts and bodies. It's such a specific aroma, bottled in its giant container, sponged off the skins of 194 people who think it must be coming from the person sitting next to them. But this is what an airplane always smells like. It is the scent of the house where the entire world lives.

"Fun—It's Heaven!"

Ford Madox Ford

THE ROOM WAS LIT BY A SKYLIGHT FROM ABOVE, SO THAT IT resembled a tank in which dim fishes swim listlessly. The walls were of varnished gray paint; an immense and lamenting Christ hung upon a cross above the empty grate; a mildewed portrait of the last Pope but one made a grim spot of white near the varnished door. On a deal chair beside the deal table the old doctor sat talking to the very old lay sister who stood before him, twisting her gnarled fingers in her wooden beads.

"Whatever it is," he said, and he waved his hand 'round to indicate the grim room. "This isn't my idea of it. That is what I told the child."

"There need be no limits to one's idea of it," the lay sister said. "What was it you told the poor child? I have not, you must remember, heard anything at all," she added. "Dicky Trout, I suppose, is killed. And he was to have married her? He was a dear young boy."

"He had just been ninety minutes in the trenches. And shot through the head! Ninety minutes! And dead! It's what they call rotten luck. They were both my godchildren." He said the words with a certain fierceness of resentment.

"I know," the lay sister said patiently.

The same resentment was in the old doctor's tone.

"What sort of work was it for me?" he asked, "to console her. What is there to say? How can you console a child of nineteen whose lover of twenty-two has been shot through the head after ninety minutes in the trenches? There is no consolation. It is the most final thing in the world. You cannot make any comments."

"There are always the consolations of religion," the lay sister said. "Believe me, they are very real."

"But how do they come in when you talk to a child like Joan about the death of a boy like Dicky Trout? What are you to say? 'The Lord giveth and the Lord . . .'"

He stopped and then began again with his fierce energy.

"Do you know what she said to me? Do you know? She said: 'It isn't possible that he won't ever have any fun again; not any fun! The lights, and the white paint, and the young girls, and the tea, and the river, and the little bands playing 'Hitchy Koo.' He wanted it so; oh, he wanted it so.' I couldn't stand it. I tell you I had to say that he would have it all again. The lights and the river and the teashops and the little bands playing 'Hitchy Koo.'"

The lay sister had nothing to say. The doctor went on:

"I'm not a very well-read man. Someone once said, 'If there had not been any God we should have had to invent one.' Who was it?"

"I think it was Voltaire," the lay sister answered. "It does not matter. What did you tell the child?"

"I'll tell you," the doctor answered. "You know her father was too busy with his regiment; her mother is a permanent invalid. I'm forever in the house. Professionally. And Joan wanted to see the places in which his last weeks were spent; his billets; the range where he fired . . . Well, I went with her, a long way into the Midlands. And we saw them: his billets and his sergeants who had known him and the range where he had fired. I think it was the range that did it.

"You see, what moved me so extraordinarily was her perpetual cry: that she wanted him to have some fun—because he wanted it so! If she had said she just wanted him back for herself—or if she had even cried! But no; she just said, over and over again, that he wanted it so! Fun! It's a curious thing for a young girl to want for her dead sweetheart; but I daresay there was nothing better or truer or more feminine that she could have wanted for him. And, just as God was invented, if He did not indeed exist—so, suddenly, Fun came into existence. On those ranges.

"Try to imagine the Mosslott Range for yourself. In the squalid suburbs of a hideous city, on a dirty, flat expanse of sordid grass, some banks of clay, like long graves. And, in them, beneath the squalid clouds, clay-colored figures reclining, intent, gazing at the banks before them, at a distance. And flat, black shapes, like the heads and shoulders of devils, peep up over the banks in front and lob away. Fun!

"And when you turned your head you saw an immense row of retorts, in silhouette. A long way off, but immense! Eighteen of them, shutting in the horizon, with plumes of dim flames running away down the wind and invisible smoke because the sky was just smoke! Fun! The proper fun for a boy of twenty-two, the sweetheart of a girl of nineteen. Well, I suppose it is all right.

"At any rate, in that *décor*, as the French would call it, Joan caught hold of my arm and cried out:

"'Oh; do you think God can forgive him . . . for practicing here to take away lives . . . every time he hit a dummy.'

"'My dear,' I said, 'God has a special pardon for soldiers. If they kill, they don't kill for themselves, but for you and me.'

"'Oh, are you sure!' she said. 'Can we be sure?'

"I don't know what it was that happened then; something cracked in me at the tones of her voice—for there, with the rifles popping away in the distance, the first thing was that a band—quite a little band—was playing. Yes, it was playing what undoubtedly was 'Hitchy Koo.'

"Now you are to understand that I have always taken a desultory interest in the uniforms of the British Army. I know that the infantry, for instance, in the reign of Queen Anne wore scarlet coats with facings, breeches, and long black gaiters. But I had a vague idea that the hat was the Kevenhuller. It was not—as you shall hear.

"For I found myself in a long street, like St. James's Street, going into the doorway of a teashop where the band was—the band that was playing 'Hitchy Koo.' And the anteroom was full of young men—fine young men in scarlet coats, with rifles and breeches and black gaiters. And their hats had cockades and were three-cornered. Kevenhuller hats I thought they were.

"Well, as I went in a young blond fellow was calling out:

"'Ypres! Stop my vitals! A man would be a mole if his blood boiled not at that name.'

"Others cried:

"'Have the rout beaten!'

"And:

"'Call out the gentlemen of the firing platoons.'

"They laughed and cheered, and their scarlet coattails whisked. I think it was 'To Wipers!' that they cried, and then there was no one there. The long white inner room was full of young men—quite young men—in that dun color, with the brass buttons. You have seen khaki, sister? Once through the grille in the door? And you saw Dicky Trout before he went? Well, then, that room was full of young men in khaki, sitting at little tables, laughing with the young girls, chaffing the waitress even—and eating éclairs.

"And Dicky Trout got up from a table and came toward me, laughing:

"'They're going to Ypres, those fellows,' he said, 'won't they make the beggars run! I was fed up with Ypres; but it's all the fun of the fair here. And Joan will be here! Fun! I tell you it's Heaven.'

"That was all I saw, just that glimpse . . . and then—it was the range again and the irregular sounds of the rifles. And Joan was talking to a sergeant who had known Dicky Trout; his eyes were full of tears.

"Well, sister, I suppose you'll say I was wrong. But that evening, in the train, I told Joan what I had seen. You'll say it was wrong. You'll say it was deluding her with false hopes. But put it how you will I believe I was right. It would not be decent if I was not right—if Heaven wasn't like that for those poor young things. God must be good to them. He must. If He were not we should have to make him. They die for you and me. It's our business to invent a fit Heaven for them. Don't say I'm wrong."

"That," the old lay sister said, "is a matter for theologians. No doubt God is rich enough to provide teashops for all who die for us. We do not know what Heaven will be like."

"And the strange thing," the doctor continued, "is not the story— you know the story—that Marlborough's men got out of their graves and fought for us at Ypres. Though it's a fine story. Damn it; it's a fine story. They couldn't lie there still and let our men be beaten back. No; the strange point for me is this:

"This morning, when I went to see Joan she was smiling as I had never seen her smile. And she said: 'You've got to go with me to the sisters. I must take the veil. I have heard a voice. But it wasn't the Kevenhuller hat they wore at Ypres. It was a proper cocked hat with a cockade—the Ramillies hat and the Ramillies tie-wig they came to be called.'

"I asked her how she could know that; I couldn't see how she could. And she answered:

"'Dicky told me. At the little table, three from the orchestra on the right. He's having such fun. They were playing, "Get Out or Get Under," and he wanted to get under the table, but I wouldn't let him. Fun! It was Heaven.'"

The old doctor paused; the lay sister said nothing.

"For myself," the doctor said at last, "I believe that Heaven will be like that. I believe that, as you say, God is a very rich man—and that He has imagination too. And I come back to that: that if there were no Heaven we should have to invent one. For what is the sense of the world without it? Here is Dicky Trout dead—and Joan taking the veil—I suppose that she may pray that Dicky has some fun."

The lay sister sighed, "I should like to hear the tune of 'Get Out and Get Under,'" she said. "I never saw a teashop in my life."

"You shall! You shall!" the doctor said. "As for the tune, you must have heard the bands playing it as the drafts go by—to Flanders. It goes . . ."

And he began to hum the jerky melody whilst the old religious nodded her head. In a room above the young girl was trying to persuade the Mother Superior that she had the vocation for that cloistral life. Her sweetheart lay dead in Flanders.

Assuredly if there were no Heaven we whom Flanders has not yet claimed must will one into existence with all the volition of united humanity.

Notes

NOTES

Notes

Notes: _____
_____
_____
_____
_____
_____
_____
_____
_____
_____
_____
_____
_____
_____
_____
_____
_____
_____
_____
_____
_____
_____
_____
_____
_____
_____
_____

Notes

NOTES

Notes

Memoranda

Notes and Memoranda

Mungo Thomson